'What do you s

Paula shook ~~her head, staring~~ at both men. It was an outrageous suggestion and yet – she couldn't deny it – wildly exciting.

'Let's take a look at her,' said the dark man, snapping the straps of her nightdress.

Paula's face glowed with embarrassment as the garment slid to the floor. Her firm breasts jutted proudly, the nipples long, brown and erect.

'Beautiful,' said the man and a shiver of desire ran through her as he cupped her swollen orbs in his big coarse hands . . .

Also available from Headline Delta

The Exhibitionists
Daring Young Maids
Maids in Heaven
Amateur Nights
Amateur Days
Bianca
Compulsion
Two Weeks in May
The Downfall of Danielle
Exposed
Indecent
Fondle in Flagrante
Fondle on Top
Fondle All Over
Hot Pursuit
High Jinks Hall
Kiss of Death
The Phallus of Osiris
Lust on the Loose
Passion in Paradise
Reluctant Lust
The Wife-Watcher Letters
Amorous Appetites
Hotel D'Amour
Intimate Positions
Ménage à Trois
My Duty, My Desire
Sinderella
The Story of Honey O
Three Women

Desires Unlimited

Samantha Austen

Delta

First published in 1997
by HEADLINE BOOK PUBLISHING

A HEADLINE DELTA paperback

10 9 8 7 6 5 4 3 2 1

ISBN 0 7472 5630 6

Typeset by CBS, Felixstowe, Suffolk

Printed and bound in Great Britain by
Cox & Wyman Ltd, Reading, Berks.

HEADLINE BOOK PUBLISHING
A division of Hodder Headline PLC
338 Euston Road
London NW1 3BH

Desires Unlimited

Chapter 1

Jo was uncertain precisely what it was that woke her from her sleep. It might have been the call of a seabird, or the crash of a wave. Perhaps it was some kind of sixth sense that told her she was no longer alone. Whatever, something had disturbed her slumbers and all at once she found herself wide awake, blinking up into the strong sunlight.

She lifted herself up onto one elbow and reached across for her watch, which was on the top of her small beach bag. She was amazed to discover that she had been asleep for nearly two hours. She looked about her. She was lying in a depression between two sand dunes, so that she was completely concealed from anyone more than a few feet away. She had chosen the spot precisely for this reason, though the beach had been quite deserted when she arrived.

She wondered idly whether she was still alone and decided to take a look. Cautiously she rose to her feet and stretched, luxuriating in the opportunity to relieve the stiffness in her limbs.

Standing there on the lonely beach, her body stretched taut, Jo made quite a sight. She had a lovely figure, slim and shapely with large, firm breasts and a trim waist. Her legs were long and slender and, as she stretched, the small bikini she wore showed off her shape beautifully. She stood five foot eight inches tall in her bare feet and she wore her dark hair to her shoulders. It framed a classically pretty face with high cheekbones, a pert nose and haunting green eyes. These gave her a look of innocent beauty that captivated every man she met.

She took a couple of steps up the sand dune and peeked over the top. On either side she could see the full length of the beach as it stretched out before her. The sand was a beautiful golden colour, the sea a deep blue. It could almost have been a continental scene and the sultry heat of the day did nothing to dispel the illusion of being far from England. She glanced both ways. To her left the beach was as deserted as ever but, as she watched, someone descended onto the sands away to her right.

Jo watched as the figure headed in her direction. She stood about twenty yards back from the beach itself and was shielded by a crop of coarse grass, so there was little likelihood of her being seen. As the lone walker came closer, she discerned it to be a young woman of about her age. She was quite small, about five foot four in height, but her figure was beautifully proportioned. She wore a beach jacket made of white towelling and carried a towel in her hand. Her hair was blonde and it seemed to catch the sunlight as she strolled along the shore.

Jo kept her eyes fixed on the approaching girl. She wondered why such an attractive woman would be alone. Surely one as lovely as that would have been able to find a companion? Then she reminded herself that she was similarly unaccompanied.

The stranger was almost alongside where Jo was hiding when she came to a halt. For a moment Jo feared that she had been discovered, but the girl made no sign of being aware she was not alone.

From this distance Jo was able to see her in some detail. She had the looks of a professional model, with full lips and large blue eyes, her hair hanging down her back in shining tresses. She glanced about her, as if ensuring that she was the only person on the beach, then she unfolded the towel and spread it out on the sand. She fussed about it, squinting up at the sky and positioning it where she would receive maximum benefit from the sun's rays. Then she reached for the sash that held her robe closed, pulling it undone and letting the garment drop from her shoulders.

As she did so, Jo gave a gasp of surprise. Beneath the robe the girl was completely naked. Jo stood transfixed, unable to take her eyes from the girl's lovely young body, drinking in every curve. Her breasts were large, with big brown areolae ringing her nipples. The hair at her crotch was as fair as that on her head, and, standing as she was with her legs slightly parted, Jo could discern the pink of her sex lips.

She was astounded at the girl's brazenness. She herself, clad as she was in a bikini, had eschewed the exposure of the public beach. Yet here was a girl who was prepared to stand entirely naked in the middle of the sands, regardless of who might happen by.

The girl stretched her beautiful frame, looking like some Greek Goddess who had just emerged from the waves. Then she lowered herself onto the towel and lay on her back, closing her eyes in the brightness of the sun's rays.

Jo slid back down to where her own towel lay in the sand, her mind filled with the image of the naked sunbather. There was something extraordinary erotic about the sight of the girl so openly and publicly displaying her body. Something that awoke a spark of arousal in Jo that she hadn't felt for some time.

Jo had found out about the beach the night before from the landlord of the small inn in which she was staying. He had explained the route to her in detail and she was grateful that she had listened carefully since it had turned out to be so secluded that she could never have found the place by herself. Apparently the beach was a closely kept secret amongst the locals and she wasn't sure why he had chosen to tell her. Perhaps he had sensed her melancholy air and had decided to try to cheer her up. Whatever it was, she reflected, it had been a generous gesture.

The holiday had indeed been intended to raise her spirits. In the weeks before, whilst her rather messy divorce had dragged on through the interminable legal proceedings, she had been feeling very low and it had been an impulse that had driven her to get out of London for a few weeks and enjoy the quiet solace of the Cornish coast.

Jo Spencer was twenty-two years old and already a divorcée. She had met her husband when she was seventeen and he was twenty-five. A whirlwind romance had followed and they had been married within six weeks. It had all seemed so glamorous at the time. He had been a roadie with a number of top rock bands and she had accompanied him on his travels, seeing the world and meeting the rich and famous. When she had tired of the moving about they had bought a flat in London where she had set up home whilst he continued to travel.

She was never certain when, precisely, she had begun to suspect his infidelity. At first there had been no specific clues, simply a tailing off of the passion with which he greeted her whenever he came home. Whereas once he would have been tearing off her clothes the moment he stepped through the door, as time went by he had appeared almost indifferent to her charms and whole days would go by with no sex at all. Then there were the other telltale signs. A smell of perfume on his clothes, the careful way his bag had been packed, and the evenings when she had tried all night to call him in his hotel room without success.

Eventually she had confronted him and a huge row had ensued. Soon afterwards he had packed his belongings and left the flat for good. A year later she had begun divorce proceedings.

The divorce had been a long and acrimonious one and she had ended up having to sell the flat and moving into rented accommodation. When at last it was settled, she had been tired and depressed. That was why she had decided to get away from it all to come to Cornwall, where she could find time to contemplate what to do with the rest of her life.

Now, as she lay on the sand, she reflected on the complete absence of sex since she had been left alone. When they had first married, she had been an eager and sensuous partner and had loved to screw at any time of the day or night. Fortunately, her husband had been an expert lover and had known precisely what she liked. He had been quite capable of giving her two or three orgasms at a time before releasing his own seed into her, leaving her more than satisfied. Since he had left, though, there had been virtually nothing, just one or two attempts with unsuitable men that had left her both unfulfilled and frustrated.

So she had put the pleasures of the flesh to the back of her mind and for a long time all thoughts of sex had left her. But now, for the first time in ages, she felt the stirrings of arousal within her. She wasn't certain why. It wasn't as if she was lesbian, though she had to admit that the naked woman had looked absolutely gorgeous. It was more the thought of the girl having the audacity to do what she was doing. To risk being discovered alone and naked in this deserted spot by a stranger. Possibly a man. For a second Jo imagined such an encounter and the reaction of the man on finding her, her charms on open display. She thought of the way his cock would harden. She licked her lips at the prospect, her hand drifting almost unconsciously down to her crotch as she visualised the scene.

All at once Jo wanted to look at the young woman again. She told herself that this was simply to confirm that she hadn't imagined what she had seen. But she knew, deep inside, that it was more than that, that she wanted a better look than the one she had had. She rose slowly to her feet, knowing that in order to do so she must move closer to the young sunbather.

The sand dunes ran all the way down to the edge of the beach and the one Jo had chosen to lie beside was a short distance back. She had taken a good look at the lie of the land when she had arrived, though, and she was aware that if she moved quietly she could get within five yards of where the girl lay and still remain concealed.

Leaving her bag and towel behind her, she began to make

her way closer to the edge of the beach, keeping to the depressions between the dunes and moving silently on the soft sand. It took her less than a minute to get to where she wanted, at the foot of the dune beyond which the girl lay. Slowly, she began to climb the dune.

Once again there was a thick growth of grass at the top of the mound of sand and Jo was able to peep through it with little chance of being seen. She was very close to the girl now, almost able to look straight down at her, and she paused to take in the young woman's charms.

The girl was lying on her back still, apparently asleep, and Jo studied her breasts. Despite their size, they retained the firmness of youth, barely sagging to the sides so that the valley between them was deep and pronounced. The large nipples were slightly conical in shape, their brown colour contrasting with the paleness of her skin. It was clear to Jo that, even if she made a habit of sunbathing *au naturel*, it was some time since she had done so. Her skin was light and smooth, with scarcely a blemish.

Jo let her eyes travel down the girl's body, noting that she lay with her knees parted about eight inches, allowing a clear view of her sex. From this range she could discern that the lips were practically devoid of hair, almost as if they had been shaved, and that her blonde pubic triangle also showed signs of being trimmed, the hairs no more than a few millimetres long. She gazed at the girl's cleft, noting the pinkness of the thick lips. She could see the girl's love bud and for a second she imagined herself sucking at the small nodule of flesh, surprised at how erotic she found the idea.

Jo wasn't sure how long she had crouched there in the sand, studying the girl's body. Ten minutes? Fifteen? It was as if she was mesmerised by the sight. So fascinated was she that she didn't notice the approaching stranger until he was only about thirty yards away.

The realisation that there was a third person on the beach came as a shock to Jo. He was walking down from the same

6

direction as the girl had come, his approach hidden from her by the vegetation at the top of the dune, the same vegetation that had prevented him from seeing Jo. Suddenly, though, a movement caught her eye, and she saw him. She stared at him, then back at the young sunbather. Where the girl lay she was obscured from his view by a slight rise in the sand, but very shortly he would be over that and he was walking directly towards her. She wondered if she should call out to the girl, warn her of her impending discovery. But what could she say? And how could she explain her own presence, concealed here in the sand and spying on the girl? Besides, there was no time to prevent him seeing her. It was only a matter of seconds before he would be upon her and the girl had been extremely careless with her beach jacket, tossing it down some yards from where she lay, so that whatever happened the man was sure to see that she was naked.

By the time all these thoughts had passed through Jo's head it was too late. The man had crested the rise and was almost upon the girl when he stopped short, staring at the lovely figure stretched out before him.

Jo watched with bated breath. The man was not much further from the girl than she was herself and she knew he was studying her body in the same way that she had. He was tall, in his early thirties she estimated. He wore a white shirt and a pair of jeans. The shirt was open at the top, revealing a broad, hairy chest. His hair was dark, cut quite short with a parting. His face was pleasant, without being classically handsome.

Suddenly the sexual chemistry of the situation seemed to transmit itself to Jo. Once again she imagined her own naked body stretched out in the gaze of this stranger and a shiver of desire ran through her as she contemplated the situation.

The man had been rooted to the spot for about thirty seconds now, his eyes wide. Suddenly he seemed to come to his senses and took a step backwards, clearly intent on retracing his steps and avoiding the girl's embarrassment.

'Hello.'

The sound of the girl's voice took Jo by surprise and she swung round to see that the sunbather had propped herself up on her elbows and was addressing the new arrival.

'I-I'm sorry,' the man stammered. 'I didn't mean to disturb you.'

'You didn't.'

Jo was amazed by the girl's demeanour. She seemed totally unworried by her nudity, addressing the man as if the encounter were a perfectly normal one.

'I'd better leave you,' said the man, backing away.

'No, don't go. After all it's a public beach. You've got as much right to be on it as I have.'

'But you're . . . I mean you haven't got any . . .'

'Clothes? No, I haven't. Does that bother you? I could put my jacket on if you like.'

'No. I mean, well . . .'

The man's face had turned scarlet. Jo watched him, astounded at the incongruity of the situation. The naked girl was showing no signs of embarrassment whatsoever, whilst the man was clearly flustered by the encounter.

'How did you find this beach?' she asked.

'I walk here every day. I've got a holiday cottage about a mile away. Normally there's nobody about.'

'I'm sorry. Did you want to be alone?'

'No. No, it's fine. It's just that you're . . .'

'Naked?'

'Yes.'

'Don't you like my body?'

'Yes. You have a lovely body.'

She smiled and Jo was struck once again by her beauty. 'What's your name?' she asked.

'James.'

'Mine's Chris. Why don't you come and sit down, James?'

'Well, I don't want to disturb you.'

'For the last time, you're not disturbing me. Please come and sit down.'

The man hesitated, clearly still nonplussed by the encounter. Then the girl flashed her smile once again and he moved forward uncertainly. She sat up and patted the spot on the towel beside her. He settled down, his face still bright red.

They began to chat, the girl leading the conversation, and soon he began to loosen up. Jo watched and listened as she gently drew him out of himself. She noticed how tactile the girl was, constantly touching him and patting him, leaning close so that her nipples brushed against his bare arm. There was no doubt that the girl was flirting with him, nor that he was beginning to respond to her, becoming bolder by the minute so that before long he had an arm about her shoulder. Jo held her breath. It could only be a matter of time before he made a move. Her body language was giving him every sign that she would not rebuff him. Once again Jo felt the familiar stirrings inside herself as the eroticism of the situation filled her thoughts.

When he made his move it was swift and certain. One minute he was talking, the next his lips had closed over hers and he was gripping her in a passionate embrace, his arms wrapped about her. The girl responded instantly, pressing herself close to him and placing her arms behind his head.

His hand went to her breasts and Jo saw the nipples harden as he caressed them, making the girl writhe with obvious passion. When the kiss finally broke they stared into each other's eyes, both clearly aroused. She was panting softly as his hands continued to knead her firm mounds.

'I want to suck you,' she said quietly.

Once again Jo shook her head in wonder. The sheer forwardness of the girl was astounding. She watched as she lifted herself up onto her knees and began undoing the man's flies. Jo craned forward to get a better look as his cock sprang into view. It was hard and stiff and she watched enviously as the girl gripped it and began working the foreskin back and forth, whilst her other hand cupped his heavy balls.

The blonde leaned forward and her hair tumbled into the man's lap, obscuring Jo's view, much to her frustration. There was no doubt what she was doing, though. The way her head began to bob up and down told Jo that the man's erection was now inside her mouth. The expression of ecstasy on his face confirmed it.

Jo was more aroused than she had been for ages. The sight of the girl fellating the stranger, her dangling breasts swaying back and forth, was unbelievably erotic. Once again she began to stroke her own crotch through her bikini bottoms, feeling the wetness inside her increase with every moment.

The man began peeling off his shirt, revealing a mass of dark hair covering his chest. At the same time the girl was easing his jeans off, still keeping her mouth clamped firmly over his cock. She pushed them down to his ankles and he kicked them aside, lying back across the towel, his hips thrusting up at her face.

Suddenly the girl sat back on her ankles and Jo was rewarded with a full frontal view of the now naked man. His body was strong and athletic, his biceps bulging, his waist slim. But it was his cock and balls that held her attention, his rod rampant and twitching, the end shiny with saliva.

'Did you like that?' she asked, a mischievous grin on her face.

'Mmmm.'

'Do you want to taste me?'

'I'd love to.'

She lay down beside him, spreading her legs as she did so and affording Jo the best view yet of her open sex. Then he rolled over between her thighs and, rising onto all fours, buried his face in her sex.

'Ahhh!'

The girl almost shouted her passion as he began to go to work on her with his tongue, making her writhe about on the towel, pressing her hips up into his face and moaning with desire. Jo was on fire with arousal now and she slipped her hand inside her bikini, seeking out her clitoris with her fingers and rubbing herself gently.

'Oh god, James,' said the girl suddenly. 'I can't wait any longer. Stick that lovely dick of yours into me now.'

The man needed no second asking. At once he lowered his body over hers, and Jo saw his hand disappear beneath him. She imagined it taking hold of his stiff rod and guiding it to the entrance to the girl's hole, then she saw his hips make a series of jabbing movements as he eased himself into her, prostrating himself over her lovely body.

He fucked her hard, grunting aloud with his exertions as his hips pumped back and forth. For her part she responded with enthusiasm, thrusting her pubis up at him, her backside lifted clear of the ground as she matched his strokes. Jo too found herself in rhythm with him, her fingers working back and forth over her slit, her eyes fixed on the copulating couple. She had never imagined that anything could be so arousing and she wished desperately that she too could have a cock inside her and enjoy some part of the ecstasy that was clearly enveloping the girl.

The man's thrusts became harder and Jo could hear the wet smack as their bodies slapped together. The girl was moaning aloud, her head back, her eyes closed, her hair spilling out behind her. Then Jo saw his buttocks tighten and she knew he was about to come.

They orgasmed simultaneously, both shouting aloud, his hips moving in jerks as he spurted his spunk into her. Jo watched in silent frustration as the two of them writhed together on the towel, locked in a tight embrace, their shouts gradually dying to moans as they collapsed together, panting with their exertions.

Jo stayed where she was for a moment longer, then slid

back down the dune, jealous and frustrated, sliding her finger out of her crack and contemplating how inadequate it was compared with the reality of a thick erection.

Chapter 2

Jo lay on the hot sand, still listening to the couple on the other side of the dune. It had been more than ten minutes now since she had witnessed their coupling and in that time they had hardly spoken. From what little had been said, though, Jo had deduced that the man was clearly embarrassed by their encounter. In fact, now that his ardour had abated, James had seemed in rather a hurry to go and, having dressed, was already in the process of saying his goodbyes to the lovely young woman with whom he had been so recently intimate.

Jo sighed. She was still highly aroused by what she had seen and once again her hand was buried inside her bikini bottom, where she was gently teasing her love bud. But her fingers just didn't seem enough after what she had witnessed and simply succeeded in prolonging her frustration.

'Enjoy the show?'

Jo jumped at the voice that suddenly sounded so close to her ear. She swung round to see the girl, still naked, standing at the top of the dune, gazing down at her. She opened her mouth to speak, but no words would come. Instead she simply stared at the young blonde.

'Well,' the girl persisted. 'Did you like what you saw?'

Still Jo was struck dumb, completely taken aback by the girl's sudden appearance.

'I can see it must have turned you on,' the new arrival continued. 'A finger's never as good as the real thing, though, is it?'

Jo looked down and realised with horror that her hand was

still down the front of her bikini bottom. She snatched it out, her face scarlet.

'Hey, no need to stop,' said the blonde. 'I don't mind.'

'What do you want?' Jo found her voice at last, though it came out more as a hoarse croak.

'Just to ask whether you'd enjoyed watching us fuck.'

'I . . . I don't know what you mean.'

'Don't give me that. You saw exactly what happened. You were watching the whole thing.'

'You knew I was there?'

'Sure.'

'You saw me?'

'Oh, for god's sake, do you think I'm blind? I knew you were there from the moment I stepped on the beach.'

'Yet you still went ahead?'

'Of course. After all, we were only screwing. Listen, I've got a bottle of wine going warm in my bag. Why don't you come and join me?'

'I'm not sure . . .'

'Of course you are. It's good stuff. French, and still ice cold. Come on.'

'I still don't think . . .'

'Well, please yourself. The invitation's there.'

With that, the girl turned and headed off down the dune.

Jo lay where she was, her mind confused. She knew it had been wrong to play the voyeur as she had and the fact that she had been caught in the act was mortifying. Yet the girl seemed so cool. As cool, in fact, as she had been when discovered by the man not much more than half an hour earlier. Even so, Jo's own behaviour had been inexcusable and she wondered whether she should simply grab her bag and make a dash for it. But that seemed a cowardly way to behave, particularly considering the other girl's nonchalance. Besides, the young blonde intrigued her. She wanted to know more about her apparently wanton behaviour.

Slowly she climbed the dune. As she crested the top she

saw that the girl was once again settled on the rug and was engaged in pouring two glasses of white wine. She smiled and beckoned when she saw Jo.

Jo made her way down to where the girl sat, holding out one of the glasses. She accepted it. It felt surprisingly cool considering how long the bag had lain in the sun. She sipped the wine, savouring its rich fruity taste.

'See, I told you it tasted good,' said the girl. 'I keep it well wrapped, you see. It's amazing how long it stays cold. Sit down.'

Jo settled down on the towel, acutely aware that only a short time before it had been the young man who had been in the same position.

'How long did you know I was there?' she asked.

'Right from the start. I came round the back of the beach to make sure nobody was there. When I saw you in the dunes I nearly chickened out. Then I thought, what the hell?'

'You knew even before you set foot on the beach?'

'Sure. That's why I stopped so close to you. I thought being watched might be more fun.'

'I don't understand.'

'Sorry. Maybe I'd better start from the beginning. What's your name, by the way?'

'Jo.'

'Mine's Chris.'

Jo took the girl's proffered hand and shook it solemnly, wondering for a second if this was some kind of odd dream. Here she was, sipping wine on the beach with a naked girl who she had just witnessed being fucked by a casual passer-by. Even now she could see the spunk dribbling from the girl's sex onto the towel beneath. Yet she showed no sign of embarrassment, lying back, propped up on her elbows, her legs slightly spread.

'What you were witnessing there, Jo, was my liberation. My shaking of the bonds of convention. Chris Peters is now a free woman.'

15

'Free from what?'

'Look, I won't bore you with the details. Suffice to say my first long-term relationship just ended. Bastard was screwing around and I never knew. Caught him at it one afternoon in my bedroom. My bedroom! The sod didn't even have the decency to use a motel to screw his floozy. Upshot was a major row, much flying crockery and little me packing up and walking out.'

'Sounds a familiar story.'

'You too?'

'Afraid so. Except I was married to mine. That makes the whole thing even more messy.'

'I'm sorry.'

'Don't be. I'm well rid of him. It's just taking a while to readjust.'

Chris picked up the bottle and refilled their glasses.

'That's the problem,' she said. 'You can't shake the whole thing out of your mind. I spent weeks on my own, cursing and crying in equal shares. And then there was the sex.'

'The sex?'

'Or perhaps I should say lack of it. I mean, a girl's got her needs, Jo. Fingers and a vibrator are all very well, but there's nothing like the real thing, don't you think?'

Jo dropped her eyes. 'I suppose so.'

'So tell me, Jo. How many men have you had since your divorce?'

Jo looked up, shocked by the intimacy of the question.

'Sorry. Bit too personal I guess.'

'No, that's all right. The answer's none, actually.'

'And how long has it been since you last got laid?'

'About a year I guess.'

'Six months for me. Oh, until just now of course.'

'Six months? You mean you don't . . .'

'Fuck complete strangers as a matter of habit? Not usually.'

'But why now?'

'I'm not sure. I just suddenly thought, life's too short. Why

16

let it stay a fantasy for the rest of my life?'

'A fantasy?'

'Sure. All my life I've had this scenario in my mind. I'm laying naked on a public beach, and some guy discovers me there. He doesn't muck about, just takes me then and there.'

'And you were re-enacting the fantasy this afternoon?'

'That's right. It wasn't quite as I'd imagined it. After all, he took a bit of persuading. But he came through in the end. Besides, being watched was an extra dimension that hadn't occurred to me.'

'So I wasn't part of the original plan?'

'No. But as soon as I saw you there, I knew you had to watch.'

'But how did you know it would happen like that? I mean anybody could have come along.'

Chris laughed. 'Actually I planned the whole thing pretty carefully.'

'But how?'

'Well I knew about this beach from when I lived here as a kid. So I've been down here every day for the last three days and checked it out. That guy's staying at a little place about half a mile away. Every day he walks down to the pub in the next village. Regular as clockwork. So you see I was pretty certain of success.'

'But what if he'd attacked you?'

'He practically did. That's the best shafting I've had for ages. Anyhow, that possibility lent a degree of risk to the whole thing. And that made it even more exciting.'

'As well as being watched?'

'Yeah, that really was a bonus. You didn't mind, did you?'

'It was a bit unexpected,' said Jo. 'But very sexy.'

'And you were really turned on?'

'Yes,' said Chris. 'Too damned turned on. It made me horny as hell.'

'Do you want to do something about it?'

Jo stared at her companion. 'What do you mean?'

17

'I could give you an orgasm.'

'But you're not a lesbian?'

'That's right. And neither are you. But that doesn't mean we can't try things. After all I'm having a good day for experimenting. You'd be my first female conquest.'

Jo eyed the girl's body, an odd thrill running through her as she contemplated the suggestion.

'No,' she said, shaking her head. 'I couldn't.'

'Why not?' asked Chris. She moved closer, kneeling up next to Jo, so close that Jo could smell her arousal. 'I'd really like to.'

'What if someone were to come along?'

Chris giggled. 'They'd probably get as much of a thrill as you did.'

Jo was silent for a moment. The closeness of the naked girl was having an unexpected effect on her and she was quite unable to rid her mind of the image of the couple fucking on the beach. When Chris reached out a hand and placed it on her knee she said nothing, but did not attempt to brush it away.

The girl came closer, her hand moving up to stroke Jo's hair. She took her cheeks between the palms of her hands and pulled her face towards her own. Their lips met.

To Jo, the contact was like an electric shock. For a second she kept her mouth closed. Then Chris pressed harder and she opened it, allowing Chris's tongue inside. All at once the girl's arms were about her, pulling her close, her breasts pressed hard against Jo's own.

The kiss was wonderful and Jo closed her eyes, suddenly thoroughly aroused by the intimate contact with this beautiful girl. She licked at the tongue in her mouth, trying to draw it further inside, the fire in her crotch increasing as she ground her lips bruisingly against Chris's.

When she felt Chris's hands fumbling with the catch of her bikini top, she tried to protest, but her voice was muffled by the kiss. The top was strapless and in no time it was off,

18

tossed aside in the sand, and she felt her breasts pressed against another woman's for the first time. It felt great, the softness of Chris's breasts an odd contrast to the hard buds of the nipples.

Suddenly Chris broke off the kiss, sitting back on her heels and gazing into Jo's eyes. She reached out and ran her fingers over Jo's breasts, sending more spasms of pleasure through her body.

'You've got gorgeous tits, Jo,' she breathed.

'So have you.'

'Lie down on the towel.'

Jo gazed uncertainly about her. 'I'm not sure . . .'

'Yes you are,' said Chris, squeezing her breasts again. 'You want it – and I want to give it to you.'

She took hold of Jo's shoulders and began pressing her backwards. For a second Jo resisted, then she allowed herself to be pushed down until she was flat on her back. She lay there, gazing down between her breasts at the young woman who seemed suddenly to be taking charge of her emotions.

When Chris reached for the waistband of her bikini bottoms, Jo made no protest. In fact she lifted her hips, allowing the brief garment to be slipped down her thighs, over her ankles and off. She stared down at her body. Her pubic hair was as dark as that on her head, forming a neat vee that pointed down towards the centre of her desires. She knew her sex lips were wet and that the swelling of her clitoris would be evident. She wondered what Chris must think of her, but was past caring now. When she felt the softness of the other girl's hand as it slid up her thigh, she found herself parting her legs even further.

'Oh!'

She gasped with surprise and desire as she felt Chris's fingers trace the length of her slit. It seemed ages since anyone had touched her down there and her response was immediate, her sex lips convulsing involuntarily at the contact.

Chris began to rub Jo's sex, taking her clitoris between

finger and thumb and teasing it out, making it still harder as she did so. Jo began to moan aloud, her hands reaching up and caressing her own bare breasts as she revelled in the deliciousness of Chris's touch.

Chris moved her hand lower, prising apart the folds of Jo's sex and probing at the entrance to her vagina. Then she slid a finger all the way in, eliciting a cry from the prostate girl.

'That feel good?' Chris asked.

'Oh god yes, Chris,' gasped Jo.

'You want some more.'

'Yes. Yes please.'

She moaned aloud as she felt a second finger penetrate her, forcing her sex still wider open as it delved into her most intimate place. She lifted her backside from the sand, pressing her open sex hard against Chris's fingers as whimpers of pleasure escaped her lips. Chris began moving her hand back and forth, sending electric shocks of pleasure through Jo's body as she revelled in the treatment she was receiving.

Suddenly the fingers were withdrawn and Jo gave a small cry of disappointment as she felt her sex lips contracting against empty air. She gazed down at her companion, a questioning look on her face, one that turned to astonishment as she saw the blonde down on all fours, her delicious breasts dangling as she brought her face closer to Jo's open cunt.

'Ah!'

Jo gasped as Chris's tongue began to lick at her inner thigh, lapping up the juices that had leaked there whilst she had been frigging her. The sensation was at once exquisite and frustrating as Jo's sex ached to be touched again.

Slowly, inexorably, Chris's tongue worked its way up over Jo's creamy white flesh, moving ever closer to the gaping pinkness of her love hole. Jo moaned with frustration, pushing her pubis up at Chris's face, willing her to go all the way.

When the tip of Chris's tongue touched her clitoris, Jo almost screamed with relief, her fingers caressing the hard knobs of her nipples as she raised her sex up and offered it to her companion. Chris took the solid little nodule between her teeth, holding it there whilst her tongue darted back and forth over it, bringing new spasms of delight from Jo. Then she slid her fingers up the inside of Jo's thighs, penetrating her with her thumbs and forcing her vagina open.

'Oh god!'

The words were almost shouted as Jo felt Chris's tongue delve into her sex, sliding deep inside her, snaking about as the girl drank the juices that flowed from her, bringing her to the very brink of ecstasy.

Jo's orgasm was loud and violent, hoarse cries ringing in the air as her naked body writhed about on the towel. Chris kept her lips locked against the dark girl's vagina, licking and sucking at her whilst she thrashed about, her breasts shaking back and forth as she pumped her hips up against Chris's face, prolonging the pleasure for as long as she was able.

At last, though, Jo began to come down, the tension slowly draining from her muscles as blessed relief swept through her. She had had no idea how badly she had needed to come, the frustrations of long abstinence suddenly relieved in that delicious act of cunnilingus.

Christ went on lapping at her sex until Jo was finally still, spread-eagled across the towel, her sex lips still twitching slightly as she slowly regained her breath. When she finally raised her head, Jo could see that Chris's chin and neck were shiny with a mixture of love juice and saliva. As she watched, the girl crawled forward onto her, her smooth, naked flesh pressing against her own. When they finally came face to face, Chris lowered her lips over Jo's, kissing her with a passion that Jo had not experienced for as long as she could remember.

Chapter 3

'Chris! Over here!'

Jo waved at the blonde girl over the heads of the other people in the wine bar. As she did so, she saw Chris turn and a smile of recognition cross her face. She began to make her way towards the table where Jo was sitting alone.

As the girl approached, Jo studied her. She was dressed in a pair of blue jeans that hugged her body beautifully, showing off the smooth contours of her hips and the slenderness of her legs. The jeans ended a good ten inches above her ankles, revealing their slim shapeliness and the daintiness of her feet, on which she wore red high-heeled shoes. On top she wore a tight, short T-shirt that left her midriff bare. Her breasts bulged delightfully, the dark outline of the nipples revealing that she wore no bra.

It was, Jo thought, the first time that she had seen Chris clothed. As she shimmied towards her, her shiny blonde hair bouncing with every step, she reflected on what a beauty she was.

'Hi, Jo.'

At once the blonde girl's dazzling smile captivated Jo, taking her mind back to their meeting on the beach. It had been almost four weeks ago that it had happened, yet the encounter had dominated her thoughts ever since, and she had found herself lying awake at night, her mind filled with the image of the naked blonde licking enthusiastically at her open sex.

But something else had been playing in Jo's mind, too. It was Chris's words when the two had first met. Her confession about the fantasy that she had nurtured for so long and that James had brought to life. She had pondered hard on the idea of a woman having such fantasies, and on the desire to make them come true. It was this that had finally prompted her to set about tracking down the young blonde.

It hadn't been difficult. She had returned to Cornwall for a long weekend and had made some discreet enquiries as to where Chris had been staying. Before long she had found out the full name and address of her seductress and had located her in the phone book. A quick call to the surprised young woman and here they were, meeting in a London wine bar.

Chris kissed Jo on the lips. It was only a peck really, but the closeness and scent of the girl recalled in a flash the passions of that hot afternoon on the beach. Jo felt a tremor run through her as the memories flooded back.

'What are you drinking?' she asked, managing to keep her voice steady.

'Gin and tonic.'

Jo got the waiter's attention and ordered two gin and tonics. Whilst they waited for them to be delivered, the two girls made small talk. Jo found herself suddenly embarrassed to be in Chris's presence after the intimacy of their first meeting, but Chris seemed quite unworried about the whole situation, chatting easily about the weather and her journey to the wine bar.

The waiter brought the drinks and retired, and Chris moved her chair closer to Jo's, her manner suddenly conspiratorial.

'So what's this all about, Jo?' she asked. 'Suddenly decided you're a lesbian after all and looking for a few tips?'

Jo blushed, embarrassed by the girl's forwardness. Despite having planned what she wanted to say to Chris, and having rehearsed it a dozen times, she suddenly found herself struggling to know where to begin.

'It's nothing like that,' she said.

'So you don't fancy me after all?'

'No. I mean yes. Well actually . . .'

Chris laughed aloud. 'Take it easy, Jo,' she said. 'It was just a joke. Now tell me, what's this about?'

'Well, you know what you did. On the beach.'

'Gave you an orgasm.'

'Shh! Not so loud!' said Jo, glancing about her. 'Anyhow, it wasn't that.'

'What then?'

'The thing with that guy, James. You said it was to fulfil a fantasy.'

'That's right.'

'Tell me about it.'

'What's to tell? I used to have this fantasy about sunbathing naked on a beach and being discovered by a complete stranger, who then fucks me. I just thought I'd try and make it come true. So I did.'

'But didn't the risk you ran put you off?'

'Certainly. But as it turned out, the risk paid off. And boy was it good. I've brought myself off just thinking about it practically every night since it happened. I only wish I'd got it on video.'

'Video!' said Jo, suddenly. 'That's an idea! And it might just work. Why didn't I think of that?'

Chris eyed her dark-haired companion. 'Listen, Jo,' she said. 'Why not just get to the point of what this is all about?'

Jo hesitated, then took a deep breath.

'Well,' she said. 'It's all about women who have fantasies. Sexual ones.'

Chris sat forward in her seat, cupping her chin in her hand. 'Go on,' she said.

'That fantasy of yours. Do you think other women have them?'

'What, do they imagine being made love to by a stranger on a beach?'

'Yes. But other things as well.'

'What kind of things?'

Jo reached into her shopping bag and brought out a small

pile of magazines. She laid them on the table. They were all women's titles, modern magazines for the modern girl and, judging from the covers, their subject matter was largely concerned with sex.

'I've been doing a bit of research,' said Jo. 'Mainly the letters pages of these magazines, although some of the articles seem relevant too.'

'What do you mean?'

'Well, take this, for instance.' Jo picked up one of the magazines and flicked through it. Then she folded the page over and began to read aloud.

'"I have a recurrent dream in which I am walking in a back street when I am surrounded by a gang of young men. At first I think they want my money, but instead they force me to remove my dress. I am wearing no underwear, so I am left standing naked in the street in front of them. Then two of them grab my arms whilst a third begins to touch me up."'

'Wow,' put in Chris. 'Great fantasy. It's even turning me on.'

'There's more. "Soon I am incredibly aroused, so that when they make me lie down in the street and spread my legs I don't hesitate. They take me one after another, giving me orgasm after orgasm. Afterwards they just leave me lying naked in the gutter, my body covered in their semen."'

'And I thought I had eccentric ideas.'

'Yes,' said Jo. 'But listen to this bit. "When I tell my boyfriend about this dream he just laughs and doesn't want to know. I think it embarrasses him. The point is, I'm obsessed with the idea and can't get it out of my mind. I even went out one night to walk the streets with no underwear on, but soon got scared and came home."'

'I'm not surprised,' said Chris. 'A lonely beach in Cornwall is one thing, but walking the streets of London . . .'

'That's not the only letter like that, though,' said Jo. 'Listen to this. "I have a fantasy that I go skinny dipping in a lake and get swept away by the current. When I finally get out I am miles from my clothes and have to walk naked through the woods. A pair of men out hunting find me but will not help me unless I surrender my body to them. Having no choice I do so and both take me then and there on the grass."'

'Gosh, these women have quite an imagination,' said Chris. 'I should read more of those mags.'

'And there's lots more,' said Jo. 'All of them desperate for some sexual excitement.'

'That's fine, Jo. But what's it got to do with us?'

'Are you working at the moment, Chris?'

'What, at this moment?'

'You know what I mean.'

'Well, I'm not in permanent employment. I'm registered at an agency, actually, but there's not much about right now.'

'Got any money put by?'

'A bit. Listen, Jo, where's this all leading to?'

Jo stared into Chris's eyes. 'I'm putting a business proposition to you, Chris. How would you like to go into partnership with me?'

'What kind of business?'

'The fantasy business.'

'Look, maybe I'm being a bit slow here, but none of this is making sense at the moment.'

'All right. Business depends on supply and demand, right?'

'Yes.'

Jo held up the magazines. 'Well, here's the demand.'

'You mean . . .'

'The women's fantasies. And these must be just the tip of the iceberg. There must be thousands of frustrated girls out there just dying for their dreams to come true. And we can make them.'

'But how?'

'Simple. We find ourselves some studs willing to play the parts and a series of suitable locations, then we advertise.'

Chris shook her head. 'It's a crazy idea.'

'Crazy, maybe. But viable just the same. Imagine if you had come across an opportunity to have your fantasy fulfilled a few weeks ago. Wouldn't you have gone for it?'

'Well, yes but . . .'

'Of course you would. So would I.'

'You've got a fantasy too?'

Jo blushed. 'Sort of.'

'Tell me.'

'It doesn't matter.'

'Come on, Jo.'

'Well . . . It's simple really. I just imagine being a naked slave at a Roman orgy.'

'And?'

'And my master forces me to have sex in all kinds of different ways with loads of men.'

'And women?'

'Yes. But look, that's not important right now. The fact is that we'd both pay to have our fantasies fulfilled, right?'

'Right.'

'Then the market must exist. Listen, Chris, I've got this whole thing worked out. We find ourselves some guys who'll do the business, then we hire an office and advertise. The initial outlay is really quite small. But I need a partner.'

Chris sat back in her chair, eyeing Jo carefully. 'You're really serious about this, aren't you?' she said.

Jo nodded.

'And how much would we charge for this service?'

'It depends what they want. I've run a few figures through my PC and I've got a pretty good idea what's required.'

Jo pulled a sheet of paper from her bag and placed it on top of the magazines. Chris picked it up and studied it for a full five minutes, occasionally asking questions about one figure or another. Jo sat watching her, nervously sipping at her drink. At last Chris put down the sheet.

'This is pretty thorough,' she said approvingly.

'Then you'll join me?'

Chris was silent for a moment, then nodded.

'Yeah,' she said. 'Besides, recruiting the staff might be lots of fun.'

Chapter 4

Jo sat down behind the desk and stared about her. The office was not large and the decor was hardly modern. In fact the whole place needed decorating. The desk had seen better days too, its surface scratched and the edges chipped, but it was solid enough to support the personal computer that sat in the middle. On one side of her was a grey metal filing cabinet they had picked up at an auction and on the other was a similar desk, the surface of which was bare. Across the room was a coat stand and a single table on which stood a kettle and some jars and cups. It wasn't exactly the executive suite, she reflected, but it was a proper office, and that was a start.

The office was on the sixth floor of a block on the west side of London. The foyer was rather dingy and the single lift creaked and wheezed to reach the top. The doorman looked as if he was part of the fixtures and, on first seeing him, Jo had been tempted to run a feather duster over him. When she and Chris had viewed the place, she had certainly had her misgivings, but one look at the rent being charged elsewhere had made her mind up and they had moved in almost at once.

Jo glanced up at the clock on the wall. It was nearly ten o'clock. Chris should have been here by now. After all, the interview was at half past. They needed time to discuss the candidates before they arrived and she valued Chris's opinion.

Jo reflected on the way her relationship with the lovely young blonde had developed over the past few weeks. Once Chris had committed herself to the project, she had proved an enthusiastic and hard-working partner. It was she who had found the office through an old friend and had suggested they visit the local auction to furnish it. Then she and Jo had spent most of the following week cleaning, painting and repairing, transforming a dingy, dusty little room into an office in which they could properly do business. Now they were ready for the next phase in bringing Jo's idea to life.

All at once there was a clatter in the corridor outside and Chris staggered in, carrying two bulging carrier bags. She dumped them on the desk and turned to face Jo.

'Jesus that lift is a nightmare,' she gasped. 'This time I really didn't think it was going to make it. It doesn't help having that doorman standing at the bottom and staring up my skirt every time I use it.'

'Maybe you should try a longer skirt, then,' giggled Jo.

It was true that her friend's skirt was extremely short, no more than a narrow band of yellow material that went round her hips, threatening to reveal her panties at any moment. The lift had no doors as such, being more like a cage, and the view from below as she ascended must have been difficult for the commissionaire to resist. Her top wasn't exactly modest, either, being tight and low-cut, revealing a wide expanse of cleavage.

Chris slumped down into the chair behind her own desk. 'Get the kettle on then, Jo,' she ordered. 'Let's start as we mean to go on.'

Jo rose and crossed to the table, where she plugged in the battered old kettle. It began to hiss loudly almost at once. Jo eyed it doubtfully.

'Do you think this place really exudes the businesslike air we were looking for?' she asked.

'No. That's why I'm late. I've been getting a few things together. Look at these.'

Chris began unpacking the bags on her desk. She pulled out half a dozen ring binders filled with papers.

'What on earth are those?' asked Jo.

'I haven't a clue. They were in a skip round the back of the building but at least they make us look established. Here, stack them on top of the filing cabinet, then take one and leave it open on your desk.'

Jo did as she asked, whilst Chris scattered more papers about their two desks. Then she produced a pair of old pen holders, complete with biros and a well full of paper clips.

'Well, the place certainly looks occupied now,' said Jo.

'And that's not all. Look at this.'

From one of the bags, Chris produced a telephone. It was an early push-button model, that had seen better days, its flex ending in bare wires.

'But we're not getting connected till Friday,' protested Jo.

'I know that. Besides, I doubt if this thing will ever be connected again. But who's to know that?'

She placed the instrument in front of her and dangled the flex between the two desks so that the end was out of sight.

'Hey presto!' she said.

Jo laughed. 'I've got to hand it to you, Chris,' she said. 'It all looks great.'

'And that's not all,' said her friend. 'All that stuff came from the skip, but I had these made up. Take a look.'

She pulled out two long triangular blocks of wood. On one face of each was a plaque. The first said 'Jo Spencer' and the second 'Chris Peters'. She placed one on each desk, then stood back to admire the effect.

'Very professional,' she said. 'And one final touch.'

She held up a sign, about a foot long. Across it was written 'Fantasy & Co'.

'That's to go on the door,' she said. 'I've already got matey downstairs putting one up in the lobby. One glance down my cleavage and he was putty in my hands.'

Jo giggled. 'You've really done a great job, Chris,' she said.

'Well, we've got to look businesslike for these interviews,' said her friend. 'Now where's that coffee?'

Twenty minutes later the two girls were ready for their first interview. They had advertised in diverse places, including actors' publications, body-building magazines and journals aimed specifically at men. They had received an encouraging number of replies and had spent many hours sifting through and singling out those they wanted to meet. Today it was a couple of men called Doug and Mark, who shared a flat in North London and had replied to an ad in one of the more upmarket men's magazines.

The two girls took their places behind their desks. Jo was feeling decidedly nervous and, judging from the tense expression on Chris's face, she guessed that her partner had similar misgivings.

'Do you think they'll come?' she asked.

'They'd bloody better,' said Chris. 'I didn't put on this skirt and blouse simply to impress you.'

'What if they're not suitable?'

'That's what this interview's for isn't it? Now hush. Look busy. I think I can hear the lift opening.'

Sure enough there was a clatter as the metal grille was pushed apart, then the sound of footsteps and low voices in the corridor. A few seconds later there was a knock on the door.

'Come in,' called Chris.

The door opened and two men stepped inside. They stood for a moment just inside the doorway, gazing about the room. Then Jo rose to her feet.

'Hi,' she said. 'I'm Jo Spencer and this is Chris Peters. We own Fantasy & Co.'

The first of the men stepped forward. 'I'm Doug,' he said. 'And this is Mark.'

As handshakes were exchanged, Jo eyed the two men carefully. Both were tall, at least six foot two inches, with Mark slightly taller than Doug. Both had broad shoulders and narrow hips and were clearly no strangers to working out. Doug had short dark hair parted at one side. His eyes were brown and intense and his face wore a disarming smile.

Mark's hair, by contrast, was long and blond, his eyes blue. His face was tanned and, Jo reflected, he wouldn't have looked out of place on Bondai beach. Both men were in their early twenties, and both were extremely good-looking.

Chris brought chairs forward for the two men whilst Jo poured coffees from a pot she had prepared earlier. The kettle was put away out of sight and she had managed to find four mugs that almost matched. When at last they were settled, the interview began.

Jo started by explaining the purpose of Fantasy & Co. As she did so, the men's eyes widened. By the time she had finished they were shaking their heads in astonishment.

'So what do you think?' she asked.

'Do you really think women will go for that?' asked Doug.

'Sure they will,' replied Chris. 'We've done our research and we think there's money to be made.'

'And our job will be to play a part?'

'That's right.'

'Let me get this straight,' said Mark. 'You actually want us to go all the way with these women?'

'If that's what they ask of you. You'll be role playing, remember, and the scenario will be explained beforehand.'

'According to your CVs, you've both worked as escorts,' said Jo.

The pair nodded.

'Didn't that involve a bit of role playing?'

'I guess so,' said Doug.

'And anything else?'

Doug smiled. 'We were sometimes called on for extra duties.'

'Well, this will be no different, except that you'll have your instructions up front, before you start.'

'So what do you think?' asked Chris.

Doug turned to his friend. 'If you can find the ladies, I guess we can perform, eh Mark?'

Mark nodded.

'Right,' said Chris. 'It just remains to inspect the merchandise. Would you mind stripping off please?'

Jo turned and stared at Chris in surprise, totally taken aback by the order. She leaned close to her partner's ear.

'You sure that's necessary?' she asked.

'Certainly. Why not? Besides, I quite fancy seeing these two hunks in the buff. Don't be such a prude, Jo.'

They turned back to the two men, who were gazing expectantly at them.

'Come on,' said Chris. 'If you want this job you'll need to show us your credentials.'

The pair exchanged a glance, then slowly rose to their feet. They began to strip.

Both removed their T-shirts first. Beneath, their chests were indeed broad, Doug's being matted with dark hair whilst Mark's was shaved and smooth. They kicked off their trainers, then pulled off their jeans. Both wore briefs and Jo found herself licking her lips as she eyed the bulges inside.

Once again the men hesitated, and Doug raised an eyebrow. Chris nodded.

They slipped down their briefs and dropped them onto the chairs. Then they stood, hands by their sides, whilst the two girls examined their naked bodies.

The men certainly had big cocks. Doug's was thick and circumcised, whilst Mark's was longer with the foreskin intact. Both had heavy scrotums, their balls dangling pendulously. Doug's pubic hair was a thick, wiry thatch whilst Mark's was fairer and less bushy.

'Turn round,' ordered Chris.

The men shuffled round until they were facing the door. They showed a pair of tight, pert behinds and muscular backs.

'The equipment looks all right to me,' said Chris. 'Now we just need to make sure it's in working order.'

Jo watched in fascinated amazement as the blonde girl rose to her feet and made her way round to the front of the desks.

'Come here,' she said.

The two men turned and moved forward. Then Jo's jaw dropped as Chris reached out and took the men's cocks in her hands.

She began to caress them, rubbing her fingers up and down and squeezing the soft flesh. Almost at once they began to thicken and lengthen in her hands. The men stood, expressionless before her, only a slight tensing of their muscles betraying their emotions as the lovely young blonde caressed their manhoods.

Chris worked easily and expertly, her hands travelling up and down the men's shafts as they began to stiffen. Slowly, as if in unison, the two cocks rose until at last they stood stiffly to attention, jutting up pink and thick from the men's groins.

'What do you think, Jo?' asked Chris. 'You reckon they'll do?'

Jo nodded, quite unable to speak for a moment as she fixed her eyes on the men's penises. Inside her, though, was a feeling she hadn't experienced since she had seen James undress on the beach. A thrill of pleasure ran through her as she remembered what she had witnessed.

Chris winked at her. 'You fancy one of these?' she asked.

Jo said nothing, but her expression told all.

'Come on, Jo,' said Chris. 'Come and feel what Doug's got to offer.'

Jo didn't move. Suddenly the air was filled with a sexual tension that had not been there only moments before. The two men eyed the girls, their stiff cocks twitching as Jo hesitated.

Jo glanced from one face to another. She hadn't expected this. It had been enough of a shock that Chris had made the men strip, but now it was clear that she intended to go a good deal further, and she obviously expected Jo to do the same. If the truth was told, she was enormously tempted. Doug and Mark were two of the most gorgeous hunks she had seen in a long time and she found herself longing to feel the hardness of Doug's cock under her fingers.

In the end it was Chris who broke the tension. She simply took Jo's hand and guided her around the desk to where the two naked men were standing, placing her hand onto Doug's shaft.

Jo closed her fingers about it, a thrill running through her as she felt it twitch. It was hot to the touch and a small drop of moisture had formed at the tip. She reached beneath with the other hand and took hold of his balls, stroking and squeezing them and bringing a soft moan from his lips.

A rustle of clothing distracted Jo and she turned to see Mark pulling Chris's top over her head. Once again Jo was able to feast her eyes on the blonde girl's lovely breasts as they fell free, the nipples already stiff with arousal. Mark dropped the top onto the floor, then closed his hands over her firm mammaries, squeezing and caressing them as she gasped with pleasure.

Then Jo felt fingers at her own blouse, beginning to undo the buttons. She looked up at Doug, who was staring intently into her eyes as his fingers worked down her front. All of a sudden she realised what was about to happen to her and was shocked to find how turned on she was. After all she barely knew Doug, yet she was allowing him to take off her top whilst she stood brazenly caressing his cock and balls.

Her bra catch was at the front and Doug found it without difficulty. He flicked it undone, revealing Jo's breasts. Whilst not as large as Chris's they were, if anything, even firmer, and her nipples too stood out stiffly.

The feel of Doug's large hands on her bare flesh sent a delicious shiver through Jo's body. She couldn't remember the last time a man had touched her so intimately. More to the point, she couldn't understand why she had waited so long to be touched again.

At that moment, she had an overwhelming desire to taste Doug's cock. She looked down at its swollen end and the bead of moisture which had grown in size and was now trickling down over the shiny purple flesh. In an instant she had dropped to her knees and, taking his heavy shaft in her hand, guided it towards her mouth. She closed her lips about him, licking at the tip and tasting his arousal. He moaned, and she felt his scrotum contract under her fingers as his stiffness increased still further. She began to suck hard, moving her head back and forth and licking at his glans at the same time.

Jo glanced out of the corner of her eye and saw that Mark had divested Chris of her skirt. Now all she wore was a pair of tiny white briefs and Jo could see a dark patch about the gusset where her wetness had leaked through. Mark ran his hand down the girl's belly, sliding his fingers under the waistband and feeling for her sex. Chris let out a stifled cry as he slid his hand still lower.

All of a sudden, Jo wanted to be naked. Keeping one hand clamped about Doug's shaft, she shrugged off her blouse and bra, releasing her grip for just long enough to let it fall to the floor. Then she resumed wanking and sucking him whilst reaching for the button at the waist of her skirt. Soon that too lay on the floor beside her.

Loud moans from Chris made Jo turn once more. The blonde was totally naked now, stretched out across her desk, her legs spread wide. Mark was on his knees, his head buried between her thighs, his tongue licking at her sex whilst she writhed beneath him.

With a shock Jo felt herself suddenly lifted from Doug's cock. He raised her until she was looking into his eyes.

'Lie face down across the desk,' he said.

A tremor of lust ran through Jo's body as she heard the words. Doug was taking control, and that was precisely what she needed. She turned and bent forward across the wooden surface, prostrating herself. The wood was hard and cold against her bare flesh and she felt her nipples harden still more as she pressed her breasts down.

Doug told hold of the waistband of Jo's panties and tugged, dragging them down her thighs and off. Then she felt a hard, masculine hand against her thigh, pressing her legs apart, and she complied at once. Jo felt extraordinarily sexy lying there, her legs spread, her cunt open, waiting to be fucked. She found herself raising her backside, offering herself to him as she felt the hardness and heat of his erection brush against the softness of her flesh.

She glanced behind her. Doug was standing, his erection in his hand, rubbing it down the crack of her behind. She felt him pause when he reached her anus, and for a second she thought he was about to bugger her. Then he moved on, and her body lurched forward as he pressed his cock against her open crack.

He paused for a second at the entrance to her vagina, then began to push. Jo gripped the edge of the table, biting her lip as she felt his pressure increase. Suddenly, he was inside her, his meaty weapon sliding home, and she groaned with pleasure and lust at the sensation.

Doug continued to force himself into her until he was buried all the way, and she could feel the roughness of his pubic hair against her sensitive flesh. It felt wonderful to be filled by a real cock again and Jo wondered how she had managed to go so long without sex.

A cry from the desk beside her made her turn, just in time to see Mark sliding his long erection into Chris's sex. The blonde girl was still stretched out on her back across the wooden surface, her legs dangling over the edge, her thighs spread wide. Jo watched as his cock disappeared inside her, bringing further excited cries from her lips.

Then, as if on cue, both men began to fuck their lovely young partners, their backsides working back and forth in unison as they thrust into their prospective employers. Jo gasped with the sheer enjoyment of it as she felt her hips rammed hard against the table edge by the insistence of Doug's assault. He fucked her with long, even strokes, his cock sliding back and forth inside her like a piston. Jo could immediately sense his control as he took her and for a second she was a professional again, noting approvingly that it was she who was being pleasured and that he was intent on ensuring her orgasm before his own. There was no doubt in her mind that such a man would be an asset to her company.

On the next desk, Mark was being similarly attentive to Chris, his large hands caressing her breasts as he pumped his hips back and forth. Chris was clearly in a state of ecstasy, her head shaking from side to side, low whimpering noises escaping her lips as she writhed beneath him. To Jo, the sight of her business partner being so thoroughly rogered served only to increase her own excitement and she turned her attention back to Doug and the wonderful fucking she was receiving from him.

All at once Jo felt a hand worming its way between her breast and the desk top and she looked across to see that Chris had stretched out her arm and was caressing her there, watching her intently as she gasped out her passion. Their eyes met and Chris made a beckoning gesture with her head, then blew her a kiss. It was clear that Doug had not failed to witness this exchange, for at once she felt him take hold of her about the waist and lift her, his cock still imbedded deep inside her. He moved her across onto Chris's desk, so that she lay at an angle to her friend, her face just above the other girl's.

For a few seconds, Jo gazed down at Chris, watching her expressions of pleasure as Mark plunged his cock into her. Then she lowered her face and her lips down over Chris's.

A new spasm of pleasure gripped Jo as she felt Chris's tongue snake into her mouth. Somehow the soft femininity of the girl, combined with the insistent thrusts of the stud behind her, seemed to double her pleasure, and she lost herself in the kiss, her hands reaching for the softness of Chris's breasts.

Jo knew she couldn't last much longer. The pleasure was much too intense and she had been on the edge of her climax for ages now. She looked into Chris's eyes. Her friend too was clearly close to coming and Jo could sense her muscles tensing as she stroked her soft flesh.

Jo's orgasm hit her suddenly, bringing a muffled cry from her lips as she was finally taken over the top. Instantly she realised that Chris was coming too, her climax possibly triggered by Jo's own. No sooner had her cunt muscles tightened about Doug's cock though, than she felt the delicious sensation of his semen pumping into her.

The office rang with their cries as the naked foursome orgasmed simultaneously, the two girls licking at one another's tongues whilst the men continued to thrust their stiff cocks into them. For Jo it was the best orgasm she had ever experienced and she revelled in the way Doug's cock twitched as he pumped his seed into her.

As last, though, they were spent. The two men withdrew their shining cocks, leaving the girls sprawled across one another, their arms flung around each other, their breasts pressed together. They continued to neck for some time, then Jo rolled off her companion to gaze up at the two men, who stood looking down at them.

Inevitably, it was Chris that spoke first.

'Well, guys,' she said, a dreamy smile on her face, 'I guess you got the job.'

Chapter 5

Chris Peters sat behind her desk studying the magazine that lay before her. The appropriate advertisement had been ringed with a red crayon and she read it through for the umpteenth time.

The heading was both bold and explicit:

'Fulfil your wildest fantasies!'

Below, in smaller type, the text went on:

'Bored with your sex life? Looking for excitement? We promise your erotic fantasies will come true. Ring, write or fax us with your own fetish and we'll make it happen. Discretion guaranteed. A souvenir video of the occasion will be yours to watch as often as you like.'

The blurb was followed by numbers and addresses.

Chris read it again, though she had it off by heart by now, then glanced across at the newly installed fax machine and telephone, willing them to spring into life. But they were silent. She shook her head, clenching her fists in frustration. Surely someone should have contacted them by now? The magazine had been on the streets for twenty-four hours already, yet they hadn't received a single response.

Not for the first time, doubts began to assail her. Perhaps this wasn't such a great idea after all. Perhaps women preferred to keep their fantasies to themselves. Maybe she and Jo had completely misread the situation.

Yet Jo had been so sure and her enthusiasm so infectious that Chris had been certain the venture would work. And Jo, despite her naiveté, was pretty shrewd when it came to business matters.

Chris sat back in her seat and thought about her new business partner. In the few weeks she had known Jo they had become very close and had discovered a real rapport that went beyond their sexual escapades. And there had been quite a few of those. Doug and Mark had introduced them to a number of other virile young men and the interviews had tended to go the same way as the first, with the two girls sampling at first hand the kind of treatment their customers would expect.

Chris couldn't remember a time when she had been so sexually active. In the past fortnight she and Jo must have been screwed by ten men at least. At first she had been worried that Jo would be deterred by the wanton way in which she herself had behaved but, once she had got over her initial inhibitions, her friend had taken to the interviews with some enthusiasm, even taking the initiative on some occasions. And there could be no doubting the intensity and authenticity of her orgasms. By the end of the first week, Chris was seeing a totally new woman in Jo. One who had begun to understand the power of her own sexuality, and to appreciate the joys of casual, uncomplicated sex with the string of hunks who had walked into their office.

The two girls had soon put enough men on their books to ensure that the venture would be successful. The idea was that once a client had signed up and agreed the details of what they required, Jo and Chris would contact as many men as were needed and call them in to be briefed. The videoing was to be done by one of the girls, whilst the other coordinated the action, at the same time doing her best to blend into the background.

There was no doubt about it, between them they had

thought of every contingency. And, now that the whole organisation was all set up and ready to go, all they needed were some customers.

All they needed, mused Chris. It sounded like a trivial requirement. But now, as she waited for the phone to ring, she realised that it wasn't trivial. Customers were a vital part of the organisation and without them all this preparation would be wasted.

Chris glanced at her watch. Nearly lunchtime. Jo would be back soon. They had agreed that there was no point in both of them manning the phone during these early stages, although the day before they had both sat in the office, convinced that their first call would come at any minute. Today, however, realising there was nothing to gain from both of them being there, Jo had decided to go to the gym, leaving Chris to mind the store. Now the morning was nearly over and not a single call had come in.

Chris heard the unmistakable creak of the lift arriving, followed by the clatter of the doors being pushed back. She looked up to see the door handle turn and Jo enter the room.

'Anything?'

She shook her head.

Jo's face fell. 'This is not exactly what we expected, is it?'

Chris smiled as reassuringly as she was able. 'Don't get despondent too soon,' she said. 'After all, it's only the second day.'

'But I would have expected something by now,' said Chris. 'Even if it was only an idle enquiry.'

'Just be patient,' said her friend. 'Come on, I'll take you out and buy you lunch.'

Jo sighed. 'Okay.'

'Well don't sound too enthusiastic.'

Jo smiled. 'Sorry, Chris,' she said. 'It's a nice idea. We can leave the phone alone for a while.'

'Maybe we should have got an answering machine.'

'Let's wait and see if we need one. Meanwhile we'll just have to be closed for lunch.'

Chris rose to her feet and grabbed her handbag. 'There's a new bistro just opened up down the street,' she said. 'What say we go down there and put away some quiche and a couple of bottles of plonk?'

'Sounds good to me,' said Jo.

They went out the door, Chris pausing to lock it before they crossed the hall to the lift. Jo pressed the button and, with a groan and a whirr, the cage began to ascend to their floor. It made its way up slowly, eventually creaking to a halt in front of them. Jo pulled open the doors.

They had just closed the doors behind them and were about to press the button for the ground floor when they heard the phone ring. For a second Chris didn't believe her ears. She turned to Jo, her eyes wide.

'Is that . . .?'

It rang again.

'The phone!' shouted Jo. 'It is! The damned thing's actually ringing!'

Chris flung open the lift and raced towards the office. She struggled with the door handle, shaking the door back and forth before she remembered it was locked. She fumbled with the key. Somehow it didn't seem to want to go into the lock. All the time the telephone was trilling away.

At last the key turned and Chris stumbled into the room with Jo close behind her. She almost fell across the desk, snatching the receiver from its cradle and jamming it against her ear.

'Fantasy and Co. Chris speaking.'

'Hello.' It was a woman and she sounded nervous. 'I wonder if you can help me?'

Chapter 6

Paula Curtis sat up in bed, suddenly wide awake. She had been deeply asleep, experiencing a strangely erotic dream. She tried to recapture the images, but they were gone. She leaned over and picked up her alarm clock. It was one o'clock in the morning. With a sigh she replaced the clock on the bedside table and shuffled across the bed to snuggle up against her husband. But there was nobody there.

Of course! He was away all this week at a business conference. She sighed. He may not be much of a lover, but at least he was a source of warmth and comfort to her in the middle of the night. She pulled the duvet about herself and rolled over.

Then she heard the sound. It was a sort of thumping noise and it seemed to be coming from downstairs.

She froze, hardly breathing, straining her ears, but all was silent. She remained listening for a full minute, then rolled over and closed her eyes once more, cursing herself for her nervousness.

Then she heard it again.

There was no doubt about it, something was moving downstairs. Perhaps it was the cat, she told herself, though she knew in her heart that she had put the animal out before coming to bed. Could she have left a window open? It seemed unlikely. She was normally so careful. Doubly so when she was alone in the house.

Slowly, reluctantly, she sat up and lowered her feet to the floor. Then she stood up and tiptoed towards the door. As she did so she glimpsed herself in the bedroom mirror. The light from the window was enough for her to discern her image.

Paula was twenty-three years old, slim, with large, firm breasts that pressed against the silk negligee she wore. The nightdress had been a present from her husband, who had bought it on a business trip to Paris. It barely covered her crotch and below it her legs were long and slender, ending in small, pretty feet. She stood about five foot three inches tall, her brown hair hanging to her shoulders.

Cautiously, she pulled open her bedroom door and listened again. All was silent now, though, and she wondered again if her imagination had been playing tricks on her. *Still*, she thought, *better go downstairs and check.*

She slipped through the doorway and onto the landing, leaning over to check for any signs of life. The house seemed silent and empty. She crept along to the top of the staircase that swept down into the entrance hall of her large house. She began to descend the stairs, making no sound in her bare feet. As she came lower she bent down to see if she could see a light showing, but there was none.

At the foot of the stairs she paused, uncertain what to do. All seemed completely silent now. Perhaps she had imagined the noises after all. Even so, she had better be certain.

She made her way across to the kitchen, opening the door and peering in. It was deserted, the back door closed and bolted. Paula headed for the foot of the stairs once more. This was silly. It had probably just been the furniture creaking or a sound from outside. *Still*, she mused, *better check the living room.*

She pushed the door open and looked in. All seemed quiet. Her hand reached for the light switch and she blinked as the room was suddenly flooded with brightness. Everything seemed to be in its place.

Then she noticed a small brown leather bag open on the floor by one of the chairs. That was odd. She couldn't remember seeing it before. She went across and picked it up, opening it and gazing inside. It was some kind of tool bag, though she had no idea where it had come from.

By the time she heard the sound behind her it was too late. The two men must have been hiding behind the door when she came in. Now they grabbed her arms and pinned them behind her whilst one of them placed a hand across her mouth.

She stared wide-eyed at the pair of them. They were big men with broad chests and powerful arms and they towered over her. They wore stockings over their heads, giving them a grotesque appearance, and they gripped her so hard she almost cried out with the pain.

'I thought you said there was nobody here,' grunted one of them to his companion.

'I didn't think there was. Bert told me the old man was away at some conference. I assumed he'd take his missis with him.'

'Well he didn't, did he?'

The man on her right, the one gagging her, pulled her face round to his.

'Listen, darling,' he hissed. 'You make a sound and I'll have to hurt you. Understand?'

Paula nodded her head vigorously.

Slowly he removed his hand from her mouth, though both kept their grip on her arms.

'Wh-what do you want?' she stammered.

'What do you think?' he asked. Beneath the stocking she could see that he had short, dark hair and he appeared quite young. Standing as he was, so close to her, she knew he could see down her cleavage and she wished she had been wearing something more decent.

'Yeah,' said his companion, whose hair was longer and fair. 'Where's the safe?'

'Safe?'

'Where you keep the money and jewels.'

'There isn't one.'

The dark-haired man twisted her arm, making her wince with the pain.

'Don't give us that, darling. We know your old man's loaded. Now where's it stashed?'

'There's a little bit of jewellery in my dresser upstairs,' she said. 'The rest is kept at the bank for security. There's nothing here worth taking.'

'I reckon she's lying,' said the dark man. 'Think we should get the truth out of her?'

'Nah,' replied his companion. 'Let's just go on casing the joint.'

'What about her?'

'You bring something to keep her quiet for a while?'

'Yeah, I reckon I can keep her out of mischief.'

'Do it then.'

Paula watched fearfully as the man reached into his pocket and pulled out something black and shiny, to which was attached a small rubber ball.

'Open up, darling,' he said, holding it in front of her face.

She shook her head, her eyes wide with consternation. But she had no choice. He took hold of her by the chin and forced her jaw open, jamming the ball into her mouth, then fastening a strap behind her head.

'Mmmf!'

Paula was unable to articulate a word with the gag in her mouth. But the man hadn't finished yet. From another pocket he produced a pair of handcuffs.

'These should keep you out of mischief,' he said with a grin.

He dragged her across to the side of the room and, forcing her hands behind her back, fastened the cuffs round one of her wrists. Then he looped the other one through the pipe of the central heating radiator and snapped it onto her other wrist.

Paula was trapped and helpless, unable to speak or to move. She watched in dismay as the two men stood back to admire their captive. She wished she had at least put on a dressing gown, aware of the inadequacy of the nightie to cover her charms. She knew that the men, too, had not failed to note her state of undress, which was made worse by the fact that one of the straps had slid from her shoulder, partly uncovering her left breast, the large brown areola showing as a half moon above the flimsy material.

The men set about searching for valuables, starting in the living room, then making their way about the house. Paula stood where she was, unable to move or protest as she listened to them moving from room to room. It took about fifteen minutes for them to search the house, after which they returned to the living room.

'Nothing,' said the first man. 'Looks like this little beauty wasn't lying.'

'Seems as if we've had a wasted evening,' said his companion. 'There's nothing here worth taking.'

'I'm not so sure.' The man moved closer to the scantily clad young woman. 'There may be something here we could have.' He reached out a hand and ran it over Paula's breast. Paula drew back slightly at the gesture, yet still she could feel her nipple hardening and she knew it must be visible through the thin material of her nightie.

'What's the idea?' said his mate.

'I was thinking that this young lady could entertain us for the rest of the evening.'

Paula stared at him, then at the second man. She could scarcely believe what she was hearing. Surely they couldn't be serious? But the expressions on the men's faces told her that they were.

'What do you think, darling?' said the dark-haired man. 'Fancy a bit of rough, do you?'

Paula shook her head violently at the suggestion, staring from one to the other. It was an outrageous idea. Yet being in the presence of these virile young men, and at their mercy, was oddly exciting. To her surprise, she was suddenly aware of a warm, wet sensation in her crotch as she contemplated what they were suggesting.

'Let's take a look at her,' said the dark man. Paula shrank back as he approached, but there was no escape. He reached out and snapped the straps on her nightie with two tugs. Then he let go and it fell to the floor.

Paula's face glowed with embarrassment as the two men surveyed her naked body. She glanced down at herself. Her firm breasts jutted proudly, the nipples semi-erect and protruding upwards, long and brown. Her pubic bush was trimmed short, the hairs no more than a few millimetres long, making a smooth dark covering for her mound and drawing attention down to the pink lips of her sex.

'Very nice,' said the man. 'Let's have a feel.'

He reached out and cupped her breasts in his large, rough hands. A shiver ran through Paula's body as he caressed her. She could feel her nipples hardening under his fingers, despite her reluctance for them to do so, and she wondered if her passion was showing on her face as he kneaded her soft flesh.

'I think she likes it,' grinned the man. 'Here, you have a go.'

His blond companion, who had been standing with his eyes fixed on Paula's naked body, now stepped forward and placed a hand on the smooth skin of her thigh.

Paula tried to protest, but the sound came out as no more than a low mumble. She knew that her position was hopeless and she was forced to stand still whilst he ran his fingers up towards her crotch.

'Mmmf!'

The girl's cry was muffled by her gag as the man's hand came in contact with her slit. He ran his large fingers along the length of it, finding her clitoris, which was already hard.

'Christ, she's wet down there,' he said to his companion.

Paula wanted to shake her head, to deny the electric effect their hands were having on her bare flesh, but she couldn't. Instead she found herself opening her legs and pressing her pubis forward against the hand that was touching her in such a delicious manner.

'Let's get that gag off,' said the dark man. 'I want this babe to suck my dick.'

The crudity of his language should have repelled her, she knew, but instead a tremor of excitement ran through her small frame as she felt his hand go to the back of her head and undo her gag.

'You-you mustn't,' she said, trying desperately to keep her voice steady as the other man continued to probe her most private place, his fingers delving deep inside her now, making the muscles of her sex convulse around them as he frigged her.

'Oh, but we must,' said the man, grinning at her. 'And you're going to enjoy it as much as we are.'

Paula wanted desperately to deny it. After all, they were taking her without asking her consent, weren't they? Yet she knew her body was giving all the consent they needed, her hips pressing forward against the man's hand as he worked his fingers in and out of her.

The dark man unzipped his jeans and let them fall to the floor. His large, circumcised cock was already half erect, standing out from his scrotum like a thick sausage. Paula found her eyes fixed on it as he worked the foreskin back and forth, watching her face as he did so.

Suddenly the other man's fingers left her crotch and were on her shoulders, forcing her downwards. She dropped to her knees, watching as the thick pinkness of his friend's cock twitched before her face.

'Open up,' he ordered.

Paula opened her mouth and he guided his cock between her lips. She closed them around it, a thrill running through her as she tasted his manhood. It had been ages since she had last sucked a man's prick. Her husband was not interested in foreplay, being content to penetrate her the moment he was hard, and she had almost forgotten the sensation of having a rampant tool in her mouth.

She felt his penis stiffen almost at once, the softness of his rod turning to an iron hardness as her sucking began to have its effect on him. She sucked hard, wishing her hands were not trapped behind her, so that she could caress his heavy balls as she worked her head back and forth.

It was almost as if the men could read her mind, for at that moment she felt the other man take hold of her wrists and suddenly her hands were free once more. She reached eagerly for the shaft that was filling her mouth so beautifully, working his foreskin back and forth as she slurped at his manhood.

She felt a pair of hands grasp her hips from behind, pulling her back until she was crouched on all fours. Then her thighs were pulled apart and, with a gasp, she felt a pair of large fingers penetrate her vagina and begin to frig her hard.

Paula had never known such pleasure, the scent and taste of cock filling her head whilst strong digits probed her love hole, sending spasms of lust through her small frame. All fear and embarrassment were forgotten as she abandoned herself to the task of bringing pleasure to these two young studs.

Suddenly the dark man stopped thrusting his hips against her face and looked across at his mate. 'This chick's really hot for it,' he said, grinning. 'Let's get her upstairs to the bedroom.'

He snatched his cock from Paula's mouth and the pair of them yanked her to her feet. She stood for a moment, glancing from one to the other. Then the dark man took her arm and began dragging her toward the door.

'What are you going to do?' she asked, stumbling as he pulled her along.

'Give you a damned good shagging,' came the reply.

'But you can't,' she protested, though she knew her voice lacked conviction.

'Try and stop us.'

By now he had reached the foot of the stairs and was dragging her up behind him. His friend followed, slapping at Paula's bare backside if she dared to lag.

They reached the bedroom and the man flung her onto the bed. Before she could move, however, he had snapped the cuffs onto her again, this time wrapping them round the centre of the metal bedstead so that her arms were pulled up above her head. Meanwhile his friend opened a drawer in her dressing table and pulled out a pair of stockings.

The two men took hold of an ankle each and pulled them down to the bottom corners of the bed. Then they tied them there with the stockings. Paula struggled for all she was worth, but was no match for the two strong men. In no time she found herself spread-eagled naked across the bed, her sex lips wide open, her breasts uncovered and unprotected.

The pair stood back to admire their work, their gazes travelling hungrily over Paula's pale young flesh. The dark man still wore no trousers and Paula watched as his stiff cock bobbed up and down in anticipation.

'Don't hurt me,' she begged in a quiet voice.

The men grinned. 'We don't intend to,' said the blond man. 'Just to have some fun with that pretty little body of yours.'

The sound of the words sent a shudder through Paula's body. But it wasn't fear that was making her tremble, it was the anticipation of what these two powerful men had in mind for her.

Once again it was the dark man who moved first, climbing onto the bed and straddling the naked captive. Taking hold of Paula's hair, he dragged her head forward and forced his erection into her mouth. She took it without complaint, immediately sucking hard at it once more. This time he was more demanding, though, thrusting his cock deep into her throat so that she almost gagged.

On the far side of the room, the second man was starting to strip. Paula found herself fascinated by the sight of him divesting himself of his clothes. The shirt came first, revealing a broad and hairless chest. Then came the jeans and finally his pants.

His cock was long and thick, still only half erect, and he

55

stood for a while, watching his friend fuck Paula's face whilst he masturbated slowly.

'Move over,' he said suddenly. 'I want her to taste my dick too.'

The first man slipped his glistening erection from Paula's mouth. She opened her lips to speak, but almost at once a second penis was pressed between her lips and she felt it swell as she resumed her sucking.

Paula was more turned on than she could ever remember being. Her whole body was alive to the sensations that the two studs were awakening in her, and she found herself raising her backside from the bed as if searching for a cock to fill it and release the delicious tension inside her.

'Ah!'

The exclamation was muffled by a mouthful of stiff erection, yet still her cry was audible as she felt her sex lips pulled apart by the dark man's fingers.

'Move over,' he said to his companion. 'I want to get inside her.'

Obligingly the man shifted his position until he was beside Paula's head, dragging her face round so that he didn't miss a stroke. Then she felt the other man climbing onto her, lowering his heavy body over hers. He had discarded his shirt by now and the thick, wiry hair on his chest felt coarse and rough against her swollen nipples.

'Oh!'

Once again she exclaimed aloud, this time at the sensation of a hard cock probing her sex lips, the bulbous end sliding up her slit as he guided it to the very centre of her pleasure.

He began to push, his glans pressing relentlessly against her vagina. Paula felt her flesh resist for a moment, then he was inside her, bringing gasps from his helpless prey as he worked his cock deeper into her with a series of short jabs.

He pushed until he could go no further and the walls of her sex felt stretched to the limit by his organ. Then he began to move his hips back and forth, screwing her gently at first, making her moan with pleasure as she struggled to concentrate on the hefty erection that filled her mouth, the man's balls slapping against her chin as he rammed into her.

Now Paula's pleasure was complete. She had never imagined she would be in a position to satisfy two men at once. Indeed she had married as a virgin and had remained faithful to her husband throughout their marriage. Yet here she now was, tied and helpless whilst two complete strangers pumped their cocks back and forth inside her without thought for her consent, and she was revelling in every second of it.

'My turn for her cunt.'

All of a sudden the cock in her mouth was withdrawn and she realised that the pair were changing round yet again. As before there was no finesse or ceremony, the blond man sliding his cock straight into her vagina whilst his companion climbed onto the bed beside her head.

This time his cock had a new taste to it. The taste of woman. The taste of Paula's own love juices that were flowing so copiously and that she now slurped from his thick shaft. It was a taste that she had never experienced before and it seemed to arouse some odd primeval instinct in her, bringing a new surge of passion as she thrashed about on the bed.

She could tell by the tension in the men that both were highly aroused now and she knew it couldn't be long until they came. The thought spurred her on once more and she thrust her hips up against the cock that filled her vagina, her sex muscles contracting about its length. As she did so, the man on top of her gave a gasp, his face contorting, the veins in his neck standing proud.

He came with a grunt, his cock twitching as his semen spurted into her. At almost the same moment, the second man also orgasmed, filling her mouth with his thick, creamy spunk. Paula's own climax followed almost at once, her cries muffled by the mouthful of sperm that she was struggling to gulp down as more spurted into her mouth.

The two men continued to pump the contents of their balls

into Paula's body as she writhed beneath them, wave after wave of pleasure sweeping through her as she gasped and moaned. By the time the two men withdrew she felt filled with their seed, her sex and mouth both running with the white fluid as she lay helpless on the bed. She looked at the two men, wondering if her ordeal was at last over. But already they were discussing how they would take her next.

Well, she thought to herself, it had all been precisely as she had specified. Fantasy and Co certainly gave you your money's worth.

Chapter 7

Paula was up on the bed, crouched on all fours, as Doug thrust his stiff erection into her, her breasts shaking back and forth with every stroke. It was clear that she was close to her climax. Doug, too, had his brow creased as he fucked the young beauty hard. Suddenly Paula cried aloud and an expression of pure ecstasy passed across her face as an orgasm swept through her, her backside pumping back and forth as yet another helping of spunk filled her already overflowing vagina.

Jo watched their performance with some satisfaction. There was no doubt that the girl was getting precisely what she had paid for, nor that her satisfaction was complete. Their first venture into the fantasy business looked like a total success. She sat back and pressed the button on the remote control, blanking out the TV screen on which she had been watching the copulating couple. Then she turned to the others.

'A pretty good start, I think,' she said.

'Damned good,' agreed Chris. 'You boys did a great job there.'

'It was quite literally a pleasure,' said Doug, and Mark nodded his agreement.

All four of them were sitting in the office, Doug and Mark opposite the two girls' desks. All had had their eyes fixed on the monitor screen. Now they turned to face one another.

'Any feedback from the customer?' asked Chris.

'Certainly,' said Jo. 'She was extremely pleased. Says it was the best night's sex of her life. She even says she might come back for more.'

'Great. And the video looks pretty good too.'

'The tricky bit was getting the camera into the bedroom,' said Jo. 'I had to get in and place it whilst she was still tied to the radiator. In the end it was okay, though. I think she'll be really happy with the results.'

'Better make sure the film gets sent off to her today,' said Chris.

'All taken care of,' said Jo. 'The courier will be here any minute. So we've got our first satisfied customer. I think we can be feeling pretty pleased with ourselves.'

'We certainly delivered what we promised,' agreed her partner. 'How did you get on with the acting part, guys?'

'It was easy,' said Doug. 'I mean the girl was obviously completely involved in the whole fantasy, so she reacted just right.'

'She was bloody gorgeous, too,' put in Mark. 'And really hot for it. We could have shagged her all night.'

'You practically did,' said Jo. 'I was worried that the videotape would run out.'

'Anyhow,' said Chris. 'She wrote us a damned good testimonial and that's the important thing. It'll make a real difference when it comes to attracting more customers.'

'Speaking of which,' said Doug. 'How are the bookings going?'

'A bit slow just at the moment,' said Chris. 'We've got two more commissions coming up next week and a couple of women called asking to come in and talk to us. I think maybe next month we should try to spread the ads a little wider, but otherwise things aren't looking too bad.'

'You gonna need us next week?' asked Mark.

'No. I think we'll break in a couple of the other guys,' said Chris. 'Try and get a handle on who's reliable and who isn't. I'll call you later in the week if anything else comes up.'

'Okay,' said Mark, rising to his feet. 'We'll be getting along then.'

'Yeah, thanks,' said Doug. 'It's certainly one of the oddest night's work I've ever done. And one of the most enjoyable.'

Once the door had closed behind the men, the two girls turned to one another, clearly pleased with themselves.

'Things are really starting to look up,' said Jo. 'I told you this was a great idea.'

Chris grinned. 'It looks like you may be right. Never underestimate the sexual desires of the average British woman. I reckon we could be onto something big here.'

'That Paula was certainly onto something big,' giggled Jo. 'Those guys can really deliver the goods.'

'I could see you were taking more than a passing interest in what was going on up on the screen.'

'It was such a turn-on. Watching those two studs in action is enough to make anyone horny.'

Chris rose from her chair and moved across to where Jo was sitting. She perched on the edge of her desk beside her. Then she reached out and ran a hand through her friend's hair.

'You could always have asked the boys to stay, you know,' she said quietly.

Jo shook her head. 'No,' she said. 'I think maybe we should try to keep our relationship with them as professional as possible. After all, that first time was just part of the audition.'

'Meanwhile, how do you get relief?'

'I'll be okay,' said Jo. 'Just need a cold shower or something.'

'Something like this?'

Chris ran her fingers down the dark girl's neck and let them slip into the top of her dress, which was cut low. She burrowed deep, seeking out Jo's nipples, cupping her breasts in her palm and squeezing them.

'What are you doing?' asked Jo.

'Nothing special.'

61

Chris began undoing the buttons that ran down the front of Jo's dress.

'You can't do that here,' said Jo.

'Why not?'

'Because you mustn't.'

'Why not?' repeated the blonde.

'Because . . .' Jo's voice trailed away and she made no attempt to stop her friend as she slowly worked her fingers down the fastenings on her dress, flicking each one undone in turn.

Jo was not wearing a bra and as the front of the garment fell open her breasts were revealed, the nipples hard and protruding. Chris stopped undoing the buttons for a moment and reached inside, taking a breast in each hand and squeezing them gently, watching Jo's face as she circled her fingers about her friend's nipples.

'We shouldn't be doing this,' murmured Jo. 'It's not very professional.' But again she offered no resistance when Chris began undoing her dress once more.

'Stand up.'

Jo looked into Chris's eyes for a second, then rose obediently to her feet, finding it easier to respond when her friend took charge so forcefully. Chris pulled the dress apart and pushed it back off her shoulders. It slid to the floor with a faint rustle. Jo was clad only in her panties now. They were brief and lacy, the waistband dipping down to form a vee at the front above which a wisp of pubic hair was just visible.

Jo felt oddly vulnerable standing there in front of her partner. She wondered what was becoming of her. Her whole outlook seemed to have changed since she met this extraordinary girl. A few weeks ago she had been celibate and had fought against her natural desires when tempted. Now here she was giving herself to another woman quite shamelessly, as if it was the most natural thing in the world. And she seemed to feel no guilt at all, so that when Chris took her by the shoulders and pressed her backwards over her desk she complied at once.

Jo lay stretched out on her back, her bottom on the edge of the desk's surface. She gazed down between her breasts at Chris as she ran her fingers over her partner's thighs, moving them in small circles, all the time closing in on her crotch. She gave a little groan, her backside squirming as she felt Chris's fingers move ever closer to the centre of her desires. She knew she was wet, and that the wetness would be showing through the thin material of her panties, but she didn't care. All she wanted was to be touched.

Chris's fingers brushed lightly against Jo's crotch, causing her to press her thighs forward in an involuntary reflex and bringing another moan from her lips. Chris smiled at the reaction, running her fingers up and down the white valley that had formed at Jo's crotch as she had opened her thighs.

'I've got something in the drawer for you, Jo,' she murmured. 'Do you want to see it?'

'Mmmm.' Jo licked her lips, running her hands up over her own breasts and toying with her nipples.

Chris reached across to the drawer in her desk and opened it. She pulled out a long, pink object. She held it up for Jo to see and the prostrate girl's eyes widened as she saw what her friend was holding. It was a dildo, thick and rubbery, complete with veins and a bulging tip. As Jo watched, Chris pressed a button and it began to buzz softly.

She placed the object on the desk beside Jo. The sound of its buzzing seemed to resound on the wooden surface, so that it was amplified, filling the room with its reverberations. The blonde reached up for the edge of Jo's panties, pulling them down in a single movement, slipping them down Jo's thighs and over her ankles.

Once the knickers were off, Chris paused for a moment and Jo knew she was admiring her naked body. She was lying flat on her back, her thighs spread. Her breasts had fallen apart slightly under their own weight but were still firm, the nipples long and hard, pointing up at the ceiling. Beneath the thin, dark triangle of pubic hair, she was aware that the lips of her sex glistened with moisture, her pink cleft wide open. As she thought of the sight she made, she felt her sex lips twitch slightly and a small bead of moisture escaped, running down her flesh and onto the desk top.

Chris picked up the dildo and slid it slowly up the inside of Jo's thigh, rubbing it lightly against the skin, moving tantalisingly close to her sex. Jo sensed her friend watching as her passion turned to frustration at the way she was being teased. Her body was in motion now, her hips thrusting upwards, her backside off the table as she blatantly offered herself for penetration. Yet still Chris avoided that final, intimate contact, keeping her on the boil until her friend could take no more.

'Oh god, Chris,' she moaned at last. 'Put it in me. I can't stand any more of this. Put it in me now.'

'Say please.'

'Please, you bitch. Please!'

Chris smiled and moved the vibrating object up Jo's thigh once more. This time, though, she didn't stop and Jo gave a cry of release as she felt the rubber press against her sex.

Chris worked the dildo up and down Jo's slit, coating the tip with a sheen of moisture. Once again, Jo could feel her sex muscles contracting as they anticipated penetration, sending her into a frenzy of desire. She almost cried with gratitude when, at last, Chris ran it down to the entrance to her sex and pressed, twisting it as she did so.

'Oh!'

Jo couldn't suppress the exclamation as the thick object slid into her, working its way deeper and deeper until it was all the way in. It felt wonderful, the vibrations sending tingles of pleasure through her body. When Chris started moving it back and forth she could barely contain her passion, hoarse cries sounding from her throat as her backside slapped down against the desk top. Chris manoeuvred the dildo expertly, twisting it as she worked it in and out, her thumb constantly brushing Jo's clitoris.

Jo came quickly and noisily, her cries echoing about the office as her body bucked and heaved on the hard, unyielding desk. Chris went on ramming the dildo into her, obviously sensing each wave of pleasure as her friend's sex lips locked about the toy, as if trying to suck it inside her.

At last, though, Jo's passion began to ebb, her thrashing becoming less violent. Chris went on manipulating the dildo, slowing her movements in time with Jo's own until the naked girl was finally still, prostrate on the desk, her breasts rising and falling as she regained her breath. Only then did Chris slide the dildo gently from her and touch the button that turned it off.

'That better?' she asked.

'Mmmm,' said Jo. 'Wonderful.'

Chapter 8

The wood was almost completely silent, the only sound the faint rustling of the leaves in the zephyr of a breeze that blew through the trees. Above, the sky was deepest blue, the sun shining fiercely down. It was hot. Very hot. The kind of sultry summer's day that drives the English out of their houses and into even hotter traffic queues, the occupants sweltering as they sit motionless amongst a hundred thousand other frustrated motorists all dreaming of a sandy beach and a cool sea.

The wood seemed a million miles from the traffic, though, the broad green branches of the trees repelling the fierceness of the sun's rays. The floor of the wood was dappled with sunlight, here and there illuminating the bright colours of a wild flower, or the green of a young sapling as it pushed its way up through the canopy.

Fiona Lee picked her way along the narrow path that led between the trees, revelling in the peace of the spot. She had been walking now for nearly fifteen minutes and had not encountered a single soul. It was as if she was alone in the world, and the contrast with the noise and the bustle of the city streets she had left behind was extreme.

Fiona loved to be alone, and to commune with nature in this way. Her tough City job gave her a hectic lifestyle that allowed her little time to herself. That was why she so valued the opportunity to get away from the hustle and bustle to somewhere like this.

She had not visited this particular place before and had

been surprised that such a tranquil and silent spot could exist so close to town. Now, as she strolled through the wood, pausing occasionally to listen to a bird's call or to watch a squirrel scramble up a tree, she felt entirely at peace with herself.

If only it wasn't so hot. She squinted up through the green canopy above her at the sun, burning relentlessly through. It was the hottest day of the summer so far and, despite the fact that she wore only a light summer dress over simple underwear, she could feel the perspiration on her face as she trekked along.

She wished she had brought a drink with her. As it was she had nothing, simply the clothes she stood up in. She had left everything else in the boot of her car, which was parked in a concealed entrance to the wood.

Suddenly a sound reached her ear. It was the sound of flowing water, a sort of bubbly, tinkling noise coming from close by. She stopped and listened again. The sound was emanating from somewhere off to her right. She knew it wasn't far away. Perhaps she could cool herself down there. She stepped off the path, pushing the bushes aside as she made her way towards the source of the noise.

She stepped carefully to avoid scratching her ankles on the vegetation. She had gone no more than a dozen yards when she found it, a spring bubbling up from beneath the ground and forming a small stream that ran away through the trees.

Fiona dropped to her knees and, cupping her hands together, caught some of the water as it came up from below. She raised her hands to her lips and sipped it. It tasted cool and sweet and she drank it down gratefully, scooping up more handfuls and pouring them into her mouth.

She remained crouched by the spring even after she had slaked her thirst, enjoying the sound of the water as it came to the surface and rushed off through the wood. It seemed like a perfect spot, shaded from the sun's rays, the pure water sparkling as it flowed away.

She wondered idly where the stream ran to. After all, it must go somewhere, she told herself. Having no other plan in mind, she decided to follow it. Rising to her feet she began to pick her way along its edge, dodging under low branches and stepping around the thick bushes as she traced its path.

Suddenly the ground dropped away in front of her and the stream disappeared. She moved forward, the sound of splashing water reaching her ears. She found herself on the edge of a steep bank, below which was a wide stretch of river. The stream she had been following emptied directly into the water and the splash she had heard was the sound of the small waterfall formed as it did so.

Fiona stared down at the river below. Its waters were crystal clear and quite deep. It was at least twenty feet wide, moving gently along at a slow pace.

All at once the water looked very inviting indeed. Fiona picked her way carefully down the bank to the edge. It was as peaceful a spot as she could imagine and she watched the water drift by, its smooth surface occasionally broken by the ripple of a fish rising to the top. Fiona crouched down and ran her fingers through the water. It felt cool after the oppressive heat of the day and looked very inviting. She decided at once to immerse her feet in it.

Rising, she kicked off her sandals, enjoying the sensation of the grass beneath her bare feet. Tentatively she placed a foot in the water. Despite the hot weather, a shiver ran through her as the cool stream closed over her ankles. The bottom of the river was soft, the sand and mud squeezing up between her toes. She moved forward so that she was standing in the stream, the water coming up to her calves.

For the next five minutes she was content simply to stand there as the water flowed about her legs, enjoying the sensation. But even that wasn't enough. What she really wanted to do was to swim. But how could she? After all she had no bathing costume.

But did that really matter, she reasoned. After all who would

69

see her in this deserted spot? She was alone wasn't she? She had had neither sight nor sound of another human being since she had entered the wood. And what harm could it do to have a swim? She need only be in for a couple of minutes. Just enough to cool off.

Suddenly her mind was made up and, turning to step back onto the bank again, she began fiddling behind her neck with the catch of her dress. She pulled down the zip and let the dress drop to her hips. Then she dragged it down and stepped out of it. She reached behind her back and flicked her bra undone, gazing about herself guiltily as she let it fall beside her dress. Then she hooked her thumbs into the waistband of her panties and pulled them down, tossing them aside on the grass.

She paused for a second, looking down at her body. Fiona was tall and slender, her breasts small but beautifully shaped, the pink nipples set high on the soft white mounds. Her hips too were slim, giving her the shape of a supermodel. Her hair was golden brown, hanging halfway down her perfectly contoured back. Standing naked beside the river, she resembled nothing more than a wood nymph, her pale, vital flesh contrasting starkly with her surroundings.

She moved down to the water's edge once again, still looking about her as if convinced she was being watched. She stepped into the river, then moved tentatively forward. The water began to work its way up her body, over her knees and up her thighs. It felt colder than ever as she stepped further out and she knew she would have to immerse herself all at once, or risk losing her nerve. She braced herself for a second, then dived forward, allowing the water to close over her head, enveloping her momentarily in a green and silent world.

She rose gracefully to the surface. She was in the centre of the river now and could barely touch the bottom with her feet. She trod water for a second, then allowed her body to float gently upward until she lay on her back, her breasts just breaking the surface as she stared up into the sunlit sky.

Fiona felt wonderful, naked and cool in these idyllic surroundings, at perfect peace with herself and her environment. She allowed herself to drift with the current, her eyes closed, her mind free of worries for the moment.

Fiona's job took her to the City of London every day, where she worked on the Stock Exchange. It was a high-powered job, involving long hours and a good deal of stress, but Fiona was good at what she did and her services were in great demand. From dawn till dusk her life was a round of deals, the evenings being spent on the telephone to foreign markets, so she seldom reached her flat before ten-thirty.

She was happy in her job, and extremely well rewarded, but it left her little time to socialise and it had been some time since she had had a steady relationship. That didn't bother her greatly, but what she did miss was the physical part of it. She had always had a strong sex drive and the lack of a man often led her to feel frustrated. She had a variety of sex toys which she used frequently, but hardly found them a replacement for the real thing. She would lie awake at night with her sexual fantasies, feeling unfulfilled and longing for a real live man. When she had seen the advertisement for Fantasy and Co it had seemed ideal.

The interview had been straightforward and businesslike. The two women who ran the company certainly knew their stuff. They had explored ideas with her in detail, finally settling on a relatively simple plan, but one that really turned her on. The agreement had been that, if everything was satisfactory, she would return and try something more outrageous.

Now here she was. Chris had been deliberately vague with her in the details of what she would do and what would happen. The idea was to make the whole thing as spontaneous as possible, and so far it was working fine. All she had been told to do was to listen for the spring, then follow it to its end. The rest she had done entirely on her own initiative, though she was aware that she must stick to the outline of the fantasy.

Now, as she lay naked in the water, the excitement inside

her began to mount. Already her nudity was turning her on and the anticipation of what was to come increased her arousal by the second. She knew too that somewhere out there was a video camera, and that she had already almost certainly been filmed displaying all. Now, as she drifted along in the cool water, she waited to see what would happen next.

Suddenly she became aware that she could no longer hear the sound of the spring emptying into the river. She opened her eyes and looked up. For a second she was confused. She didn't recognise the spot at all. Where before there had been lush grass running down to the edge of the river, now she was surrounded by muddy banks at least six feet high. She looked behind her, and was just in time to catch a final glimpse of her dress on the river bank as she was carried round the bend. The current must be stronger than she had at first thought and in her few moments of reverie it had swept her away from where she had entered the water and was now carrying her downstream.

She struck out for the bank but, when she reached it, soon discovered that it was far too steep to climb. She swam across the river and tried the other side, but without success. She tried swimming against the current. She was a strong swimmer, and in no danger, but she was quite unable to make any progress. There was only one thing for it. She had to let the current carry her downstream until she could find a place where she could get out of the water.

She relaxed and at once the water pulled her along, the high banks rushing by on either side as she searched for a good landing point. For some time there was nothing, but then the river swung round a bend and she came in sight of a bridge, beyond which was a gap in the bank. She swam over to the right-hand side, letting the current carry her under the bridge, then striking out for the gap.

She nearly missed it. But for the tree root that projected from the bank right beside it she would have been carried past. A last despairing lunge at the root allowed her to get a firm grasp on it, then she was able to haul herself out of the water and up to the grass above, where she collapsed on the ground, gasping with the exertion.

Fiona looked about her. She was naked, and a long way from her clothes. She really was in trouble now and she knew it. But for the moment she merely lay where she was, getting her breath back. Then, she knew, she had to make a plan.

Chapter 9

'But where the hell is she?'

Jo almost shouted into her mobile phone, her face creased with anxiety. This was a serious mess. Their business was scarcely launched and suddenly things were going badly wrong. She held the instrument close to her ear as she listened to Mark's reply.

'We're not sure,' his voice crackled. 'We thought we had loads of time to set the log across the river, but there's been no sign of her. Are you sure she turned up?'

'Of course I'm sure,' said Jo. 'I was down by the spring and I followed her to the river. I tell you she went swimming just as planned, at about two o'clock.'

'Two o'clock?' Mark's voice was incredulous. 'You said two-thirty.'

'I said she'd be out of the water by two-thirty, you idiot,' groaned Jo. 'She must have gone past before you even got there. Oh hell, this is a real cock-up.'

'Well if she went past us, she must have got out somewhere further downstream,' reasoned Mark. 'I thought we had that covered.'

'Let's hope to god we did,' replied Jo. 'Chris went down that end. I'll give her a call. Meanwhile stay right where you are. And keep your video camera handy.'

She pressed the button that broke the connection, then shook her head. This was really bad news. They had intended to keep Fiona within the bounds of the forest. That was why Mark had been despatched to put the branch across the river in such a place that she could easily have climbed out. Now she could be anywhere, and she was their responsibility. She punched in the number of Chris's phone and listened impatiently for an answer.

'Chris here.'

'Oh, thank god, Chris. Where the hell are you?'

'Just where we agreed. So Mark didn't make it?'

'You know?'

Chris laughed. 'Of course I know. I knew the moment our customer emerged from the river as naked as the day she was born. And on the wrong side of the bridge.'

'Oh, thank goodness she's all right.'

'Well, I guess that depends on your definition of the words all right,' said Chris. 'She's not exactly well placed at the moment.'

'What do you mean?'

'The trouble is, the forest is fenced just here. Across the road from the bridge there's no way back in.'

'What, no way at all?'

'There are gates about half a mile apart. They're normally kept padlocked, but I managed to get keys to two of them by persuading the local keeper that I was a bird watcher. They're not exactly convenient, though. The nearest one is a couple of hundred yards up to the left, and she'll probably want to go to the right when she reaches the bridge and cross the river, because that's the side her clothes are on.'

'What if she does?'

'She'll have a long way to go. And she'll be on a public road.'

'Is it busy?'

'No. But it's not exactly quiet either.'

'So she might get caught?'

'It's quite possible.'

'Damn. We really didn't need this,' cursed Jo.

'Who knows,' replied Chris. 'It was her idea to be naked in

76

a compromising position. She might even enjoy it.'

'Let's hope so,' said Jo. 'Otherwise, I'm afraid this commission might be our last.'

Chapter 10

Fiona lay where she was for some time, the sun drying out her body as she regained her strength. It had been more of a struggle than she had realised in the water and she was surprised at how tired she was. She was young and fit, though, and it wasn't long before she began to feel recovered.

When she had fully regained her breath, she climbed to her feet and looked about her. She was certainly in a predicament. Totally nude and a good three-quarters of a mile from her clothes. And would she be able to find her way back? The banks of the river had been thick with bushes, making its path difficult to follow. She had a long walk ahead of her, during which she would be totally vulnerable to anyone she encountered.

The thought dismayed her yet, at the same time, the idea was oddly thrilling. To be naked and exposed in a public place was exactly her fantasy. She ran a hand down her stomach and over her dark pubic mound, her fingers feeling for her clitoris. It was hard and slippery with wetness and she caressed it gently, a tremor running through her as her body responded to her touch.

She stood for a good minute, rubbing her love bud, loving the sensation it gave her. And the more she rubbed, the more aroused she became, so that the prospect of the naked walk back to her clothes became increasingly exciting to her. She began slowly to walk back along the river, still caressing herself.

The first problem was the bridge, and she surveyed it

carefully. It spanned the river some twenty feet above her, the supports dropping vertically into the river, leaving no way to go under it. Her only route back to the wood was to climb up and cross it, and that would mean exposing herself on the road. She stared down at her body. Her nipples were hard, her fingers glistening with wetness as she teased her love button. She imagined the sight she would make to anyone encountering her, and another spasm of lust shook her. It was time to move on.

Forsaking her masturbating, she climbed up the embankment until her eyes came level with the bridge parapet. A metalled road ran across it, with the wood continuing on the far side. As she stood there she heard the sound of a car approaching and ducked down just as it passed by. She remained crouched low, making sure it was some distance away before she raised her head again.

She had to get across, but she had to pick her moment carefully. The road was wide and she knew she would be exposed for twenty seconds or more by the time she had scaled the bridge wall.

The sound of another car met her ears and she dropped down once again. The vehicle swished past no more than a few feet from where she was. She waited until the coast was clear, then straightened up once more.

She looked right and left, listening hard. There was neither sight nor sound of traffic. Dare she go now? She hesitated. Once she had crossed the wall she would be committed, she knew. There was no turning back and, if a car approached at speed, no avoiding being seen. She took one final look. Then, taking a deep breath, she began to hoist herself up onto the bridge.

Once on top of the wall she paused again, her eyes searching about her. To any casual observer she knew she would have made an extraordinary sight, this slim, beautiful young woman standing totally naked by the roadside, her young skin taking on a golden hue in the afternoon sunshine. Just for a second she remained where she was, striking a pose, her hands on her hips, her legs slightly spread. Then she was on the move again.

She jumped down onto the verge and headed off across the road. The tarmac felt hot and hard beneath her bare feet and, as she crossed to the centre of the wide road, she began to feel very exposed indeed, her head darting nervously from side to side.

She reached the far side safely and ran gratefully toward the trees. Then she pulled up, her jaw dropping in dismay. Running along the edge of the wood, its green staves almost invisible from any distance, was a tall fence. It was all of ten feet high, the metal staves running vertically about six inches apart. Fiona stood at the foot, gazing up at it, knowing for certain that she wouldn't be able to climb it. She had to find another way in.

She glanced behind her. Should she go back? The cover of the embankment looked very tempting from her current position of total exposure. But to return would serve no purpose. She must at least cross over the bridge.

She turned to her right and began to run, following the edge of the wood, searching for a place to enter it. The fence seemed to go on and on, with no sign of a break, except where the river split it. She reached the other side of the bridge, then decided to take refuge beside it again whilst she considered what to do next. She crossed the road once more and jumped onto the wall, then stopped short. The land fell away on this side of the bridge, leaving a drop of about fifteen feet. Even if she was able to get down, she'd never climb up again. A feeling of panic began to grip her. She seemed to be trapped on this open, unfriendly road.

She ran to the other side once more and continued her journey along the fence, searching desperately for a way in.

Then she heard the car approaching.

It was coming from behind her and seemed to be approaching at speed, the swishing sound of the tyres on the road growing louder by the second. Fiona glanced about herself, but there was no chance of concealment. She had to run on.

The car was just around the bend behind her now and she glanced back as it came into view. It was a small hatchback, about a hundred and fifty yards behind her, and it instantly began to slow.

Fiona wondered at the sight she must make, her pert, white behind on full view as she ran along the road ahead of the slowing car. She was beginning to tire now and the car was coming closer and closer.

She heard a wolf whistle and glanced behind once more. There were four young men in the car and all were watching her, their windows wound down as they grinned at the naked girl.

They pulled alongside her, still whistling and calling. Fiona ran on, aware of the way her breasts bounced with every stride and of the delight this was bringing to her audience. She tried not to look at them, her mind concentrated on finding a way off this confounded road.

Suddenly she sighted what she was looking for. About a hundred yards ahead was a gate in the fence, and it was open. She gave a gasp of relief. If only she could reach that, she could gain the relative safety of the wood. She tried to run faster, but the car remained alongside, the men reaching out of the windows trying to grope her as she ran.

'Pull over,' one of the men shouted to the car's driver. 'Stop just ahead and we can head her off.'

Fiona glanced to one side and, to her dismay, she saw the car accelerate ahead of her, then brake to a halt. But there was still hope. They had stopped just beyond the gate and clearly hadn't seen it yet. They leapt from the vehicle and spread out across the road, prepared to stop her.

'Come on, darling,' one of them shouted.

The gate was less than twenty yards away now, with the men another ten yards beyond it. Fiona ran on, praying they would not notice it until it was too late.

Ten yards, five. They were moving towards her now, preparing to catch her. Then she veered sideways and was through.

The men shouted with rage as she clanged the gate shut. There was a bolt on it, with a padlock hanging open. She knew she had to secure it. There was no way she could escape the men if they got through and tried to chase her. She slammed the bolt across just as they crashed against the gate on the other side, and began fumbling with the lock.

They reached through the bars, grabbing her breasts, squeezing them and pinching the nipples. Other hands forced their way between her legs, their fingers probing her vagina. But Fiona knew that that was what would save her. So intent were the men on groping her naked body they failed to notice what she was doing until it was too late. She looped the end of the padlock through the bolt and snapped it shut. Then she wrenched herself from their grasp and jumped backwards to where she was just out of range of their hands.

The men realised what had happened, and roared with dismay. But there was nothing they could do about it. The naked young woman they had been pursuing was just out of range, and the gate was holding fast.

Now that the immediate danger was over, Fiona was calm once more. She stood, taking up the pose she had done on the bridge parapet, her hands on her hips, legs spread slightly, staring back at the men. All of a sudden the arousal had returned and the opportunity to flaunt her naked body to these four randy strangers was strangely thrilling.

'Come on, darling,' shouted one of the men. 'Let us in. We weren't going to hurt you.'

'Yeah,' shouted another. 'We just wanted a bit of fun.'

'Bit of fun eh?' responded Fiona. 'Sorry fellas, I only fuck with men, not boys.'

'Go on,' shouted another. 'I know you want it. Your cunt's wet as hell.'

He held up a finger, which moments earlier had been inside her.

'No chance,' said Fiona. She felt unbelievably sexy standing there, showing off her breasts and sex so blatantly. She almost fancied the idea of screwing the men then and there. But she knew she had to move on. Before she went, though, she decided to tease them just a little bit more.

She moved her hands up to her breasts and began to caress them. The nipples were already erect and she teased them with her fingers, her eyes fixed on the wide-eyed men.

'You see, guys, I can get all the pleasure I need from my own hands,' she said. 'I don't need you.'

So saying she ran a hand down her body and, widening her stance slightly, she slid a finger into her own vagina. The men's jaws dropped as they watched her caress herself, bending her knees slightly as she pressed her fingers deep inside her. She looked up at them, the expression on her face one of pure arousal. Then she turned slowly and walked away, still fingering herself, oblivious to their pleas that she return.

Fiona had other things on her mind.

She set off through the forest. The path from the gate was wide and well-defined and she had no trouble following it through the trees. She had dried out completely now and the sensation of the sun on her naked flesh felt good. In fact she was feeling very sexy, a feeling that had been enhanced by her encounter with the young men in the car. Her flesh still tingled where they had touched her and her fingers strayed occasionally to her sex as she walked along, seeking out her hard little love bud and caressing it gently.

She knew she had to stay as close as possible to the river in order to be sure of finding her clothes and so she was forced to stray from the path occasionally in order to keep it in sight. This involved picking her way between the trees and she had to take care to avoid the bushes and branches that threatened to scratch her bare skin.

She had been walking for about ten minutes when she reached a grassy clearing. She paused there, leaning back against a tree, listening to the sounds of the wood. Beside her the river splashed past and above wood pigeons cooed in the trees. This really was a beautiful place, she thought. If not for her nudity and the urgency to find her clothes and restore her modesty she would have remained in this spot for some time, basking in the sun's rays.

She glanced down at her body, noting the pinkness of her nipples, which stood out stiffly erect from her breasts. She toyed idly with them, rolling the hard flesh between finger and thumb, her caresses sending pulses of pleasure through her body. She ran her other hand down over her short pubic curls, once again seeking out her clitoris and easing it from between the folds of her sex. She gave a little gasp as she rubbed her fingers back and forth over it. It was a delicious sensation and she found herself spreading her legs wider, pressing her body back against the harsh bark of the tree and thrusting her hips forward as her excitement grew.

She slipped a finger into her vagina, then another. It felt good. Suddenly a new urgency began to overtake her. A desire to bring herself to orgasm here, in this quiet spot.

She began to work her fingers back and forth with renewed vigour, her excitement increasing with every stroke. She was moaning now, her eyes closed, her legs spread wide, her knees bent as she thrust her pubis forward onto her hand, the wetness from her vagina escaping and trickling down to her wrists. As she did so she felt her orgasm building inside her and her limbs began to stiffen in anticipation.

Suddenly a flash of reflected sunlight caught her eye on the far side of the clearing. She froze at once, the hands she had been using to caress her body now hugged close to her skin in an attempt to cover her breasts and crotch. Another flash. Something metallic was moving in the bushes less than ten yards away from her.

'Who's there?' she called nervously.

There was silence.

'I know you're there,' she called again.

Once again there was no sound. Then, slowly, a figure emerged from the bushes.

It was a man. It was difficult to tell his age as he had a dark, bushy beard. On his nose were a pair of metal-rimmed circular glasses. He was quite tall and slim, wearing a khaki shirt and matching trousers. Round his neck hung a camera.

'What are you doing here?' she asked.

'I might ask you the same question.' His voice was deeper than she had expected, with no particular accent. 'This is a private wood you know. What are you doing here?'

'I . . . I was just walking.'

'Do you often walk about naked?'

'I lost my clothes.' Fiona found her confidence deserting her in the face of the man's assertive manner. Normally she would have been less submissive, but her nakedness put her at a considerable disadvantage. She hugged her breasts tight, aware that she was blushing.

'Nevertheless you're trespassing.'

'What are you doing here then?' she asked.

'I'm the gamekeeper. I was doing a little bird-watching. Then I discovered one bird I hadn't expected. Fortunately I had my camera with me.'

Fiona gasped. 'You took photographs of me?'

'Certainly.'

'But you had no right.'

'I had every right. You're trespassing, I'm not. And you were making quite an exhibition of yourself.'

Fiona's colour deepened. 'You were watching?'

'Naturally. It's not every day one gets the chance to see a beautiful girl masturbating, let alone to photograph it.'

'What will you do with the photos?'

'Don't worry, my dear. I won't be sending them to the

86

tabloids. They'll simply be for my pleasure and that of a few select friends.'

'But you have no right.'

'I think we've explored that argument. Now, what are we going to do about you?'

'About me?'

'Yes. Strictly speaking it's my duty to hand trespassers over to the police. I'm sure they'd be most interested in arresting you.'

'You wouldn't do that would you?'

'It depends. What would you do if I just let you go?'

'I'd find my clothes and leave at once.'

'And where are your clothes?'

'They're by the river. Somewhere up ahead.'

'Which river?'

'That one,' she said. She went to point to the other side of the clearing. Then, realising this would mean uncovering herself, nodded her head instead.

'Are you certain? Three rivers meet in this wood you know. Tell me how you got to the river.'

She described where she had parked her car and the route she had taken into the wood. Then she told him how she had been washed downstream and had clambered out on the other side of the bridge. When she had finished he shook his head.

'As I thought, you're following the wrong river. This one is far too shallow to swim in. Take a look if you don't believe me.'

Fiona eyed him suspiciously for a moment.

'Go ahead, take a look.'

She straightened up from where she had been leaning and walked across to the edge of the clearing, aware that she was presenting him with a perfect view of her backside as she did so. She peered over the bank. Sure enough the water was only a few inches deep. She turned back to him.

'I don't understand it,' she said. 'I followed it from the road.'

'You should have walked all the way back to the bridge after you entered the wood,' he said. 'This one joins the main river a bit further downstream. The more you follow it, the further it's taking you from your clothes.'

Fiona was flabbergasted. Things were worse than she had thought. She cursed herself for her stupidity.

'So,' the man said. 'You're trespassing, you're stark-naked, and you don't know where you are. What are you going to do?'

Fiona eyed him. It was clear that he held all the cards, and that she was in a serious predicament.

'Can you help me?' she said at last.

'What's in it for me?'

Fiona felt an odd sensation in her stomach as he said the words. There was no mistaking his intention. And equally no mistaking that she would have to comply with his demands. This idea sent a new tremor through her and she felt the muscles of her sex suddenly convulse.

'What do you want?' she asked.

'To photograph you.'

She stared at him. 'You want me to pose for you? Like this?'

'That's what I said.'

'But I couldn't.'

'Why not?'

She opened her mouth to answer, then closed it again. Why not indeed? After all, being seen by the young men in the car had been a real turn-on. The thought of men looking at pictures of her naked was equally thrilling. And it would, at least, get her out of her predicament.

'How many would you take?' she asked.

He grinned, sensing victory. 'A couple of rolls,' he said.

Fiona took a deep breath.

'All right,' she said. 'What do you want me to do?'

'Take your hands away for a start.'

She stared at him for a moment, then slowly lowered her

hands to her sides. He let his eyes roam over her lovely young body, taking in the firm breasts with their upward pointing nipples, the flatness of her stomach and the prominence of her pubic mound, the dark curls barely covering the pink slit below.

'Lean against the tree facing the trunk,' he said. 'Then thrust back your arse and look over your shoulder at me.'

She did as she was asked, pressing her breasts against the rough bark and pushing her backside at him, her head turned towards the camera.

Snap!

'Good. Now press yourself against the tree. Hug it, as if it was a lover, then throw your head back and let your hair hang down.'

Snap!

'Right. Turn and face me. Thrust your breasts forward and open your legs. Offer yourself to me.'

Snap!

'Now down on all fours. I want to see those delicious tits of yours dangle. Stick your arse out.'

Snap!

The session went on, him shouting the orders whilst she obeyed. And the longer it went on, the sexier Fiona felt. He began posing her himself, moving her limbs into the position he wanted. As he did so his hands would brush against her breasts, lingering momentarily on the rubbery flesh of her teats. Then he began positioning her thighs, and his fingers or thumbs would inevitably brush against her slit, bringing a small gasp from her when they did so.

Soon Fiona was even more turned on than ever. It was as if the camera was making love to her, and she responded with genuine enthusiasm, cavorting in front of the lens, exposing more with each shot until he had her flat on her back, her legs spread wide, her backside clear of the ground as she thrust her open vagina up at the lens, the lips parted to expose the wetness inside.

When at last he put the camera down she remained where she was, making no attempt to cover herself and leaving her legs apart. He sat down beside her and, without speaking, began to stroke her inner thighs. Fiona simply lay and watched him. She wanted to be fucked now and she knew that he knew it. So she remained as she was, her naked body spread-eagled on the ground, waiting for him to make the move.

He shifted his hand higher up her thigh, watching her face. She said nothing, but she knew the expression of frustration on her face told him all he needed to know. When he touched her sex lips she simply moaned, her hips gyrating slightly.

He probed a finger into her and her response was electric, a sudden jolt shaking her body as the muscles of her vagina tightened about his probing digit. As he fingered her, his other hand strayed up to her breasts and he began to stroke them, squeezing and kneading them. Fiona lay with her eyes closed, the occasional groan escaping from her throat as she writhed about under his touch. She was aroused to the point of no return now and knew that if he didn't screw her soon she'd simply come under the ministrations of his fingers.

But she wanted to be fucked. To have reached this state of arousal and not experienced a cock within her would simply not be enough. Suddenly she could resist it no more and she rose to her knees, her hands reaching for his fly.

He sat back on the ground, passive now as she worked urgently to undo his trousers. She yanked down the zip and reached inside, dragging his rampant tool from its confinement. It was a truncheon of a cock, the thick shaft jutting straight up from his groin, the foreskin stretched back so the eye in the end was exposed, glistening with his own lubrication.

Fiona took it into her mouth at once, sucking greedily at it, her hands kneading his heavy balls. Now it was his turn to groan with pleasure as she went down on him, savouring the taste and smell of his arousal, her head darting back and forth as she fellated him with enthusiasm, her breasts swinging below her as she did so.

All of a sudden he grasped her shoulders and pushed her head back. She stared up at him, her expression one of wanton abandon.

'I want to be fucked now,' she said.

'Lie on your back and spread your legs.'

She gave his cock one final squeeze and lay back on the grass. Then she slowly opened her thighs, revealing to him the object of his desires.

He knelt between her legs, looking down at her, his cock occasionally bobbing up and down as his own arousal pulsed through him. She watched as he grasped his shaft and began slowly to masturbate, his eyes travelling over her naked flesh. She was almost gasping with desire now. The longer he hesitated, the more agitated she became, her vaginal muscles convulsing rhythmically, as if tightening around an invisible erection.

At last he moved forward, his body suspended over hers. She stared up into his eyes as she felt him guide his cock towards her honey pot. Then he was pressing himself to her, his cock nuzzling against the entrance.

'Mmmm.'

He entered her with a series of short jabs, each one taking him further and further inside. He slid in easily, his meaty weapon stretching her deliciously until his pubic bone was pressed against hers and they were totally united. Then he began to move, his hips pumping gently back and forth inside the moaning girl.

He placed a hand on her breast, his rough fingers squeezing the soft globe as he closed his mouth over hers. His lips were soft and they parted to allow his tongue to snake into her mouth. She wrapped her arms around his neck, pulling him down to her whilst she pressed her hips up against his, her cunt alternately gripping and releasing the thick cock that plunged relentlessly into her.

Suddenly he rolled over, his penis slipping from her. Fiona looked up in surprise to see him lying on his back, his heavy erection standing proud, glistening with her juices.

'Get on top,' he ordered.

Fiona scrambled eagerly to her feet and straddled his body, her fingers rubbing her clitoris as she contemplated how their positions were reversed. Then she dropped to her knees, moving forward until she was directly over his manhood.

She lowered herself slowly. Still toying with her love bud with one hand whilst the other grabbed his bulging tip and guided it to her sex. She slipped it into her, whimpering quietly as she did so, then she lowered her body until she was sitting on him, his cock once again buried within her.

This time it was Fiona's turn to do the work and she set about her task with relish, moving her body up and down as she took her pleasure from him.

Fiona tossed her hair back, gazing up into the sunshine, loving its warmth on her bare breasts as they bounced up and down with every stroke. She had never felt so abandoned. Naked and carefree in this open place, with a man whose name she didn't even know, she felt totally liberated. This was what she had paid Fantasy and Co for – and they were delivering with bonuses. She gazed down at the man's face. He had his eyes closed, his forehead creased as if in pain. But she recognised the expression as one of pure ecstasy and she ground herself down onto him with new vigour as she sensed the approach of his orgasm.

He came suddenly, his cock jerking within her as she felt the spurts of semen gushing into her. It felt wonderful to have a man's seed fill her once more, and her own orgasm came at once, her cries ringing through the trees as her body shook with pleasure.

Fiona continued to thrust her hips against his until she had milked all the sperm she could from him and her sex was running with the hot, viscous fluid. Only then did she begin to slow, her own orgasm gradually losing its intensity as she came down, until at last she was still, staring down at his face, aware that her own was running with sweat.

She wondered how far away her clothes were. It didn't matter really. Suddenly she was in no hurry.

Chapter 11

Jo sat in the office, her eyes fixed on the TV monitor as she completed the editing of Fiona's video. On the screen the naked girl was walking through the forest with her bearded companion. As they approached the camera zoomed in on her crotch, revealing the stream of semen that trickled down her thigh. The edit was nearly finished now. All Jo had to do was the final part where, on finding Fiona's clothes, the man had draped her forward over a tree trunk and taken her from behind. Then Jo's work would be completed for the day.

This, their fifth exercise to date, had been quite a success. Fiona had telephoned her only the evening before, full of praise at the service she had received from Fantasy and Co. Ironically, the one part of the project that had nearly caused a disaster had come in for particular attention.

'Having that car full of yobs chase me was a stroke of genius,' Fiona had said. 'The timing was impeccable. A few more seconds and they'd have caught me. I nearly came then and there at the thought of it.'

'We aim to make it a special experience,' said Jo.

She scarcely dared contemplate what would have happened if the young men had caught her. Perhaps she would have enjoyed it, being gangbanged at the roadside by a bunch of youngsters. The trouble was it would have been difficult to explain how that would have fitted with Fiona's original fantasy of being discovered naked by a bird-watcher and forced to pose for his camera.

Even the photos had provided a little extra fun for this

extraordinary exhibitionist. She had insisted on taking the film to the developer herself and had even gone through the pictures with the shop assistant, picking out particularly lewd shots for enlargement. By the time she had left the shop, the young man's pants had been bulging noticeably.

As Jo completed the editing, she contemplated their success to date. Five well-satisfied customers behind them and already the appointments book was filling up. At this rate they would need to employ a secretary in the near future, as she and Chris were spending more and more time out in the field armed with their video cameras.

Jo watched as Fiona enjoyed yet another orgasm, then the screen went blank. She pressed the button on the recorder and the tape slipped from the machine. Jo labelled it and placed it in a box, which itself went into a brown envelope.

She was just finishing the address on the envelope when the door opened and a man entered. She recognised him at once as Ed, the bearded man she had just been watching fuck Fiona. Ed had been commissioned for the one-off job from a model agency, after Fiona had insisted that her bird-watcher be bearded. Jo was quite surprised to see him still around, since she had paid him off that morning.

'You still here?' she asked.

'Hi. Yes, I've just been down the gym and I remembered I'd left my bag behind. I won't be a minute. How did the video look?'

'It's okay.'

'It must be quite hard work trying to stay hidden whilst you're filming.'

'We're getting better at it. Where did you leave your bag?'

'Just behind Chris's desk.'

He pulled out the bag. Then, to Jo's mild irritation, sat down in her partner's chair.

'So, you must have quite a business going here,' he said.

'It's coming along,' said Jo.

'That chick you set me up with was quite something. I

96

wouldn't mind meeting her again.'

'Well, you won't. The whole point of this thing is that it's a fantasy, divorced from real life. It wasn't you that was screwing her, it was a fictitious bird-watcher.'

'Still, we seemed to hit it off pretty well.'

'Only because you were part of the fantasy. Don't get the idea that, just because you fucked her, there's something between you.'

'That's for me to find out, isn't it?' he asked. 'Is that the video?'

He reached across for the packet, but Jo snatched it off the desk.

'Leave it, Ed,' she said. 'You've done your bit and you've been paid. That's an end to it.'

'I could deliver the video for you.'

'Absolutely not.'

From the beginning Jo and Chris had realised that the essence of the business must be discretion. The names and addresses of the clients were confidential, only to be seen by the two girls. The videos were edited by them and the master tapes were kept locked in the safe. The men were ordered to ask no questions of the clients, except where they coincided with the scenario of the fantasy. Now it seemed it would be necessary to reinforce that message to Ed.

'Listen, Ed,' she said. 'When we took you on for this job, it was agreed that you would ask no questions. You performed well and got paid for it. Next time your type is called for, we'll keep you in mind. But keep your nose out of the rest of the business. All right?'

'Okay,' he said. 'Keep your hair on. I was just interested, that's all.'

'Well, I've got a lot of work to do, so if you don't mind I'd like to get on with it.'

Ed rose reluctantly to his feet. 'I can take a hint,' he said.

'Good. Nothing personal, but your job here's complete now, and mine isn't.'

Ed went to the door, then turned.

'You're a pretty good-looking chick, Jo,' he said. 'Any time you fancy working out one of your own fantasies . . .'

'I'll call,' she said. 'Goodbye, Ed.'

'And good riddance,' she murmured as he closed the door. 'If ever I have a fantasy involving a complete clod, you'll be the one.'

She sat for a moment, reflecting on what had happened. She really should be more careful. If Ed had got hold of the packet he'd have seen Fiona's address at once and the whole thing would have been blown. From now on the appointments book would be kept in the safe as well as the videos.

She pulled out her diary and checked her schedule. Tomorrow's customer was called Diane, and she was a very different kettle of fish from the submissive Paula and Fiona. She picked up the phone. Time to call up Doug and Mark and make sure they were fully briefed for the job.

Chapter 12

Doug stood in the small, windowless room, eyeing his reflection rather dubiously in the mirror. He wondered what his friends would say if they could see him now.

His outfit was like nothing he had ever worn before. His only real concession to modesty was a black leather posing pouch with silver studs running down the front. About his neck was a stiff leather collar and his face was covered by a leather mask that had two small holes for his eyes and another for his mouth. About his wrists and ankles he wore bands, also of studded leather, bearing metal clips which had been joined so that his wrists were fastened behind his back and his ankles were locked together.

Doug shifted uncomfortably. He had been waiting in the room for nearly an hour now and his legs were beginning to ache. Jo's instructions had been quite specific, however. He was to remain standing where he was until told to do otherwise. The quiet whirr above his head told him that the video surveillance camera attached to the ceiling was scanning the room once more, so he dare not move.

He wondered what this particular fantasy could be about. Jo and Chris had simply said that he was to do exactly as he was told without protest. He knew that Mark was similarly incarcerated nearby, but that hardly offered him any comfort.

All at once he heard the sound of footsteps in the corridor outside and he stiffened as he heard them halt outside the door. Then a key turned in the lock and it swung open.

His jaw dropped when he saw Jo. She too was clad entirely

in black leather. Her torso was trapped in a tight corset, which lifted her bare breasts and separated them, making them bulge upwards, the dark nipples prominent. Below she had on the briefest of G-strings, the back no more than a cord that was lost in the cheek of her behind. From the bottom of the corset came suspenders which held up a pair of black fishnet stockings. On her feet she wore high stiletto heels that clacked on the floor as she walked.

'Come out, slave,' she ordered. 'Your mistress awaits you.'

Doug staggered rather than walked through the door. The bands at his ankles were joined by a chain no more than a foot long, which made walking extremely awkward. Outside he found himself in a long corridor with plush carpets on the floor and oak panelling along the walls. He had been brought to the house blindfold and this was his first opportunity to appreciate the luxurious surroundings in which he had been imprisoned.

He had little time to appreciate the decor, however, as Jo was urging him along the passage as quickly as he was able. She had produced a leather horsewhip from her belt and was flicking the backs of his legs with it, each blow stinging him and urging him onward.

They descended a flight of stairs into a wide hallway, then passed through another door into a large reception room, the walls hung with expensive oil paintings. Here he was told to wait whilst his jailer walked forward to a large pair of double doors at one end. She tapped on the door.

'Come!'

The woman's voice was strident, echoing about the room.

Jo flung the doors open and beckoned to Doug. The young man stepped forward tentatively, looking to right and left.

The sight before him brought him up short. He had been expecting another elaborately decorated room. Instead, the one into which he was being taken was draped all about with black cloths, even the windows were covered. The only light came from concealed bulbs in the ceiling, each one casting a small pool of light on the ground beneath it.

All about the walls were chains and manacles. Cabinets held rows of whips and canes, and other instruments were displayed, the purpose of which he could only guess at. In the centre of the room was a low, wide stage, atop which was a divan draped in black in keeping with rest of the room. Reclining on this was a woman.

She was like no woman Doug had ever seen before. Her hair was long and black, hanging down almost to the floor. Her face was elaborately made up, especially about the eyes, which were green and piercing, seeming to glitter in the light from the bulb above her. She wore a strapless black silk dress that raised her magnificent breasts, accentuating a deep valley of cleavage. The dress clung to her body like a second skin. It was long, stretching almost to her ankles, with a slit that ran all the way up one side, held together by strips of material at the hips, waist and bust. It was obvious she wore nothing underneath.

She lay on her right side, her left leg stretched forward. At her feet sat a young man. He was slim and rather effeminate looking with long curly hair. He wore only a jockstrap sparkling with sequins. He was holding the woman's foot in his hands and kissing her ankles, running his fingers over the patent leather of her sharp high heels. To the side stood a similarly dressed man who held a large fan in his hand which he was waving up and down.

Doug simply stood, staring at the scene. It was like something out of a comic book, though there was nothing comic about this lady. A cold feeling gripped his stomach as he stared into those cruel eyes.

Whack!

Jo's whip sang through the air and caught Doug just below the buttocks, making him jump with surprise.

'Kneel before your mistress!' she ordered.

Doug dropped to his knees at once, his body shaking slightly as he gazed up at the woman.

She shook her leg impatiently and her young attendant released her foot. Then she rose. She was a tall woman and in the heels she fairly towered over Jo as she stepped down from the platform.

'What have we here?' Her voice was icy, sending a shiver down Doug's spine.

'A slave for punishment, mistress,' said Jo.

'What misdemeanour has he committed?'

'He was caught fucking one of the chambermaids below stairs.'

'Was he indeed?' The woman moved forward until she was standing right in front of the kneeling Doug, so close that he could smell not just the musky perfume she wore but also the scent of woman beneath. She took his chin in her hand, yanking his face up to stare into her own. Her fingernails were long, like talons, and painted black.

'Aren't you aware that the female staff are off limits to slaves?' she asked.

'Yes.'

Whack!

The whip descended across his back.

'Yes, mistress!' barked Jo.

'Yes, mistress.'

The woman walked round behind him, her heels clicking on the wooden floor. Doug felt the hairs on the back of his head bristle as he sensed her eyes upon him.

'He's not much of a specimen,' said the woman. 'What could she have seen in him?'

'I believe he is well endowed, mistress,' replied Jo.

'Is that so? Perhaps we'd better see. Secure him to the post.'

Doug felt a tug at his collar and rose to his feet. The woman pulled him round to face her, still gripping the leather band. Once again he shivered as her eyes met his.

Suddenly he was being dragged to the centre of the room, where two posts stood side by side. Chains hung from the top of the posts and he watched warily as Jo released his wrists from behind him and attached them to these chains. Then she pulled down on the ends and his hands were dragged up above his head until they were stretched tight.

Once his arms were secure, Jo undid the chains at his ankles, pulling his legs apart and attaching the bands to rings set in the floor.

Doug was helpless now, his hands stretched above his head, his legs held apart. He stood, eyeing his mistress and jailer with apprehension, not knowing what to expect next.

'Nigel, come here.'

The young man who had earlier been caressing the woman's foot rose to his feet and crossed to where the two women stood.

'What do you think of this specimen?' asked the woman.

'Very beefy,' he replied.

'Yes, but you like a bit of rough, don't you, Nigel?'

'You know me too well, mistress.'

'Would you like to look at his tackle?'

'Yes please, mistress.'

'Go ahead then.'

Doug watched with foreboding as the man approached. He had a slim, wiry body, virtually hairless, and he eyed Doug's crotch with interest.

He reached out and closed his fist about the waistband of the posing pouch. Then, without warning, he tugged hard and the cord snapped at once. He flung the skimpy garment to one side.

Doug was naked now, his thick, circumcised organ and heavy balls revealed to those present. He watched the young man with trepidation.

'Hmm,' said the woman. 'Not bad at all. Would you like to suck him, Nigel?'

'Yes, please, mistress.'

'I've got a better idea. Where's that chambermaid? The one he was so keen to get his cock into?'

103

'She's in the cells, mistress,' said Jo.

'Bring her here.'

Jo nodded to Nigel, who looked decidedly sulky at having been refused the opportunity to taste Doug's cock. He gave a little bow to his mistress, then headed for the door.

It was five minutes before he returned, during which time Doug was left to sweat whilst the dominatrix returned to her couch, reclining elegantly whilst her other slave fanned her.

The return of Nigel was heralded by the sound of voices outside, one of them female, speaking in indignant tones.

'I tell you, you can't take me in there like this. I've done nothing wrong!'

The door crashed open and Nigel ran in looking rather smug. Behind him were Mark and Chris.

Doug stared at them both. Mark was dressed in a similar manner to himself, with straps and leather briefs. Chris, however, was almost naked, being clad in only a ragged skirt which scarcely came as low as her crotch. Her breasts were bare. Around her neck was a collar similar to his own, but smaller. Her arms were cuffed at the wrists and the elbows, which had the effect of thrusting her breasts forward. Mark held a lead attached to her collar and he dragged her to the centre of the room where he forced her to her knees.

'So this is the little bitch that cavorts with my slaves,' barked the mistress. 'Come here, slut.'

Mark released his hold on her lead and Chris rose slowly to her feet.

'On your knees!' ordered Mark.

The hapless girl fell to her knees once more, then shuffled awkwardly across to the edge of the stage. With some difficulty she managed to climb onto it and moved to where the woman was reclining.

She stuck out a foot.

'Kiss my feet, slut!' she ordered.

Slowly Chris bent forward and placed her lips on the shiny leather.

'Clean my shoe,' said the woman. 'With your tongue.'

Chris glanced up at her, then slowly protruded her tongue, licking tentatively at the leather.

'Clean it all over.'

As Doug watched Chris bend forward, revealing the pert globes of her behind, he felt the first stirrings of lust. Glancing down at his cock, he could see that it had begun to swell. He tried to clear his mind of lustful thoughts, but his eyes kept straying to Chris's backside and his penis stiffened a little more.

Chris was made to lick every inch of the woman's shoes. Only when not a speck of dirt remained was she allowed to stop.

'Now, slut,' said the woman. 'What were you doing giving your body to that oaf?'

'I-I couldn't help it,' stammered Chris. 'He was too strong for me. He just took me.'

'Nevertheless, you know my staff are to remain celibate unless I decree they may satisfy their carnal desires. And then they must do it in the manner of my choosing.'

'Yes, mistress. I'm sorry, mistress.'

'Silence! For this act of wantonness you will receive twelve strokes. And the slave who fucked you will have fifty.'

'No, mistress!' cried Chris. 'Fifty will kill him!'

'That's his problem.'

'Please . . .'

'Do I understand you have feelings for this man?'

'Yes, mistress.'

'Is he such a good fuck?'

Chris lowered her eyes. 'Yes, mistress.'

The woman studied her for a while, then a grin spread across her face.

'We'll see how powerful a lover he is,' she said. 'He will witness your punishment from where he is. Meanwhile this young lady will stimulate him.' She nodded in Jo's direction.

'You, little slut, will be tied to the other post,' she went on, turning back to Chris. 'If he can spunk on you from that distance I shall spare him. Then you and he will become entertainment slaves, giving exhibitions of fucking for my friends. Otherwise he receives the whipping and you will spend the next year in one of my dungeons. Tie her!'

At the sound of these words Mark stepped forward and grabbed Chris's lead once more. He dragged her from the stage across to the second of the two bondage posts.

There was a metal ring set no more than eighteen inches from the floor on this post. Mark released Chris's wrists and attached them to this ring, one arm wrapping round each side of the post. Then her feet were secured to the ground in a similar way to Doug's, her ankles wide apart. This left her almost bent over double, her backside high in the air, her arms hugging the post, her cheek hard against the wood. She was staring directly at Doug, the distance between her face and his cock about six feet. Doug knew it would take a massive orgasm to project his seed that far, and he eyed his still half-erect cock with some doubt.

Meanwhile, Nigel had taken a whip from one of the racks on the wall and was taking practice strokes. The swish of the leather through the air made Doug shiver. Apparently satisfied with the chastiser he had chosen, the effeminate young slave walked across to where the girl was tethered.

Rip!

In a single movement he reduced Chris's skirt to a useless rag, tossing it aside. She was totally nude now, her breasts dangling temptingly, the skin on her backside stretched tight.

Suddenly Doug felt a small, soft hand on his thigh. He swung round to see that Jo had moved up behind him. She stood close, her bare nipples brushing his skin, her hand sliding up and cupping his balls. At once he felt a renewed stiffness in his member as she stroked the puckered skin of his scrotum.

Nigel had moved up behind Chris now and she gazed back at him apprehensively as he took two more practice strokes. Then he tapped her backside twice and drew back his arm.

Swish! Whack!

The whip came down across Chris's buttocks with a loud crack and she screamed loud. Doug watched her closely. He couldn't decide how much was an act and how much was true pain. He knew the whips were made of a light plastic which should reduce the amount of damage they did, but there was no mistaking the crack of whip against bare flesh, and he suspected the blow must smart quite a lot.

Swish! Whack!

The whip came down a second time on Chris's exposed buttocks, rocking her body forward and bringing another cry from her. At the same time Doug felt Jo's hand close about his penis and begin working the foreskin back and forth. He gave a quiet groan.

Swish! Whack!
Swish! Whack!

As he watched the naked girl's punishment, Doug felt his arousal growing. He couldn't explain it, but the sight of the lovely young woman, bound and helpless, being lashed in front of these onlookers seemed suddenly incredibly erotic, and his cock stood up proudly from his groin.

Swish! Whack!
Swish! Whack!

Tears were flowing from Chris's eyes and once again Doug wondered how much the punishment was actually hurting. There was no doubting the force of the blows as they fell and he imagined how red her buttocks must be as the whipping continued.

Swish! Whack!
Swish! Whack!

Jo was wanking him hard now, her fist flying up and down his shaft. He eyed her pink breasts, so deliciously pushed upwards and outwards by the corset. The nipples were stiff and hard and he longed to be allowed to suck one.

Swish! Whack!
Swish! Whack!

The onslaught was relentless, and there was no mistaking the look of anguish in Chris's eyes. Doug had been counting and he knew there were only two more strokes to come. He knew too that Chris had the willpower to withstand them.

Swish! Whack!

Only one more to go now, and still Jo worked on Doug's erection, her fingers groping for his balls as she worked the foreskin back and forth. He could feel his muscles beginning to tense, yet he knew he must hold back for a bit longer if he was to succeed in spurting his semen as far as the tethered girl.

Swish! Whack!

The final blow fell, cracking into Chris's bare flesh and rocking her forward. Then Nigel flung the whip aside and for a moment there was silence, broken only by the sobs of the girl and the short gasps coming from Doug. Nigel turned to his mistress, who had watched the beating with avid interest. She was leaning forward in her seat, her hand gently caressing her crotch through the thin material of her dress.

'Use her as you like,' she said, a slight smile on her face.

Nigel grinned, then reached for his waistband and pulled down the jockstrap. His cock was surprisingly large for one with so slight a frame, and it was already erect, standing like a thick, pink flagpole. He eyed Doug's body, and for a second the captive feared that he was to be the object of the young man's attentions. But then he turned to Chris, moving round in front of her, his cock standing just in front of her face.

Doug watched as Chris opened her mouth and took him inside, the tears still flowing down her cheeks. She began to suck him, her jaws forced wide by the thickness of his organ. Once again Doug felt his orgasm approach and had to fight to control himself as he watched the naked girl fellate the young man.

He didn't remain long in her mouth, though, just enough to lubricate his stiff organ. Then he withdrew, his erection shiny with Chris's saliva, and walked round behind her.

He moved in close, taking hold of Chris's inflamed bottom cheeks. Doug looked on, fully expecting him to fuck her, but the expression on Chris's face told him otherwise.

She gave a little cry as Nigel forced his cock into her backside. Doug watched her bite her lip, clearly struggling to relax her sphincter as Nigel eased himself into her rear passage. He buried himself little by little, twisting his shaft with his fist as he pressed onwards, shoving himself inside until he could go no further and her arse cheeks were pressed against his groin.

He began to move his hips back and forth, pumping his cock into Chris's rectum. Doug was uncertain whether Chris's cries were of pain or arousal, then he realised that Nigel had an arm about her waist and was teasing her clitoris, and he knew the girl was turned on.

The atmosphere was electric. The dominatrix, Mark and the slave with the fan all looked on with fascination. Doug wondered at the sight they must make, his own body tethered and naked, his hips thrust forward as Jo wanked him hard, whilst in front of him was Chris's flushed face, her breath coming in hoarse gasps as Nigel buggered her.

Nigel came first, a triumphant shout ringing round the room as his sperm gushed into Chris's behind. This time Doug knew he could hold back no longer and he climaxed with a gasp, watching as a thick gob of semen spurted from the end of his cock. It described a high arc through the air, then splashed onto Chris's upturned face. A second followed, then a third. By now Chris had her mouth open, catching what she could in it and licking it from her cheeks and chin. Doug felt a pair of lips against his cheek as Jo congratulated him for his prowess, whilst his prick continued to ejaculate blobs of thick, white fluid which splashed down onto the floor.

As Doug's passion began to abate he saw that Chris too was coming, her body shaking in silent passion as her hips ground down on Nigel's fingers.

A cracking sound from across the room caught Doug's

attention and his eyebrows rose as he saw that Mark was crouching down on all fours in front of the mistress. She had hiked her dress up to her waist, revealing a cunt entirely shaved of hair, which Mark was licking eagerly at whilst she brought her whip down across his back.

Doug estimated it was an hour since he had been brought into the room. He knew the woman had booked them for a whole day and night. He knew too that there were more dungeons and torture chambers set up below stairs.

He only hoped they all had the stamina to last out.

Chapter 13

Ed Mercer sat in his room, brooding, his bearded face sullen. He checked his watch, then glanced across at the telephone. It remained silent, despite his willing it to ring. What the hell was going on with the agency? They hadn't found him a job for more than a week now and his cash was beginning to run short. The rent was due soon and both the gas and electricity bills were standing on the mantelpiece. Why weren't they finding him any jobs?

He grabbed the receiver and punched in a number, listening impatiently as the ringing tone sounded in his ear.

'Ace Model Agency,' said the female voice at the other end.

'Sandra please.'

'May I ask who's calling?'

'It's Ed of course. Don't you know my voice?'

'Ed who?'

'Ed Mercer,' he shouted. 'I'm on the bloody books.'

'Hold the line please, Mr Mercer.'

At once the girl's voice was replaced by the sound of soft music. Ed fumed at the phone. That bloody receptionist always had been a toffee-nosed bitch. He had disliked her ever since she had declined a date with him, preferring the company of her smart-aleck boyfriend, the schoolteacher. A schoolteacher for Christ's sake. Here he was offering her one of the finest bodies in London and she preferred some skinny academic.

Ed glanced across at the full-length mirror on the wall opposite. He rose to his feet and stood admiring his physique. Even dressed in shirt and jeans as he was, there was no doubting his physical prowess and he tightened his left bicep, watching with satisfaction the way it stretched the fabric of his shirt.

There was a click, then a voice came on the other end of the line.

'Sandra speaking.'

'Sandra, it's Ed.'

'Yes? Hello, Ed, what do you want?'

'What do you think I want? I want a bloody job, Sandra.'

'Ed, I told you yesterday, there's nothing for you.'

'There must be something.'

'No. There's just no call at the moment.'

'Everyone else seems to have work.'

'Yeah, well, maybe they try harder.'

Ed's face darkened. 'Just what the hell's that supposed to mean, Sandra?'

'It doesn't matter, Ed.'

'No, come on, Sandra. You must have meant something.'

'It's nothing. I'm sorry I spoke.'

'Sandra, if there's a problem I want to know.'

'Well, for a start there's the beard.'

Ed stared at the receiver in amazement. 'What do you mean, the beard? What's wrong with my beard?'

Ed was proud of his beard. He thought it made him look more manly, set him apart from the other men at the agency. They were nothing more than a bunch of queens in Ed's eyes.

'There's nothing wrong with your beard,' said Sandra defensively. 'It's just not fashionable, that's all.'

'George Michael's got a beard. So has Paul McCartney.'

'And neither of them works for a modelling agency. The trouble is, Ed, I can only get you specialist character parts. And there's not too many of them around.'

'I'm not shaving it off.'

'Suit yourself. Anyhow, it's not just the beard.'

'What else then? Don't tell me my eyebrows are too bushy.'

'Don't be silly.'

'What then?'

'If you must know, it's your attitude.'

'What the hell's wrong with my attitude?'

'For a start, you fly off the handle at the first mention of any criticism,' said Sandra, keeping her voice low. 'But that's not all.'

'What else then?'

'We've had complaints, Ed.'

'Who from?'

'That fashion shoot you did two weeks ago for that outdoor clothes firm. Apparently you kept criticising the photographer.'

'I was only trying to help. The idiot didn't know what he was doing.'

'But he was the photographer, Ed. You're just the model. You're paid to do as you're told. Anyhow, that wasn't the only complaint.'

'Who else?'

'That new company, Fantasy. The girl there said you were trying to find out the names of their clients.'

'It was just this girl. She really fancied me, I could tell, but they wouldn't give me her name. Just unnecessary bloody bureaucracy.'

'Look, Ed,' Sandra argued. 'You have to remember that they're the boss and you're just an employee. We just can't afford to have you intimidating our clients, particularly a new one like Fantasy. They could turn out to be a real good customer.'

'Are you saying it's my bloody fault that those buggers don't recognise talent when they see it?'

'Ed, I can't afford to keep you on my books if you keep upsetting the clients.'

'Screw your fucking books then,' shouted Ed. 'There are other agencies around. Ones that recognise true talent. I don't need a two-bit outfit like yours.'

And with that he slammed the receiver down.

Ed flung himself into his chair, fuming. Damn! He hadn't

113

meant to say that. Even if Sandra's agency was incapable of recognising his many talents, they were at least a source of income. And now he had thrown that source away, just when he needed it.

That bitch at Fantasy and Co, he brooded. It was all her fault. Going behind his back like that. Just who the hell did she think she was? For two pins he'd tell the world about her sordid business.

That was a thought! He might be able to sell the story to one of the Sunday tabloids. SOCIETY GIRLS RUN SEX COMPANY, that ought to make a good headline. He could earn a couple of hundred exposing the women who got their rocks off on what Fantasy did.

Then another thought struck him. The reason the whole thing was confidential was to make sure the women's husbands and friends didn't find out. The whole business was based on secrecy. So if he could find out who Fantasy's customers were, he might be able to persuade them to part with some money in order to keep his mouth shut. Even better, if he had hold of one of those videos, who knew what they might pay to get it back. It could be a real earner. All he had to do was find a way to get hold of not only one of the videos, but also the address to which it was being sent.

He grimaced. The trouble with that plan was that he'd not only need to get hold of the bookings diary, but also the master video tapes. And then he'd have to match the one to the other. It was going to be a hell of a task.

Then another thought struck him. The video he had seen on her office desk. It had had an address on it, awaiting delivery. That was the one time when both tape and address were in the same place. If he could just intercept the tape at that point the whole thing would be easy. All he needed was to work out a way to get hold of it.

For the first time that day a smile spread across Ed's face as he began to make his plans.

Chapter 14

Jo looked up as the door to the office opened and Chris came in. The blonde was dressed in a short summer dress that showed off her figure beautifully. Not for the first time Jo reflected on how attractive her partner was. Once again Jo had the video equipment set up on her desk and was busy editing a tape.

'Is that yesterday's tape?' asked Chris.

'Yes. I wanted to get it done this morning, otherwise we're going to fall behind.'

'How does it look?'

'Great. The guy we hired to do it seems to know his stuff. The pictures look really good. Take a look.'

Chris came round the desk to stand beside her partner. On the screen was an imagine of herself, totally naked and tied spread-eagled on her back to a large wooden frame. As she watched, the woman who had played the mistress attached nipple clamps to her breasts whilst Jo, wearing only a black strap-on dildo, positioned herself between her legs and began to ease the long, thick phallus into her vagina.

'She was certainly into the kinky stuff, wasn't she?' remarked Chris.

'So were you by the look of it. I lost count of the number of times you came.'

Chris grinned. 'Yeah. I never knew I could get turned on by a whipping.'

'How's your backside today?'

'Not too bad. That whip doesn't do any real damage. It

hurts a bit, though. And it didn't half turn my backside red. It's still too sore to wear panties.'

'Really? Let's see.' Jo reached for her friend's dress, lifting up the hem and exposing her backside. Faint red stripes were still visible across the smooth white globes of her behind. She traced one with her finger.

'That hurt?'

'A little.'

'What about your tits? Those clamps looked pretty vicious.'

'Yeah, they're a bit sore too.'

'No bra then?'

'No.'

'Good.'

With that Jo reached up the back of her friend's dress and pulled down the zip in a single movement. Then she pulled the dress down to her friend's waist.

'Let's have a look.'

Chris turned and Jo felt for her breasts. The nipples were indeed swollen, and Chris winced slightly as Jo's fingers toyed with them.

'Gently,' she remonstrated.

Jo pulled her closer and closed her lips over the pink buds, sucking gently whilst her tongue licked at them.

'Mmmm. That's better,' sighed Chris.

On the screen, Chris was still tied helpless to the frame. Jo watched from the corner of her eye as her other self plunged the dildo into her friend's sex, the great black object sliding in and out, making a stark contrast to the girl's light skin. As she watched she took hold of Chris's dress again, pulling it down over her hips and off.

She took her mouth from her friend's breast and sat back a second to admire her body. Naked, the fair-haired girl was gorgeous, her lovely breasts enhanced by the swollen nipples. Jo ran her hand down her stomach, enjoying the smoothness of her flesh.

'The pictures are good, aren't they?' she said.

'Mmmm.'

'Do you like watching yourself being fucked by me, Chris?'

'Yeah.'

Jo took hold of Chris's hips and turned her so that she faced the screen. Then she pressed on her back, forcing her to bend forward over the desk. She traced the girl's spine with her finger, running it down to the crack in her behind, then further, seeking out the tight little hole of her anus.

'Oh!'

Chris gave a little cry as Jo wormed her fingers into her friend's backside, twisting it as she penetrated her.

'How was having Nigel's cock in your arse?' she asked.

'Really strange,' gasped the naked girl. 'But a real turn-on. Especially with everyone watching.'

'He made you come,' said Jo, still twisting her finger.

'Yeah.'

Jo slipped her other hand between Chris's legs, feeling for the soft folds of her sex. It was hot and moist down there and she ran her fingers along the girl's slit, enjoying the way the muscles of her sex convulsed as she stroked her. She slipped a finger into Chris's vagina, smiling as she heard her friend gasp with arousal.

'Just watch the video,' she said.

Chris had little choice, sprawled face down as she was across Jo's desk, her face only inches from the monitor. On the screen, Jo continued to fuck her, her backside pumping back and forth as she thrust the thick strap-on into her helpless friend. At the same time the mistress tugged at two thin chains attached to the nipple clamps, alternately stretching the flesh of her breasts.

Jo slipped a second digit into Chris's sex, working her hand back and forth whilst the finger of her other hand remained deep in her friend's anus. She could sense Chris's arousal increasing with every second, the tension in her lovely young body transmitting itself to her through her fingertips. She

117

looked up at the girl's face. Her attention was fixed on the screen where the images of herself and the mistress had been joined by Mark. As she watched, the young man dropped his briefs and thrust his stiff cock unceremoniously into Chris's mouth. At once the girl began sucking him eagerly, the slurping sounds coming through the audio track.

Jo moved her fingers back and forth vigorously. Chris was becoming more animated by the second, as was her alter ego on the screen, who was threatening to break the bonds that held her, her body thrashing back and forth, her cries of pleasure barely muffled by her mouthful of stiff cock. Jo was having difficulty keeping her fingers inside her friend as the girl thrust her hips hard against the edge of the desk, her breasts slapping loudly against its surface.

The cries from the screen indicated that the tethered beauty was coming, cries cut short by the spunk that Mark was pumping into her mouth. Jo guessed that the scene would be enough to send her partner over the top, and she was right. Chris came violently and noisily, her cries of passion drowning out the soundtrack as her sex muscles tightened about Jo's fingers. Jo frigged her friend as hard as she was able, prolonging the orgasm with her double penetration for as long as possible as Chris writhed and moaned on her desk.

When, at last, her friend was still, Jo withdrew her fingers, smearing the wetness on them across the flesh of Chris's behind. The girl lay where she was, panting, her body glistening with sweat. It was some time before she raised her head and turned to her companion.

'That was unexpected,' she said.

Jo grinned. 'I've wanted to bring you off for a while. Then when you came in with no undies I couldn't resist it.'

Chris rose to her feet, leaning down and kissing Jo on the lips. 'You've come a long way from the demure little thing on the beach,' she said.

'That's your bad influence,' laughed Jo.

'Hang on. This whole enterprise was your idea.'

'I guess we both must have corrupted each other.'

Leaving her dress where it lay, Chris wandered round the desk and dropped into her own chair.

'Seriously, though,' she said. 'The lady with the whip took quite some pleasing.'

'Yeah. Definitely our most ambitious job yet. But also our most lucrative. She was very generous.'

'And how are bookings going?'

'Great. We're booked three days a week for the next month. And that's capacity as far as things go at the moment. We need the breaks to edit the videos and handle all the admin. In fact I think we should advertise for a secretary.'

'She'll have to be broad-minded,' said Chris, stretching out her long legs and placing her feet on her desk. Jo couldn't help admiring her lovely body. Having her naked in the office was something of a distraction, but one she was prepared to put up with.

'Meanwhile,' said Jo. 'We've got to find ourselves a gang of bikers by next week.'

'Couldn't Sandra at the agency help?'

'Not really. Most of her guys are ultra careful with their bodies, and that means riding a bike is out.'

'Maybe we should find some real bikers,' suggested Chris.

'Isn't that a little dangerous?'

'Not really. I used to go out with a biker, you know. His name was Gerry. He had a Harley Davidson, leather jacket, reflecting sunglasses, the lot. Scared the pants off anyone who saw him. The joke was that he wasn't like that at all. In fact he was a real pussycat underneath it all. Trouble was he was more interested in the bike than me, so I left him.'

'Do you think he might be able to help?'

'It's possible. I've probably still got his number.'

Chris pulled open a drawer and rummaged inside. She pulled out a notebook and began riffling through the pages.

'Here we are!' she exclaimed at last. 'I'll give him a call and see if he's there.' Then she paused, reaching into the drawer once more and pulling out the vibrator she had used on Jo the week before.

'On second thoughts,' she said. 'I might just make use of this first.'

'You're not horny again already?'

'Of course. You don't mind do you? It's just that the way you've been staring at my body is getting me going again.'

'Sorry. I can't help it. You're such a turn-on when you're naked. Go ahead and use it.'

Chris spread her legs to either side of the desk and raised her backside from the chair. She switched on the vibrator and ran it up and down the lips of her sex. Then, twisting it as she did so, she began pressing it into her vagina.

Jo watched, her eyes fixed on her friend's breasts and sex.

'Better hurry,' she said. 'Doug and Mark will be here soon.'

'That's all right,' grinned Chris. 'I'll have enough stamina to take them on as well.'

And she began to work the dildo back and forth inside her.

Chapter 15

Jo peered anxiously down the dark alleyway in front of her, then turned back to Chris. 'Are you sure this is the right place?'

'Gerry said Bolton Street. And that's what this street's called.'

'It doesn't look very lively.'

'Well, according to Gerry it's where the biker club is.'

'But it might have moved. You said Gerry gave it up a couple of years ago.'

'Yeah, but he was pretty certain they still met here. Come on, we'll take a look.'

Jo hung back for a moment, still unsure. After all, Chris hadn't seen Gerry for years. How did she know she could trust him?

Tracking down Chris's biker ex-boyfriend hadn't been as easy as expected. The number in her address book proved to be well out of date, but she had found others and had spent nearly an hour ringing round until she had finally located him, now settled down with a girlfriend and baby in the country.

Once they did contact him, though, he had proved a useful source of information. He still retained a number of friends from his younger days. It had been his suggestion that they try the club to which they were headed that night. The trouble was that it didn't exactly look a salubrious spot and Jo felt decidedly nervous as they made their way down the quiet lane.

'Ah, that's more like it,' said Chris suddenly. 'Look down here, Jo.'

Jo's eyes followed the direction in which Chris was pointing. At the far end of the lane was a driveway that opened into a wide space. It was there that the motorcycles were parked. Dozens of them, all gleaming chrome with long, high handlebars and brightly coloured fuel tanks.

'I guess this is the place,' said Chris.

'But where's the club?' asked Jo.

'Gerry said it was in a cellar. It must be that place there, let's take a look.'

The two girls made their way across to the building beside the bike park. Its windows were dark and there was no sign of life at all. In the centre was a green door, the paint peeling from it. Chris walked up to it and knocked loudly.

They waited, but there was no answer. She knocked again, with similar results.

'I wonder if it's unlocked,' said Chris. She reached down and tried the handle. The door opened. 'Great, we're in,' she said.

'We can't just walk in,' said Jo.

'There's not much else we can do,' said her friend. 'Come on.'

She stepped through the door, with Chris behind her. They found themselves in a darkened hallway. To their right was a flight of stone stairs, leading downwards.

'That must be the way,' said Chris, and began to descend.

Jo was decidedly uneasy as they made their way down. She felt almost like a burglar sneaking into the building. As they descended the stairs, though, a sound met her ears. It was the sound of music, rock music, though it seemed very distant.

'Do you hear that?' she said to Chris.

'Yeah. I guess we're headed in the right direction.'

They fumbled their way down the steps and, at the bottom, came up against a door.

'I suppose it's in there,' said Chris.

'Should we knock?'

'No. Let's just go in.'

Chris turned the door handle and pushed. Almost at once they were struck by a wall of noise. Heavy, jarring rock music that almost deafened them. What kind of soundproofing the door had Jo didn't know, but it was certainly effective.

Chris stepped into the room with Jo close behind her. The atmosphere was thick with smoke and the lighting was dim. The dark corridor had given them the opportunity to accustom their eyes to the darkness, however, and they gazed about at the scene.

All around the walls were tables and chairs, most of which were occupied. Nearly all the occupants were men, large, burly looking fellows with thick arms bedecked with tattoos. All wore denim waistcoats and most had long hair. There were a few women too, dressed in jeans and tight tops, as well as the apparently mandatory waistcoats.

Jo stood slightly behind Chris, intimidated by the many pairs of eyes that had fixed on her and her companion the moment they had walked in the door.

Suddenly the music stopped and the room was silent. Then a chair scraped back and a man rose to his feet. He was well over six feet tall, with broad shoulders and biceps like hams. He strode across to where the two girls were standing. He had dark, fierce eyes and he towered above them, his arms folded.

'Yes?'

'I . . . er, Gerry sent us.'

For a second the man's eyes narrowed, then a broad grin spread across his face.

'You must be Chris and Jo,' he said. 'Gerry told me to expect you. I'm Jet. Welcome to the Vipers' hideout.'

And with that he reached out a burly arm and shook them both by the hand.

Jet ushered the two girls across to a table and a bottle of beer was placed in front of each. Jo took a swig from hers, suddenly realising how dry her throat was. Other members of the gang gathered around them. Jo noted that their waistcoats all carried a similar design on the back, a representation of a snake poised as if to strike. *Hence the Vipers*, she thought.

Jet introduced the bikers to the girls. There were too many for Jo to take in the names, but all had nicknames such as Snake, Dragon or Shark. All shook her gravely by the hand, their manners impeccable.

When, at last, the greetings were complete, Jet sat down at the table.

'Now,' he said. 'Gerry told me you have a job for us. Tell us what you've got in mind.'

Chris began by explaining the purpose of Fantasy and Co. The men's eyes widened as she described some of the scenarios they had set up.

'And they actually pay for this kind of thing?' asked Jet in amazement.

'Yes. They pay very well,' said Chris. 'After all, we offer total discretion and we make the whole thing as realistic as possible. It's got to be just right, you see.'

Jet gave a low whistle. 'That's certainly some business you're in,' he said. 'So where do we come in?'

'We've got a customer with a fantasy about bikers.'

'What kind of fantasy?'

'A fantasy about being picked up by a bike gang, who then have their way with her.'

'And you want us to do it?'

'That's about it.'

Jet shook his head. 'Listen, we're not on *Candid Camera* or something are we?'

Chris laughed. 'No, we're on the level. Are you game?'

'I guess so. What do you think, fellas?'

There was a general nodding of assent.

'What about us girls?' said one of the female bikers.

'You're included if you want to be.'

'Just try and stop us.'

'So tell us the details.'

Chris began to explain her plan to the bikers. Jo, who knew it all already, wandered across to the makeshift bar at the side of the room, where she was given another beer by one of the bikers. He was a tall, slim man who introduced himself as Tiger. Soon they were joined by one of the girls, whose name was Vixen.

'So, Tiger,' the girl said. 'You gonna join in this bit of fun?'

He grinned at her. 'That all right by you, baby?'

She placed an arm round him. 'Sure,' she said. 'You know I'm game for anything.' She turned to Jo. 'You ever been on a bike?'

Jo shook her head.

'You wanna come for a spin with Tiger and me?'

Jo looked at her. There was an edge of amusement in Vixen's voice, the hint of a shared joke, and Jo caught a glance between the two bikers. She sensed that she was being tested and that to refuse would be to fail the test.

'All right,' she said.

The girl smiled and winked at her companion. Then she took Jo's hand and led her towards the door. Jo glanced over her shoulder at Chris, but her partner was deep in conversation with the bikers and had clearly not noticed her departure.

They climbed the stairs and went out into the parking area. The night was warm and the air felt fresh after the stuffiness of the cellar.

'You come on my chopper,' said Vixen. 'Tiger'll follow us.'

Jo stared at Vixen's machine. It was large and black, with shiny chrome handlebars set high up, so that as Vixen straddled it she sat straight in the saddle, her hands at the level of her face. She kicked the starter and the engine came to life with a throaty roar.

'Hop on,' she said.

Jo was wearing a short, tight dress, quite unsuitable for riding a motorcycle, but she sensed that this was part of the test and she was determined not to show any weakness. She hitched up her hem, aware of Tiger's eyes on her brief white panties, and climbed aboard behind Vixen.

The girl dropped the clutch and Jo was forced to grab her round her waist as the machine leapt forward, sliding across the parking area and raising a shower of gravel behind it. Then they were on the road and roaring away with Tiger in hot pursuit.

The ride was one of the most exhilarating experiences of Jo's life. There was something almost sexual about the sensation of having so much power throbbing between her legs as the bike fairly flew along the road, the wind streaming through her hair. Vixen handled the machine like an expert, leaning low into the bends, then squeezing a handful of throttle, occasionally raising the front wheel from the ground as the rear tyre dug into the tarmac.

They rode on for what seemed like miles and Tiger was always close on their tail, grinning broadly at Jo every time she glanced back at him.

All at once they slowed down, then swung left off the tarmac and onto a gravel road, the bike sliding sideways as Vixen wound on the power. Jo looked about her and realised that they were in a municipal park, racing along a narrow track.

Ahead was a playground area and suddenly Vixen was changing down through the gears, the wheels skidding slightly as they slowed. She swung the machine onto a patch of concrete beside a slide, then kicked down the stand and killed the machine. Almost simultaneously Tiger pulled up beside her and did the same.

After the roar of the bikes' engines, the silence seemed to overwhelm Jo and she shook her head, as if trying to regain her senses.

Tiger climbed from his machine and Vixen did the same, swinging her leg forward over the fuel tank. She turned to Jo, who was still astride the saddle.

'Well, what do you think?'

'Fantastic. You ride as though you were born in the saddle, Vixen.'

'And did it give you a thrill?'

'Oh boy, yes.'

'What about down there?' Vixen reached down and slid her hand under Jo's crotch, cupping her sex. 'Did it make you wet?'

Jo gave a gasp of surprise at the intimacy of the touch. Vixen slipped her hand back and forth, her fingers tracing Jo's slit through the thin panties.

'She feel hot?' asked Tiger, grinning.

'She sure does. That power's a real turn-on isn't it, baby?'

'I . . .' Jo found herself at a loss for words as the girl continued to caress her. She hadn't realised it, but the ride had made her wet and had stimulated her clitoris into a hard nut. She knew that Vixen could feel it through her pants and she knew the soft moans that were escaping her lips would give away her arousal to the two bikers.

As Vixen continued to stimulate Jo's sex, Tiger moved in behind her, his hands sliding round her waist and then up to cup her breasts, his fingers squeezing them through the fabric. Jo wore no bra and the thinness of the material allowed him to feel the hardness of her nipples. He kissed her shoulder, then ran his lips lightly up her neck, his tongue snaking into her ear and making her sigh with pleasure.

'You're a pretty little plaything,' said Vixen quietly. 'We'd like to play with you some more, if that's okay.'

'What if someone comes?' Jo knew it was a feeble remark and she wished she hadn't said it. Clearly Tiger and Vixen didn't give a damn if someone came by.

Suddenly Tiger had hold of her arms, forcing them back behind her and holding them tight. Jo was helpless now and she stared into Vixen's face as the girl watched her struggle. Jo knew that she was in no danger, that this was all part of their game, and she felt a sudden thrill at the forcible way they were taking her. She struggled a bit more, but did not cry out.

'It's no good fighting it, pretty one,' said Vixen. 'You're ours now.'

She slid her hand from under Jo's crotch and up to the buttons that ran down the front of her dress. One by one she flicked them undone until it was open all the way to Jo's waist. Still she said nothing, but when Vixen leaned forward and, pulling the dress open, closed her lips over Jo's nipple, the girl emitted a low moan.

Vixen sucked greedily at Jo's swollen teats as her hands returned to the buttons, unfastening the dress all the way to the bottom. When the last button was undone, Tiger took hold of the garment and pulled it off her shoulders, tossing it aside onto the grass. Jo was clad only in her brief panties and a pair of black hold-up stockings now, her pale flesh almost translucent in the moonlight.

'Turn her round,' said Vixen.

Tiger grabbed Jo under the arms and dragged her round. She was forced to raise her legs and swing them over the seat as he turned her to face backwards on the bike. Then he took hold of her wrists and placed her hands on the handlebars.

'Hold those and don't let go,' he ordered.

Jo obeyed. There was something deeply exciting about the way the two bikers were taking control of her, using her like some kind of sex doll, whilst she complied with their desires. Their very demeanour spoke to Jo of dominance and she was happy to do as they demanded of her, letting them use her body as they wished.

Vixen took hold of her ankles and pulled her along the saddle until her arms were stretched up above and behind her, still gripping the handlebars. Then her hands went to Jo's panties. Pulling them down in a single movement and discarding them beside her dress.

Jo glanced down at her naked body. She was stretched across the motorcycle, her breasts pulled almost oval, her feet resting on the passenger footrests so that her sex was wide open. The two bikers stepped back to admire their plaything and she gazed back at them, her chest rising and falling as her arousal increased.

'Ever been fucked on a chopper?' asked Vixen.

Jo shook her head.

'There's always a first time.' With that she turned to Tiger and reached for his fly.

She slipped it down and reached inside for his cock. Jo watched with interest as she pulled it out. It was already half erect, its thick stem jutting from his jeans. Vixen took it in her hands and, dropping to her knees, guided it into her mouth.

Jo watched longingly as the girl sucked him to erection. She too wanted to suck his cock, to taste his manhood and feel the power of his erection between her lips. She too wanted to finger her own sex, which was becoming hotter by the second. She was almost screaming with desire as she lay there but she knew she had to play their game, so she remained where she was, occasionally glancing nervously about lest someone should come by.

Vixen sucked loud and long at Tiger's cock, her head working back and forth until his shaft was stiff as a ramrod, standing upward from his fly, the tip glistening with saliva. Then she rose to her feet, her hand still masturbating him gently, and led him across to the naked Jo.

Jo was perfectly positioned to be fucked, her feet tucked back, her backside projecting over the edge of the bike seat. Vixen moved Tiger into position between her spread thighs, then guided his cock towards her open vagina.

The prostrate girl gave a gasp of passion as she felt his weapon pressing between her sex lips. Vixen smiled at the reaction, feeling for Jo's clitoris and rubbing it gently whilst she eased Tiger's rod into her. Jo moaned softly as she felt her sex forced open by the heavy erection that was sliding ever deeper inside her, stretching her wonderfully. He pushed on until she felt his hips pressing against the inside of her thighs, and she knew he was all the way in.

Tiger wasted no time on foreplay, beginning at once to move his hips back and forth, clearly as aroused as Jo and anxious to have her. Now that his pubis was hard against Jo's, Vixen removed her hand from Jo's love bud and moved up to stare into her face. She began to toy with the naked girl's breasts, leaning forward and sucking at the hard, brown nipples as her companion rammed his cock into her with increasing gusto.

Jo felt extraordinarily aroused, lying naked and pale across the gleaming black machine whilst the two bikers screwed her. Every thrust from Tiger's cock brought a new grunt of pleasure from her as she lay there, her breasts bouncing back and forth whilst Vixen sucked hungrily at them.

Tiger and Jo came simultaneously, the first spurt of his semen inside her triggering a delicious orgasm in the young woman. Vixen sucked and squeezed her breasts as her body writhed beneath her, small cries of ecstasy escaping from her lips as wave after wave of pleasure coursed through her.

Tiger continued to fuck her until every last drop of his spunk had been deposited inside her. Then he withdrew, tucking his still-glistening cock into his pants whilst Jo lay gasping on the bike, her head thrown back, her firm young breasts rising and falling with every breath. Vixen moved close to her, taking her chin in her hand and kissing her on the lips.

'You're all right, Jo,' she said. 'I think we're going to enjoy working for Fantasy and Co.'

Chapter 16

Belinda cursed silently at the group of motorcyclists ahead of her on the highway. She had been following them for some miles now and they seemed determined to block any attempts by her to pass, weaving back and forth across the road, riding three abreast and constantly swinging across the path of her vehicle, causing her to brake to avoid them. She had sounded her horn at them a number of times, but their reaction had simply been to sound their own back, laughing at her efforts to pass.

It wasn't as if she was in a hurry. It was simply the deliberate way in which they seemed to be hogging the road that was annoying her, and the longer they stayed there, the crosser she became. The trouble was that they had so much more power than she did and the moment they saw her close on them they would simply speed up, leaving her angry and frustrated.

All at once one of them ran dangerously close to her, waving two fingers in the air as he did so, and Belinda decided she had had enough. Ramming the gear lever into third, she stood on the throttle and pulled across to the right hand side of the road. She was past half a dozen of the machines before they even saw her coming. A grin creased her face as she watched them stare at her in surprise.

The road ahead was clear and she shifted up into fourth, pressing her foot flat to the floor once again. She was past more then half of them now and making good progress.

She was nearly clear of the group when it happened.

Suddenly one of the lead bikers swung across the road in front of her. She was going a good deal faster than him and for a second a collision looked inevitable. She slammed on her brakes, the tyres screeching as her wheels locked up. In the end it was very close indeed, the bike just brushing her wing mirror as the rider pulled back. Belinda leaned on the horn, emitting a long blast as she brought her vehicle back under control.

In no time she was surrounded by motorcycles, the riders shaking their fists and shouting at her, hemming her in and causing her to reduce her speed considerably. She sounded her horn again, but to no avail. They had formed a tight cordon about her car and there was no way to shift them.

Then she realised they were slowing her down, gradually reducing their speed and forcing her to do the same. Up ahead she could see a track leading off the main road and she realised with a shock that that was where she was being taken.

They signalled a left turn. Belinda knew that she must either turn with them, or collide with the bikes on her right. They had effectively left her no choice but to follow them and she turned off the road, her car bumping up the gravel track. She checked her mirror. Soon her car would be lost to sight from the road behind her and she began to feel a twinge of apprehension as she gazed round at the denim-clad gang.

They drove on for about half a mile, then slowed in unison, so that Belinda was forced, once again, to follow suit. They brought her to a halt, standing their bikes in front and behind her car so that she was unable to drive away in either direction.

Belinda sat in her car. For a moment she contemplated locking the doors, but knew that would simply be a sign of weakness. Besides, they could easily break the windows and she didn't want her car damaged. She decided the best tactic would be to confront them, so she climbed from the vehicle, slamming the door and standing with her hands on her hips, glaring at the group of bikers.

132

'Just what the hell do you think you're playing at?' she asked angrily.

'We might as well ask you the same question,' retorted a tall, dark biker. 'You nearly had Jag off his bike there.'

'You were driving atrociously,' said Belinda. 'You were all over the road. It was lucky I didn't hit one of you earlier.'

'It was just a bit of fun,' said the large man. 'We weren't doing any harm. It was just you that got uptight.'

'Of course I got uptight. You were blocking the road with your silly antics.'

'We just take up a lot of space, that's all. Besides, nobody was hurt in the end.'

'Well don't you think it's time you grew up?'

'Why bother? Life's just a hassle. Maybe it's you that needs to loosen up a bit.'

'What does that mean?'

'Well, you car drivers have no idea how much fun the open road can be. When did you ever ride a bike?'

'I wouldn't want to.'

'How would you know when you haven't tried? Come on, I'll show you.'

'Don't be stupid. Besides I've got places to go.'

'Like where?'

'Just places.'

'Well, let them wait. Take a break from real life and let your hair down. You're only young once.'

'Don't be silly. I couldn't.'

The man shrugged. 'If you want to chicken out, I guess that's up to you.'

'I'm not chickening out,' she insisted, suddenly stung by the remark. 'I never chickened out of anything in my life.'

'Well come on then.'

Belinda eyed him. The suggestion was a crazy one. She was a professional woman. She didn't have time to go dashing about on the back of a motorcycle with a gang of dropouts. Nevertheless, seen at close quarters they weren't nearly as intimidating as she'd expected. In fact, the one who had been doing the talking was really quite dishy.

'What about my car?' she asked, realising that the statement was tantamount to acquiescing.

'It'll be safe enough here.'

'I don't know.'

'Yes you do. Live a little.'

'Would we go far?'

'Not that far. Now, you coming or not?'

Belinda gazed around at the bikers. She couldn't believe she was even considering the idea. After all, she wasn't a biker. She was a very successful advertising executive, on her way to spend a weekend at her country cottage. It would be unthinkable for her to go off with this rabble. At the same time, though, there was something strangely attractive about these coarse, unruly men and women. Something that stirred primeval thoughts inside her. Something that appealed to her most primitive instincts.

She glanced down at herself. She was dressed okay for a bike ride, tight jeans encasing her long, shapely legs and a simple blouse that strained to contain her large, bulging breasts. She shook back her long, flaming red locks and looked the biker in the eye.

'Okay, Mr Biker,' she said, 'Show me what that machine of yours can do.'

'Call me Jet,' he said. 'Climb aboard.'

He straddled his machine. It was a heavy American-built bike with a tear-drop tank and a huge engine that snarled into life as he kicked the starter. Belinda climbed into the seat behind him and grasped his waist. She could feel his muscles through the denim waistcoat he wore and the smell of maleness about him sent a tingle of excitement through her.

He opened the throttle and dropped the clutch and the machine sped away, the other bikes following in their wake. He leaned the bike over on the soft gravel and the rear wheel skidded round through a hundred and eighty degrees. Then they were racing back towards the other bikers.

They appeared to be on a direct collision course with one of the other bikes and Belinda let out an involuntary scream as the two cycles swerved apart at the last second, narrowly missing one another. Then they were heading down the track, leaving her car in a cloud of dust. In no time they had reached the highway and were speeding away.

Like Jo had been, Belinda found herself thrilled by the speed and power of the machine as they roared along, leaving the others far behind. She clung tightly to Jet, leaning with him into the corners and laughing aloud as he weaved his way in and out of the white lines in the middle of the road.

They rode on for five or six miles, with Belinda revelling in the experience. It was as if she was leaving normal life behind, her troubles momentarily forgotten.

All at once they began to slow. She peered out from behind Jet and saw that they were approaching another track, not unlike the one where she had left her car. They swerved off the highway and down the track, which was lined on either side by trees.

'Where are we going?' shouted Belinda.

'You'll see.'

They thundered along at breakneck speed, the trees and bushes flashing past as they penetrated deeper and deeper into the wood. Then, suddenly, the trees parted and they were in the middle of a wide, grassy clearing. As they crossed the grass, Belinda saw that there were a number of bikes parked on the far side, with groups of bikers standing round them or sitting on the grass. At the far end a makeshift stage had been erected where a group of musicians was playing.

'What's going on?' she asked.

'Just a little get-together,' called Jet over his shoulder. 'We have them every now and then.'

'I thought rival biker gangs were always fighting one another.'

'We're rivals all right, but we don't fight. That's a myth got up by the press.'

They came to a halt beside the other machines and climbed off. Behind them the rest of the Vipers were arriving and parking their bikes.

'Come on,' said Jet. 'I'll get you a beer. What's your name, by the way?'

'Belinda.'

'Come on then, Belinda.'

He took her hand and led her across to where a large icebox stood. He handed a couple of pound coins to a man who stood beside it, then opened the lid and pulled out two bottles of beer, snapping off the caps and handing one to Belinda. She took a swig. It was cool and refreshing and she gulped it down.

'What happens next?' she asked.

Jet called to a heavily bearded man, who was sitting on the edge of the stage.

'What's going on, Django?'

The man grinned. 'The chicks are gonna have a wet T-shirt contest,' he said. 'You Vipers better find a contestant.'

Jet grinned back. 'Sounds like a good idea. Let's go tell the others.'

He took Belinda back to where the rest of the Vipers were gathered. They too had helped themselves to beers and were standing in a circle chatting.

'What's cooking, Jet?' asked one of the men.

'Wet T-shirt competition. Which of you girls is gonna represent us? How about you, Vixen?'

'Fuck off, Jet. You know I'm not a blockbuster,' said one of the girls. Belinda eyed her. She was certainly lovely looking beneath the rough clothes, but her breasts were no more than average.

'Those bastards always do this to us,' said another of the girls. 'They know we'll never beat Moll.'

'What happens to the winner?' asked Belinda.

'Free crate of beer,' said Jet.

'Hey, wait a minute,' said the girl called Vixen. 'What about her?'

Belinda stared at her. 'Me?'

'Yeah. You're pretty well stacked. We could make you an honorary Viper.'

Belinda shook her head. 'No,' she said. 'I couldn't.'

'Why not, Belinda?' asked Jet. 'That's not padding in there is it?'

'Certainly not,' said Belinda indignantly. She was immensely proud of her breasts and was fond of wearing tops that showed them off at their best.

'C'mon, baby,' said another of the bikers. 'I reckon you'd give Moll a real run for her money.'

'It's out of the question,' said Belinda.

'I think Jet's right,' said Vixen. 'She must be wearing falsies. Otherwise why's she so shy?'

'It's not true,' said a red-faced Belinda.

'Then prove it.'

Belinda looked around at the bikers. The whole idea was unthinkable. How could she, Belinda, the sensible, serious businesswoman, take part in a wet T-shirt competition with a bunch of scruffy bikers? It was crazy.

But was it really so crazy? Hadn't she already stepped outside the bounds of normality by allowing herself to come with them to this place? Was she really such a prude as to turn down the suggestion flat? She shook her head in confusion, unable to believe that she was even contemplating the idea. Yet she was, and the more she thought about it, the more she was unable to find an argument against it. There was another factor too, though it was one she was reluctant to admit even to herself. The fact was that the idea of the contest was oddly thrilling to her. But how on earth would she summon up the courage?

'What about it, baby?' said Jet, putting an arm around her. 'I think you'd be great.'

'But I haven't got a T-shirt,' said Belinda, only too aware of the feebleness of the excuse.

'That's no problem, I have,' said Vixen. She opened a small pannier on the side of her machine and pulled out a clean white T-shirt, which she tossed to Belinda.

'But I . . .'

'But what?' asked Vixen. 'You said you needed a T-shirt. Well now you've got one.'

Belinda knew she was trapped. She opened her mouth to protest once more, then closed it again. It was no good arguing, she was going to have to go through with it.

'All right,' she said quietly.

'That's settled then,' said Jet. 'Belinda's going to represent the Vipers.'

'Come with us,' said Vixen, beckoning to Belinda. 'We'll show you the ropes.'

Still in a daze, Belinda followed Vixen and the other female bikers across to the edge of the clearing. They took her into a group of trees behind some bushes.

'You ever do one of these things before?' asked Vixen.

Belinda shook her head.

'It's no big deal. You've just got to be confident. Get your kit off.'

'What, everything?'

'Down to your knickers. Come on, don't be shy, kid.'

Slowly Belinda began to undress. She kicked off her shoes, then peeled her jeans from her long, slim legs. Next she pulled off her blouse. Now all she wore was matching bra and briefs. She hesitated for a moment, looking round at the biker girls, who were watching her expectantly. Then, her face reddening, she reached up her back and undid the catch on her bra.

She allowed it to slip down her arms and drop to the ground. Then she stood, her arms hanging at her side, whilst they took her in.

Vixen gave a little whistle. 'Boy, those are perfect.'

Belinda's breasts were indeed lovely to behold. Firm and

138

plump they jutted proudly from her chest with barely a hint of sag. The nipples were large and brown. They were not even partially erect, yet still came to thick points that looked designed to accommodate a lover's lips. Belinda stood, feeling pale and conspicuous as the bikers studied her body. She wished she had worn a more substantial pair of panties. The ones she had on sat low on her hips and were made of sheer, thin material through which her pubic hair could clearly be discerned.

She reached for the T-shirt, pulling it over her head. It fitted quite snugly, so that her breasts pressed against the material, her nipples perfectly outlined. She dragged the hem down as low as she was able, but still it barely reached her crotch, so that the whiteness of her panties showed with every move she made.

'Will I do?' she asked.

Vixen inspected her critically, then gave a nod.

'You'll do,' she said approvingly. 'Let's go.'

As they emerged from the trees, Belinda saw that all the bikers had gravitated towards the stage, where the band was still beating out its music. Then she saw the other competitors. They were dressed just as she was, in white T-shirts and knickers. There were three of them. All three had beautiful figures, their legs shapely, their waists slim. And all three bulged invitingly from their T-shirts. Belinda glanced down at her own chest and, for the first time, found herself feeling competitive. All at once she wanted to win the competition and she began to eye the other girls critically.

Jet came across and put his arm about her. 'You look great, kid,' he said. 'Go and show them who's boss.'

She smiled shyly at him. 'I'll do my best,' she said.

The music had stopped now, and a man climbed onto the stage. Like all the bikers he was clad in denim, a large beer paunch hanging over the waistline of his jeans.

'Right, guys,' he called. 'My name's Bud and I'm running this show. I think it's time for some action. We've got four little beauties here and an impartial gang of judges, yourselves.'

At this a cheer went up from the watching bikers.

'Let's have the first contestant then,' he went on. 'It's Flash from the Devils.'

For a moment none of the four girls moved. Then two burly bikers stepped forward and, amid much catcalling and whistling, dragged the first girl onto the stage. Flash was tall and willowy, her body curving smoothly in at the waist. She had long, dark hair that hung down her back. She stood, her pretty face wearing a slightly nervous expression, as the man on the stage described her charms to the onlookers.

'Now,' he said at last. 'Let's see what she's really made of.'

From the front of the audience a man stepped out carrying a large bucket of water. Before Flash had a chance to turn away he had flung it over her, soaking her completely and making her squeal with the cold. Another cheer went up from the onlookers as she staggered to the front of the stage.

The water had done what was required of it. The whiteness of the T-shirt's material had been rendered virtually transparent by the soaking and the paleness of Flash's breasts was now clearly visible, the darker flesh of her nipples contrasting starkly.

Flash was made to turn on the spot whilst the catcalling men admired her body. Then it was the next girl's turn.

The second contestant was called Suki. She was smaller than Flash and had an hourglass figure, with a trim waist opening to large hips. She too looked nervous and shied away the moment the bucket of water appeared. There was no escaping it, however, and in no time she too was drenched and her lovely pert breasts were on view to those watching.

The third contestant stood beside Belinda without speaking. By elimination this had to be Moll. Belinda had already guessed as much, though, from the way her breasts pressed against the material of her T-shirt. Suki and Flash had certainly been generously endowed, but there was no doubt that Moll was something special and Belinda began

140

to doubt whether she really would win the contest.

Moll was called up onto the stage. At once the shouts and whistles doubled in volume. She was much more confident than her two predecessors, blowing kisses to the crowd and striking provocative poses on the stage. She didn't flinch when the water was flung over her, laughing and pressing her chest forward as her magnificent breasts became suddenly visible through the thin material.

Moll strutted up and down the stage, grinning at the crowd, placing a hand on one hip and laughing aloud at the lewd comments they shouted. Belinda watched her with some apprehension. Clearly she was not going to be easy to beat.

All at once, Belinda realised that her turn had arrived. The crowd shouted their approval as she shuffled nervously onto the stage. As she looked out at the rowdy bikers she suddenly felt a sense of unreality. Could this really be her, standing before a group of bikers wearing only a T-shirt and a pair of very brief briefs? By rights she should be relaxing at her country retreat, not putting on a lewd show for these young men and women.

But at the same time she felt a genuine excitement at what she was doing. Somewhere, deep inside, a base desire was being satisfied by her exhibitionism. The idea of all these strangers ogling her body was a real turn-on. Especially since she knew she had a gorgeous figure, one which would excite all the men watching.

So engrossed was she in her audience that Belinda almost forgot the man with the bucket. She was reminded well enough, though, by the freezing cold water that was suddenly poured over her, drenching her completely.

Once again a cry of approval arose from the onlookers. Belinda glanced down at herself to see that, as with the girls who had gone ahead of her, her breasts were now quite visible through the wet material. There was another effect, too. One that made her face glow even redder. The icy coldness of the water had caused her nipples to harden, so that they pressed against the clinging T-shirt, forming solid knobs of brown flesh.

Belinda's first instinct was to cover herself. To place her hands across her breasts and hide her nakedness. But then Jet caught her eye and she thought of the honour of the Vipers, and the confidence which Moll had displayed. At once she remembered her determination to acquit herself well in the competition, together with the way the girl bikers had supported her, and she determined to do her best.

She placed her hands on her hips, smiling at the onlookers, who cheered her reaction. Like Moll, she started to strut up and down the stage, pressing her chest forward and catching the eye of those below her, winking suggestively at them. More applause arose as she shook her shoulders, making her breasts quiver in the most delightful manner. With a shock Belinda realised that she was enjoying herself tremendously and that each cheer was increasing her arousal.

Bud started clapping his hands and indicated to Belinda that she must take her place alongside the other contestants, who had stood back from the edge of the stage whilst she had been parading. She gave a final wave to the ecstatic bikers, then stepped back to take up her place beside Moll.

Bud took charge again. He began calling up each girl in turn, extolling her beauty and urging even more applause. Moll was, once again, in her element, laughing at his comments and pressing her body against his. Not to be outdone, when it came to her turn, Belinda grabbed him and planted her lips over his, probing her tongue into his mouth and rubbing her breasts against him. By the time she broke away she was feeling even more horny and she threw a defiant glance at Moll as she took her place in the line-up once more.

Bud called for silence and announced a preliminary vote. The rules were that a gang couldn't vote for their own contestant. One by one the girls were brought forward and the men raised their hands. Suki and Flash took about a third of the votes between them, the rest were almost equally divided between Moll and Belinda, with Belinda slightly ahead.

Suki and Flash were ushered off the stage, amid much cheering from the audience. Then Bud called for silence once more.

'Okay,' he said. 'It's between Moll and Belinda now. I want you girls to show us what you've got. The biggest cheer wins it.'

At once Moll went into a dance routine, shimmying across the stage and striking the most evocative poses, much to the delight of those watching. Not to be outdone, Belinda too began to move. She had always been an excellent dancer, and now she put her skills to good use, her body moving smoothly to a silent rhythm.

For a while there was nothing between the two girls as they showed off their bodies to the excited crowd. First one would get a cheer, then the other. Then Belinda noticed that Moll had stopped dancing and had moved to the front of the stage. She stood with her hands on her hips, watching Belinda.

Belinda too stopped and went across to stand in front of Moll. The two girls faced each other whilst the crowd shouted to them. At first Belinda couldn't make out what they were saying. Then she heard the words, 'Get them off,' and she knew what was being asked.

Slowly, simultaneously, the two girls reached for the hem of their T-shirts. Both grasped the material and pulled it up to just beneath their breasts, revealing their midriffs and bringing fresh cries of approval from below. Then Moll winked at Belinda and both girls dragged the sodden garments over their heads and off, tossing them far out into the crowd.

Belinda eyed Moll's breasts. They were indeed magnificent, with large areolae, the nipples forming hard brown buds. She glanced down at her own chest, noting how her nipples still protruded from her firm mounds. The audience were hysterical now and she knew what they were asking for.

Moll looked down at them, shaking her head and laughing. It was at that moment that Belinda realised there was only one way to win this competition.

She turned to face her audience, scanning their faces, her hands still planted on her hips. Gradually the cheering died away and an air of expectancy settled over the crowd. Belinda glanced across at Moll, then out at the sea of eager faces. She shivered slightly as contemplation of what she was about to do sent a sudden thrill through her.

She reached for the waistband of her panties, hooking her thumbs into the elastic. She paused for a second then, taking a deep breath, she yanked down the skimpy garment, waving it round her head a couple of times before tossing it out over the crowd. Then she stood, legs apart, hands on hips, her body totally nude.

The crowd went mad.

Chapter 17

Belinda stared out at the cheering bikers, savouring their adulation as they took in all her charms. It felt wonderful to be so publicly naked and the applause was like a physical force caressing her lovely young body. Bud placed an arm about her, taking her wrist and raising an arm above her head, bringing further shouts of delight from the onlookers.

'The winner!' he announced.

As he turned away to pick up Belinda's prize, Moll sauntered across to her, still clad in only her knickers. She placed an arm around Belinda's waist and pulled her close, pressing her lips to Belinda's. Belinda was quite taken by surprise by the gesture, even more so when she felt Moll's tongue prise her lips apart and delve into her mouth. She had never kissed a woman in so intimate a manner before and was surprised by the effect it had on her. She was even more surprised when Moll cupped her breast, her fingers closing over the hard teat.

The woman began to caress Belinda's breasts whilst her own pressed against the naked girl's skin. Suddenly the passion of the kiss threatened to overcome Belinda and she wrapped her arms about Moll's neck, pulling her body close. She closed her eyes, her entire body tingling with arousal as Moll continued to toy with her nipple.

As they embraced, Belinda felt Moll's other hand begin to move down her body, sliding over the smooth curve of her flank until her fingers were running through Belinda's pubic bush. Belinda knew she should stop the girl, but she was simply

145

overwhelmed by the excitement and passion of the kiss.

When Moll found Belinda's clitoris she sent a jolt through her entire body. The biker girl's touch was light, yet firm. Her slim fingers encircling Belinda's love bud and teasing it erect. Belinda moaned softly at the touch, her hips starting to move in a circular motion, pressing forward against Moll's fingers. All at once nothing seemed to matter to her but the delicious sensations that the girl was arousing in her. The whole of her being seemed to be centred in her crotch, where Moll's hands worked so expertly.

The orgasm took Belinda by surprise. One second she had been in full control of herself, the next she was crying aloud as the strongest climax she had ever experienced swept through her. She clung hard to Moll, her pubis thrusting against her hand, as she allowed the exquisite pleasure to overcome her. Moll worked her fingers back and forth, her tongue still deep in Belinda's mouth, prolonging the orgasm for as long as she was able.

Gradually Belinda began to come down from her peak. As she did so she began to realise that the roaring sound in her ears was coming from below. She opened her eyes to see the rows of bikers, their faces swathed in grins, and the enormity of what she had done began to dawn on her. She wanted then to turn away, to hide herself from the men's gazes, but Moll kept a firm grip on her, showing Belinda's body off to the crowd and indicating the wetness that had leaked onto her fingers.

Then Bud was approaching with the crate of beer, holding it out to her. Moll released her grip on the dazed girl and jumped down from the stage, leaving her alone. Belinda took the crate from Bud, still barely aware of what she was doing. Then she was staggering off the stage and down to where Jet and the rest of the Vipers were waiting for her.

'Well done, baby.'

'You were the best.'

'What a show!'

The bikers gathered round her, slapping her on the back and kissing her cheeks. Someone took the beer crate from her, then thrust an open bottle into her hand. Belinda looked at them, still slightly dazed by her experience. Jet moved close and put his arm about her waist.

'That was real sexy,' he said.

'I . . . I don't usually do that sort of thing,' she stammered.

'Well you should. Gorgeous chicks like you were made to show off their bodies.'

She looked around herself. 'Where are my clothes?'

'Never mind that. I've got something better for you. Vixen!'

The crowd parted and Vixen came through. She was holding something made of blue denim cloth in her hand. She held it out to Belinda.

'Here,' she said. 'We reckon you've earned this.'

Belinda took it from her. It was a denim waistcoat with a snake embroidered on the back.

'Go ahead,' said Jet. 'Put it on. This makes you an honorary Viper.

Belinda stared at the garment, then round at the watching bikers. She knew that such honours were not bestowed lightly and she smiled rather shyly.

'Thanks,' she said.

She pulled on the waistcoat and a low cheer went up from the Vipers. She looked down at herself. Somehow, wearing only that simple garment she looked even more sexy than when she had been naked. She considered fastening the buttons, then decided against it, allowing her breasts to part the blue cloth.

The party continued, the bikers swigging their beer and laughing and joking together. The band began to play again and Jet grabbed Belinda's hand, dragging her onto the dance floor. Gradually Belinda's inhibitions began to fall away and she threw herself into the dance, strutting back and forth, her breasts bouncing delightfully as she gyrated about the clearing.

The band changed tempo, going into a slower number with a heavy, moody downbeat. As it did so, Jet pulled her to him, placing his arms about her and pulling her close. Belinda wrapped hers about his neck, pressing herself against him, enjoying the feel of his strong body beneath the rough denim that chafed against her bare flesh.

When he kissed her she responded at once, turning her face up to his and opening her mouth wide, her lips crushed against his own. His hand slid under her waistcoat and closed over her breast and she felt her nipples pucker to hardness. She gave a little moan as he squeezed her smooth, soft flesh, his hands strong yet gentle. When he pressed his leg between her own she accommodated him at once, shivering as she felt the roughness of his jeans press hard against her bare crotch. At the same time his other hand slipped down to her backside, taking a handful of her pert buttocks and pressing her close against him.

He broke away and gazed down into her eyes. She was panting slightly, her hips rubbing up and down the blue denim, the moisture in her staining it a darker colour.

'I want you,' he said quietly.

'And I want you.'

He glanced over her shoulder and gave a nod. All of a sudden there were two more Vipers standing close behind her. They took hold of her arms, grasping them firmly and pulling her from his grip. She threw him an inquisitive look, uncertain what was happening. He winked at her, then once again nodded to his cohorts, who took her arms and placed them about their necks.

They lifted her in a chair lift, wrapping their arms around her waist from either side and placing a hand under each thigh. When they pulled her up they spread her legs wide, offering a perfect view of her glistening sex to all the bikers. Belinda stared down at herself. She had never felt so exposed, her breasts jutting proudly forward, her thighs pulled apart.

They carried her through the crowd of bikers, like some

sacrificial maiden being taken to the altar. She caught the men's eyes as she was taken past, blushing red at the thought of what was to happen. It was an extraordinary situation, being carried away naked by these powerful strangers in the sure knowledge that she was in their power and that they would do what they wished with her. She wondered if they expected her to struggle. To fight for her honour. But she was beyond that now. The whole afternoon had seen a build-up of the sexual tensions inside her, relieved only by the brief pleasure that Moll's fingers had given her. Now she wanted only to be fucked. To feel the pleasure of a thick cock deep within her, and as they carried her away from the gathering and into the woods she moaned softly in anticipation of what was to come.

They carried her to a small clearing, where they laid her down on the grass, her legs still spread wide. She watched as the Vipers filed in behind, forming a semicircle about her.

Vixen moved first, beckoning to one of the other girl bikers. The two dropped down on either side of the prostrate Belinda and, leaning forward, closed their mouths on her breasts.

'Oh!'

Belinda cried aloud at the delicious sensation of the two women sucking at her nipples. They took hold of her arms and held her down whilst they slurped noisily at her, bringing her nipples to long, hard points then rubbing the saliva in with their fingers. Belinda lay, her arms outstretched, her eyes tight shut as she revelled in their caresses. Then another hand touched her. A larger, rougher hand that slid up the inside of her thigh toward the very centre of her desires.

She opened her eyes and peered down between the mounds of her breasts. Then she gave a gasp. Jet was kneeling between her thighs, one hand running up towards her sex whilst the other grasped a thick, meaty penis that projected from his fly, its tip alternately appearing and disappearing as he worked his foreskin back and forth.

He found her clitoris, his thumb encircling it whilst she moaned and writhed beneath him. Then he moved forward and she felt him seek out the entrance to her place of pleasure.

When he slipped his cock into her she almost came then and there. The sensation of being penetrated whilst her breasts were being simultaneously stimulated was almost too much and she shoved her hips forward, urging him deeper. He pressed himself in, little by little, each new push stretching her wider and renewing her cries of passion.

He fucked her with slow, even movements, his backside moving up and down as he stared into her face. Belinda moaned her pleasure, her head shaking from side to side, struggling to free her arms, which were still pinned down by the two girls. It was like nothing she had ever experienced, naked in the open air, her erect nipples being teased and sucked by two women whilst this burly young man in scruffy jeans rammed his cock into her. And all the time the other Vipers were watching.

She stared round at them. All the men had bulges at their crotches. One or two had freed their erections from their jeans and were stroking themselves. To her left another of the biker girls had dropped to her knees and was busily sucking the man next to her.

Jet's screwing was becoming more urgent now, his tempo increasing with every stroke. Belinda too could feel the passion rising in her and she bit her lips as she tried to stifle the cries of lust that constantly escaped her. She was responding to his every thrust, her backside banging against the grass as their torsos slapped together.

He came with a gasp, his body shuddering as his seed began to spurt deep into her vagina. The sensation of the hot viscous liquid entering her cunt was the trigger for Belinda's own climax, her screams ringing in the air as the release of orgasm overcame her. The two girls clung hard to her writhing, bucking body whilst Jet continued to empty his balls into her.

Belinda's orgasm went on and on, as she relished every stroke from the strong young man on top of her. At last though, he began to slow and she sensed he was coming down, his

150

body collapsing onto hers as the last of his semen leaked from him. He lay for a moment, his weight almost crushing her, then rolled aside, leaving her gasping for breath.

She was given no time to recover, though. No sooner had Jet pulled out than the two girls were dragging her up off her back. They pulled her to her knees, then forced her forward on all fours. Immediately she felt another cock pressing against her vagina. She turned in surprise to see one of the Vipers kneeling behind her, guiding his cock towards her already dribbling sex.

Belinda, held down as she was, couldn't have prevented his assault if she'd wanted to. But the moment she felt his shaft slide into her she realised that she didn't want to, and she pressed her backside up, spreading her legs to facilitate his access.

He wasted no time, starting to thrust into her at once, his belly slapping against the tight flesh of her backside. Belinda gasped as she felt her passions rekindled, the muscles of her sex tightening about the new invader.

Then, with a shock, she realised that another cock was bobbing in front of her face. She looked up to see the man whom the girl had been sucking earlier. He was kneeling in front of her whilst the biker girl guided his weapon towards Belinda's mouth.

She took him inside, suddenly overwhelmed by the taste and smell of man as he began eagerly to fuck her face. For Belinda the sensation was incredible, having two rampant cocks inside her at once, both insistently thrusting into her. She began to suck hard at the knob that slipped in and out of her mouth, whilst she tightened her cunt about the other. She was rewarded by gasps of pleasure from both men as they renewed the violence of their actions.

The two came simultaneously, spurting their semen into Belinda's mouth and cunt whilst she shouted her own pleasure, the thick, white liquid escaping from her mouth and dribbling down her chin as she struggled to swallow it. Even as she sucked the last of the semen from his still-throbbing cock she felt yet another violate her from behind as a fourth biker began taking his pleasure in her.

On the far side of the clearing, still disguised in her biker's kit and helmet, Jo zoomed the camera lens in on the naked, wanton beauty, who was clearly loving the gangbang she had asked for. Taking her hand from the camera she slid it down between her legs and rubbed her crotch.

She couldn't remember when she had last desired a fucking so much.

Chapter 18

Ed Mercer took another sip at his coffee, then stared down at the magazine in his hand. A beautiful blonde girl stared back. She was lying on a sun-drenched beach as naked as the day she was born, her legs slightly spread as she gazed seductively at the camera. He flicked to the next page, where the same girl was leaning back against a palm tree, one hand caressing her large, firm breast whilst the other was placed low on her hips. Ed studied the picture carefully, taking in every inch of the girl's gorgeous body.

Suddenly a movement on the other side of the road caught his eye and he looked across. A motorcycle had pulled up outside the building opposite and he watched with interest as the man climbed off. As he turned away, Ed studied his back eagerly. Then his expression turned to disappointment as he saw the lovingly embroidered picture of the snake on the biker's waistcoat. Clearly this man was no motorcycle courier. He watched as the man stepped through the front door of the building and headed for the lift. He wondered idly if he might be headed for the office of Fantasy and Co. He doubted it. After all there were plenty more offices in the building.

Ed sighed. He had been in this café for three days now, watching the door to the building where the girls had their office. He had seen them come and go, along with the two hunky men who he knew were part of their organisation. What he was watching for, though, was couriers. Those ubiquitous leather-jacketed motorcyclists who rode through the streets of London, weaving in and out of the traffic as they hurried letters and packages to their destinations. He knew that the girls of Fantasy and Co used such men to deliver the videos to their clients and it was precisely one of those videos that he wanted to get his hands on. That was why he had sat here for so long.

If truth were told, he had actually seen plenty of couriers in the last three days. Each time one had pulled up outside the office Ed had abandoned his coffee and magazine and run across to intercept them.

'Fantasy and Co?' he would gasp as he reached them. But every time he was rewarded by a blank look and a shake of the head.

He knew, though, that if he was patient, eventually he must find the one he was after. It was just a case of waiting for long enough. But after three days of fruitless searching he was beginning to wonder how long it would be before he finally found the one he sought.

He took another sip of coffee and turned the page of his magazine. This time the naked beauty had her arm wrapped about the waist of a bronzed hunk leaning against a surf board. He felt his cock stir in his pants as he imagined himself as the young man in the picture about to fuck this brazen beauty.

Then the sound of another motorcycle met his ears and he looked up once more. The rider was clad all in black and his machine bore the unmistakable panniers of a despatch rider. Ed was on his feet and out the door before the machine had even drawn to a halt.

The man kicked down the stand of the bike and dismounted. He was of stocky build, and had the words 'Ace Couriers' inscribed on the back of his jacket. As he turned towards the building Ed intercepted him.

'Fantasy and Co?' he asked breathlessly.

'What?' The man placed two fingers inside the front of his helmet and pulled the padding away from his ear.

'Fantasy and Co. Is that where you're going?'

'What's it to you?'

'I've got it here.' Ed reached into his jacket and pulled out a packet.

The man eyed him suspiciously. 'I was told the sixth floor.'

'Yeah, I know, but I brought it down for you.'

'Why?'

'The lift's out of order. And this one's really urgent. Wanted to make sure you got it.'

The man sniffed. 'I can climb stairs you know. Still, I'm not surprised about the lift. I've been to this place before. Bloody thing belongs in a museum. Let's have it, then.'

He reached out a hand and Ed gave him the packet. He studied the address.

'You sure this is right? It says Croydon and I was told Tunbridge Wells.'

'Change of plan. That's not a problem is it?'

The man shrugged. 'Makes no odds to me.'

And, tucking the package into his jacket, he strode back towards his bike.

Ed watched him ride away with a sense of rising excitement. Phase one of his plan had worked perfectly. Now it was time to put phase two into operation.

He strode back across the road to the café. The package he had given the man contained a video tape he was returning to the video library. The owner might be mildly surprised to receive it from the courier, but Ed felt confident that he wouldn't raise too many suspicions.

He swigged down the last of his coffee and picked up the bag that was resting beside his chair. From it he pulled a black leather jacket and a motorcycle crash helmet. He shrugged on the jacket and pulled the helmet over his head, buckling the strap. Then, dropping his magazine into the bag, he set off across the road.

There was a small mirror at the back of the lift, and Ed studied his appearance as it creaked slowly upward. He had been reluctant to shave off his beard, but it had been necessary to prevent his being recognised. That, together with the glasses he wore beneath the helmet disguised his appearance sufficiently, he felt, to keep him safe from recognition.

The lift reached the sixth floor and he pulled the door open, stepping out onto the landing. Opposite was the door behind which Fantasy and Co did their business. He paused for a second outside, then knocked.

'Come in.'

He stepped into the office. There, sitting at their desks, were the two girls who ran the business. To his surprise, though, there was a third person in the room. It was the tall biker he had seen enter the building earlier with the snake on his back. The blonde girl was busy writing a cheque out, which she handed to him. Ed turned to the other girl.

'Ace Couriers,' he said.

The girl stared at him, and for a second he feared he had been recognised. Then she reached into the drawer of her desk and pulled out a package.

'This is it,' she said. 'It needs to get there this afternoon.'

Ed studied the address. 'No problem,' he said. And turned to go.

'Hang on a minute!' This time it was the blonde speaking.

He froze, not looking back. 'Yes?'

'Where the hell were you trained?'

His heart sank, but he kept his voice steady. 'What's the problem?'

'Your helmet. Next time take it off when you come in the office. For all we know you could be bank robber.'

'Sorry,' he mumbled.

Then he was out of the office and heading for the lift.

He was about to slam the door when another figure appeared on the landing. It was the biker.

'Hang on,' he said. 'I'm going down.'

The man climbed into the lift beside him. Ed shut the door and the lift creaked slowly into life.

'What are you riding?'

156

'What?' The question took Ed somewhat by surprise.

'What bike are you riding?'

'Me? Oh, er . . .' Ed struggled to think of a make of motorcycle. The man obviously knew the girls and he didn't want to give anything away, least of all the identity of his machine.

'A Honda,' he said at last.

'What cc?'

'Er . . . A five hundred?'

To his relief the biker nodded. 'Twin or four cylinder?'

'I'm not sure.'

'Oh come on, man, you must know that.'

Ed thought desperately, trying to find an answer. The lift seemed to be moving more slowly than ever, creeping from floor to floor.

'It's a friend's machine,' he said at last. 'I'm borrowing it whilst mine's being fixed.'

'And you haven't got round to counting the exhausts?'

Ed grinned weakly. 'I've been a bit busy.'

The lift came gently to a halt, and Ed offered a silent prayer of thanks as he slid the door open. He stepped out into the street with the biker beside him.

'Well where is it then?'

'What?'

'Your bike.' The biker pointed to his machine. 'There's mine, but I can't see yours.'

'I parked it round the corner.'

'Why? There's nothing to stop you leaving it here. Anyhow you couriers never normally seem bothered by parking restrictions.'

'Listen,' said Ed. 'I'm in a hurry. I'll see you.'

And he hurried off down the street, clutching the package.

Upstairs in the office, Jo turned to her partner.

'Did you notice anything familiar about that courier?'

'No. Why, did you?'

'I'm not sure,' said Jo. 'I just had the impression I'd seen him before.'

'Perhaps you have. He's not the first courier we've had in here.'

'Yeah. Maybe you're right. How are you getting on with preparations for tomorrow?'

'The Underground thing? I think it'll be okay.'

'It's our toughest one yet isn't it? I mean a girl who wants to expose herself to a stranger on the tube, then get fucked in some alleyway. There's a real risk of getting caught.'

'Yeah, but if we do it on a quiet lane later on at night I think it'll be all right.'

'You'll have to make sure she picks the right guy.'

'That's taken care of. He'll be wearing a carnation.'

'That's a bit corny isn't it?'

'Corny it may be. But it's simple and it'll work. Meanwhile let's talk about how we're going to handle the cameras.'

And the two friends huddled together in earnest discussion.

Chapter 19

As the tube train rumbled through the long tunnel, Jo checked her watch for the tenth time. It was eleven fifteen, and they were almost exactly on time. She glanced about the carriage. It was right at the back of the train and there were few people on board. At the far end sat Chris, carrying the small briefcase that contained the hidden camera. Further down, Mark was carrying a second camera. Everything was prepared. For her part, Jo had merely to observe and ensure all went to plan.

She looked across at Doug. He was standing by the door, studying the advertising poster above it. He looked unusually smart this evening, dressed as he was in a charcoal grey suit, the red carnation in his buttonhole looking particularly distinctive.

Jo ran through the plan in her mind once more. The customer was due to board the train in four stations' time. She would be wearing a short, grey mackintosh and nothing else. Her fantasy was to expose her naked body to a stranger on a train and subsequently to seduce the man, allowing him to fuck her in some public place. Jo and Chris had already done their research and had found a quiet alleyway where they had concealed a mattress earlier in the evening. Mark was to keep guard whilst Doug satisfied their client's desires.

Jo smiled with quiet satisfaction. The plan was perfect. They had studied all angles and decided that nothing could possibly go wrong. Now it was just a case of waiting for the client to board.

The train began to slow down as they approached another station and Jo checked the map. Only three more stops after this one, then they were in business.

The train halted with a jerk and the doors slid open. As they had expected, the station was virtually deserted at that time of night, but there was a single figure on the platform. As luck would have it, he stepped into their carriage and Jo glanced idly at him. Then her jaw dropped.

He was wearing a red carnation in his buttonhole.

For a second Jo suspected a trick and glanced about at her friends. But they were looking as surprised as she was. The man himself seemed unconcerned, taking a seat beside the door and pulling out a newspaper. Jo stared at him, then across at Doug. If anything, the newcomer's flower was brighter and more prominent than Doug's. She quickly made her way down to where Chris was sitting.

'Did you see that?' she asked.

'Of course I did. What are we going to do? If she gets on she might flash at the wrong guy. Then we'll really be in trouble.'

'Just our luck to pick the only tube train in London with two carnations.'

'We've got to make certain there's only one before we pick up our customer.'

'Perhaps he'll get off before she gets on.'

'Yeah, and perhaps not. No, Jo, you'll have to do something to make sure she doesn't pick the wrong one.'

'Me? What the hell can I do?'

Chris thought for a moment. Then her face brightened. 'Do the same as the customer.'

'What?'

'Give him a quick flash. Then chat him up. Seduce him if necessary. Just get that flower out of his buttonhole.'

'But I can't flash him. I'm not wearing a coat.'

'In that dress you won't need one. Just get rid of your bra and pants and undo a few buttons top and bottom.'

Jo glanced down at her dress. It was a simple one-piece affair, plunging at the neck and with a very short skirt that showed a vast expanse of thigh. She had to concur, if reluctantly, that with the buttons running up the front it was tailor made for what Chris had in mind for her.

Still she shook her head. 'I can't,' she repeated.

'Yes you can. You've got to. Now quickly, get your undies off.'

'What, here?'

'Where else? They don't equip these things with dressing rooms, you know.'

'Why can't you do it?'

'One, because I'm filming, and two because I'm wearing jeans. Come on Jo, we're running out of time. Give me your bra and pants.'

'He'll see me.'

'No he won't. He's reading a paper and nobody else is watching.'

'But . . .'

'But nothing. She'll be getting on soon. Hurry up.'

Even as she spoke the train began slowing down once more and they clattered into another station. Jo looked hopefully at the man with the carnation, but he didn't move. Then the doors closed and they were pulling away again. She sighed and reached down the back of her dress for her bra strap.

She pulled the right strap off her shoulder and, with a bit of manoeuvring, down her arm. Then it was a simple matter to pull the bra through her left armhole and off. She passed it to Chris, who tucked it into her bag whilst Jo reached under her skirt and pulled down her panties, stepping out of them and handing them to her friend. It seemed odd to be without them. The air felt strangely cool against her bare sex and she shivered, partly with cold but mainly in anticipation of what was to come. She checked the tube map again. Their customer would be getting on at the next stop but one. There wasn't much time.

161

She rose to her feet, but Chris grabbed her hand and pulled her back.

'Not quite ready yet,' she said.

She reached up and undid the top two buttons of Jo's dress, then the bottom one. This left her breasts almost exposed, so that the act of merely bending forward would reveal their full glory. As for the skirt, the slightest movement would cause the material to part, uncovering her dark pubic triangle.

'Right,' said Chris. 'Go for it.'

'It is a far, far better thing that I do now,' intoned Jo as she stood up.

Her heart beating hard, Jo made her way down the carriage to where the man was sitting. Already the train was slowing once more and she knew she had to act fast.

She stopped just in front of him, positioning herself close so that she knew that if he looked up he would be rewarded by a glimpse of her bare crotch through the slit at the front of her dress. Taking a deep breath, she spoke.

'That's a lovely flower in your buttonhole.'

The man looked up in surprise. He was quite handsome, Jo thought. In his mid thirties, his hair receding a little but good-looking nevertheless. He was taken quite by surprise by the lovely young woman standing in front of him. At first his face held an expression of mild irritation, then his eyes widened and she knew he had realised she was without panties. Jo smiled.

'May I smell it?'

'I beg your pardon?'

'The flower. May I smell it?'

'I . . . er . . . Yes. If you like.'

Jo leaned forward towards him. As she did so the front of her dress fell open, exposing her delicious breasts, the nipples brown and hard. The man was spellbound, staring down at her creamy orbs whilst she moved her face so close to his that her hair brushed his face.

'Mmmm,' she said. 'It's lovely. Do you always wear one?'

'Pardon?'

'The flower. Do you always have one in your buttonhole?'

'Oh. No, I've been to a wedding, that's all.'

She took the seat beside him, placing a hand on his knee. 'I bet it would go really well with this dress,' she said. 'Can I try it?'

'Try what?'

'Try the flower on. Is there something the matter?'

'Yes. I mean no!' The man's face had turned a deep shade of scarlet.

'Where shall I wear it, down my cleavage?'

'Er . . . If you like.'

'You put it there.'

'Me?'

'Sure. Go ahead.'

A sheen of sweat broke out on the man's brow as he gaped at the wide expanse of cleavage Jo was pressing in his direction. His hand shook slightly as he reached for the flower. Jo watched with growing impatience as he fumbled with it. Already the train was slowing down and she knew their customer would be waiting on the platform.

The man plucked the carnation from his buttonhole at the moment the train emerged into the lights of the station. As he reached towards Jo's breasts, the doors rumbled open and Jo spotted the slim, petite brunette who she knew was their customer.

The feel of the man's fingers on the soft flesh of her breasts brought her back to her senses. She looked down and watched him slip the stalk into the cleft.

'Do you think it goes?' she asked with an air of innocence.

The man nodded dumbly.

Jo stared into his eyes. Now that she had the carnation, her mission was accomplished. Yet she felt she owed him a little more. She had never been a prick teaser and the bulge at his crotch told her that this man's prick was decidedly excited by her little performance so far. She ran her hand over it, feeling it twitch as she squeezed it gently.

'My, but you're excited,' she remarked.

He nodded.

All at once, Jo made up her mind. She had started this seduction and now she must see it through. After all, Chris and the boys could see to their customer. Right now she was far more interested in the hard rod under her fingers.

She extended a hand and grasped the man at the back of the neck. Then she pulled his face towards hers, placing her mouth over his and delving her tongue between his lips. For a second he resisted, his body stiff. Then he relaxed, wrapping his arms about her and reciprocating with a passion that quite took her breath away.

Jo glanced over his shoulder at Chris. It was clear that her friend's attention was elsewhere and as Jo followed her gaze she realised that the brunette had allowed the short coat she was wearing to fall open and she stood facing Doug. Beneath the coat she wore only a suspender belt and stockings and Jo felt her pulse quicken as she took in the girl's small, pert breasts, perfectly rounded like ripe oranges, the nipples hard and brown. She let her eyes drift down the slim body to the trim waist and the dark pubic bush that sprouted from a prominent mound. There was no doubt that the young woman was extremely beautiful and the expression on her face as she displayed her body was one of pure lust.

Suddenly Jo felt a hand slide down inside her dress, the fingers closing over her breast, and she was reminded once more of her own situation. The man's hands were large, his grip firm, and she gave a little sigh as she felt her nipples respond to his touch. She knew she wanted him. The whole thing had begun as a diversion, but now her fires were lit and the smell and taste of this virile man were arousing her more than she had expected.

He broke their kiss and gazed into her eyes.

'Where are you getting off?' he asked.

'Wherever you are.'

He smiled. 'Next stop's mine.'

'And mine then.'

Jo looked across at the other couple. Doug had moved closer to the young woman, his arms wrapped about her inside the coat so that her naked flesh was pressed against him as he kissed her. Jo knew that they too would be getting off at the next stop for their rendezvous in the alley that she and Chris had prepared for them.

Once again the train began to slow. The man remained seated beside her for a short time, still caressing her breasts. Then he took her by the hand and rose to his feet, pulling her up with him. As they approached the door she saw his surprise at discovering the other couple still locked in a passionate embrace, the girl's coat pushed right back so that her nudity was obvious, her pale breasts pressed hard against Doug's broad chest.

The train came to a halt and the pair drew apart, the girl nonchalantly pulling her coat together, though not before everyone watching was able to get a good look at her considerable charms. Then the door slid open and Jo and her companion stepped out onto the platform.

They walked towards the exit, their arms wrapped about one another. Behind them Jo could hear the clack of the other girl's heels on the platform, but she did not turn round. She wondered what Chris would be thinking of her and what she was doing. Well, she mused, it had been Chris's idea in the first place. And it was strictly for business reasons after all, though glancing at the man beside her she couldn't help thinking that this was the kind of business she enjoyed.

As they passed through the station gates he turned to her.

'I can't take you back to my place,' he said softly.

She smiled. 'That's okay. Let's find somewhere quiet.'

He took her arm and led her up the road. Behind them she could still hear the other couple following. Up ahead was the alleyway where she and Chris had planted the mattress. It seemed to be there that the man was leading her. Indeed, as they reached it he made to turn in. Jo hesitated, pulling back. That was the one place they couldn't use.

'No,' she said. 'Not in there.'

'Why not? We'll not be disturbed.'

'There's a little park further on,' she said. 'The grass will be softer.'

In fact she and Chris had rejected the park on the grounds that it was a little too public and the risk of discovery was greater, but in this instance Jo didn't feel as if she had much of a choice. The man nodded his assent and they walked on, leaving the coast clear for Doug and his escort.

The park was set back slightly from the road. The pair stole inside quietly. It consisted mainly of a wide stretch of grass, but off to their left was a small clump of bushes and it was towards these he led her. He had wrapped his arm about her waist and he held her close to him as they walked, the scent of his aftershave filling her nostrils.

They reached the bushy area, picking their way between the shrubs into the centre where a tall tree stood. The man swung Jo round and pushed her back against the trunk, pressing his body against her and planting his lips on hers once more. As they kissed, his hands dropped to her breasts, pulling the material of her dress aside and grasping her succulent orbs, once again causing her nipples to pucker to hardness as he rubbed his hand over them.

Jo moaned quietly. Whilst her current situation had been quite unexpected, she was thoroughly aroused now, and anxious to feel this tall stranger's flesh against her own. When he began to undo the remaining buttons of her dress she made no objection, drawing back slightly to allow his fingers room to unfasten them easily.

When he reached the bottom button the dress fell open and he stood back to admire Jo's body. Her skin appeared pale in the moonlight, her firm breasts jutting forward proudly, forcing the material aside. He reached up for her shoulders, pushing the dress back over them, and Jo lowered her arms to allow it to fall to the floor. Then his hands were on her once again, caressing her breasts and delving down between her legs. As she felt his fingers run through her pubic thatch, she parted her legs slightly, gasping as he wormed his way between her thighs and slid his finger into the warm moistness of her sex. He twisted it, watching the passion on her face as he did so.

'You like that?' he asked.

'Mmmm.'

He began moving his hand, frigging her gently, and she felt her vagina tighten about his fingers. The contact felt wonderful and Jo found herself becoming more turned on by the second, her hips suddenly thrusting forward against his insistent finger whilst she pressed her lips bruisingly against his.

All at once she had to touch him. She groped blindly for his fly, feeling the hardness of his erection through the material and tugging at the zip. She reached inside, her hand closing about his thick pole, squeezing it and feeling it throb beneath her fingers. Pulling her lips away from his she dropped to her knees in the grass, sighing with disappointment as his fingers slid out of her. She pulled his erection out of his pants and stared at it. It was heavy and knobbly, with a bulbous end, and she worked his foreskin back and forth gently, watching as the purple knob was exposed and then covered again. Then, leaning forward, she took him into her mouth.

This time it was his turn to gasp as she sucked hard at his manhood, her fingers caressing his large, heavy balls as she did so. His knob twitched uncontrollably as she fellated him and for a moment she was afraid he was going to come then and there. She withdrew her head and gazed up at him.

'You ready for me?' she asked, her face split by a mischievous grin. He nodded silently.

'How do you want me?'

'From behind.'

At once Jo dropped onto all fours and turned away from

him, spreading her legs and thrusting her behind back at him, presenting him with perfect access to her sex. He reached down, running his fingers over the crack of her backside, pausing to stroke the tight star of her anus before moving his fingers lower and sliding them into her vagina. Jo gave a small cry as she felt herself so intimately penetrated.

'Oh shit,' she moaned. 'Just fuck me would you?'

At once the fingers were withdrawn and replaced by something else. Something large and hard with a wet, slippery end that retraced the route his fingers had taken. Jo groaned with frustration as he held off, barely touching her as he masturbated slowly. Then his cock was pressing against her sex, bringing new cries from her lips as it slipped into her.

He pressed it all the way home, grasping hold of her hips and forcing his way further and further into her until his manhood was completely buried within her vagina.

She moaned aloud as he began to move, drawing his hips back then ramming them forward, making her breasts quiver deliciously as he did so. He fucked her with an easy grace, the sensation of his throbbing erection plunging into her bringing Jo to new heights of arousal with every stroke. She clenched her fists, grabbing handfuls of the thick grass in her attempts to steady herself against his onslaught, her lower lip clenched between her teeth as she fought to prevent herself from crying aloud.

He slid his hands about her waist and she gave a start as he found her clitoris. It was hard as a nut, protruding between her sex lips like a glistening pink bud, and her body shook with pleasure as he caressed it, circling it with his finger whilst still thrusting his cock deep inside her.

Jo's mind was dominated by the pleasure he was giving her, her whole being concentrated on the wonderful sensation he was producing with his penis and his fingers. His motions were growing more violent now and she fought to retain her balance as he rammed his hips hard against her backside.

They came simultaneously, he groaning with delight as his

cock twitched inside her, each pulse bringing another gob of sperm from its tip that jetted deep inside her, intensifying the pleasure of her own climax as her sex muscles convulsed about him, sucking his seed deep into her.

They remained locked together in the bushes, he a dark shadowy figure, she pale and naked, both gasping with lust as their orgasms washed over them, their motions slowing now. He went on pumping until he had deposited the last of his seed deep inside her, then withdrew. Jo collapsed onto the grass, gasping for breath, her sex muscles still twitching, forcing a dribble of spunk out onto her thighs. She rolled over and gazed up at the man, who was standing over her buttoning up his pants.

'Do you want your carnation back?' she asked quietly.

He smiled, his teeth showing white in the moonlight.

'Keep it,' he said. 'I reckon you've earned it. Do you want me to walk you home?'

She shook her head. 'I'll be all right.'

He dropped to his knees and kissed her on the lips, his fingers playing with her breasts.

'I'll be off then.'

She watched him make his way through the bushes until he was out of sight. Then she rose to her feet, stretching her limbs luxuriously. It had been an unexpected encounter and the thrill of being fucked in the open air by a stranger had invigorated her. But now she had other things to think about. With an effort she brought her mind back to the real business of the evening. The woman on the train. For a second she felt guilty at abandoning her friends. But there had been nothing else for it, she told herself. What she had done had been simply to respond to the call of duty. It would have been disastrous if the woman had chosen the wrong man to display to, although on this occasion she suspected things might have worked out all right. Still, it was time to get back to her colleagues and find out if all was going well.

She pulled her dress on and, still buttoning it, set off back in the direction of the station. As she approached the alley she could discern a dark figure partly concealed in the entrance. It was Chris.

'How's it going?' she whispered.

Chris did not speak, simply nodded down the alley.

Jo squinted into the darkness and gradually the scene became clear to her. Mark was crouched behind a dustbin, the video camera in his hand. In front of him the petite young woman was stretched out on her back totally naked. Crouched between her thighs was Doug, also nude, his face buried in her crotch. The girl was making small bleating sounds, her backside rising and falling, her breasts quivering as he licked her. As Jo watched she gave a little cry and a shudder ran through her small frame, indicating that she had climaxed.

'That's her fourth orgasm,' whispered Chris. 'One with his fingers, one with his cock and two with his tongue. I reckon Doug's going to need reinforcements soon.'

But even as they watched the girl was pulling Doug down on her once more and Jo saw the length and stiffness of his cock as he slipped it into her.

'It looks like he's still got some stamina left,' she grinned.

Chapter 20

Ed sat back in his chair, his eyes fixed on the flickering television, an expression of delight on his face. On the screen, a naked Belinda was lying prostrate on the grass whilst Jet rogered her with some vigour. Two other bikers, both girls, were holding her down and simultaneously playing with her lovely breasts. Ed ran his hand down over his crotch. There was no doubt that this was one sexy woman and he felt his cock swell as he watched her antics.

He checked the second video machine. The record light was on and it was connected to the first by a pair of wires. With any luck the copy would be virtually perfect. Then the next stage of the scheme would go into operation. He smiled with satisfaction as he contemplated his plan. He'd soon show those damned women who was the one with the brains. And he'd make them squirm before he let them off the hook. Perhaps he'd even demand to fuck the brunette. She wouldn't dare refuse. The prospect of their gorgeous customer finding out her tape had fallen into the wrong hands would be enough to make her see things his way.

The sound of Belinda's cries distracted him once more and he watched as she writhed about beneath the biker, the pair of them enjoying noisy climaxes. The man withdrew but almost at once she was poised to suck at another of the bikers whilst yet another was penetrating her from behind.

Ed eased his stiff cock from his pants and began working his foreskin back and forth, his eyes fixed on the action. He really needed a woman. He imagined himself fucking Jo, spreading her naked over her desk and ramming his stiff organ into her. He'd show her what a real man could do. She'd soon regret the way she'd dismissed him and bad-mouthed him to the agency. She could have a mouthful of his spunk in return. That would teach her.

All of a sudden the idea of Jo sucking him off, coupled with the sight of Belinda doing precisely that to the biker, became too much for him and a jet of spunk shot from the end of his cock, splashing down onto the carpet. Another followed, then another, and he groaned with pleasure, his hand still jerking back and forth as he milked himself dry. The spurts continued, their force diminishing, until a final dribble emerged from the end of his penis and ran down his shaft. He gave a sigh of satisfaction and sat back in his chair.

As soon as the video ended, he'd compose the letter he was going to send with it.

Jo placed the telephone receiver back in its cradle and stared at the instrument with a puzzled look on her face.

'What's up?' asked Chris.

'That was Belinda. Says she hasn't had the video yet.'

Chris sat up, an expression of concern immediately creasing her features.

'But she must have done. It went out the day before yesterday. I saw you hand it over to the courier.'

'I know. I just don't understand it.'

The two girls were seated behind their desks. When the phone rang, they had been discussing the close call they had had on the tube the night before. Now that incident was momentarily forgotten as they contemplated this latest problem.

'You sure you addressed it right?' asked Chris.

'I'm certain. I'm always really careful about that. Besides I've got the receipt in my drawer.'

She opened the drawer and pulled out the carbon copy, scanning the address.

'It's fine,' she said at last. 'No mistakes.'

'We'd better contact the courier firm then,' said Chris, reaching for the phone.

Ten minutes later she replaced the receiver and shook her head.

'Something very fishy's going on' she said.

'What did they say?'

'That the courier picked up the package all right, but not from this office.'

'What?'

'Apparently he was intercepted in the street. Some guy gave him a package, claiming it was the one he was to collect, so he took it.'

'But what about the guy who did collect the video?'

'He must have been a stooge. Probably the same guy.'

'You mean someone's got a copy of Belinda's video?'

'Worse than that. He's got her address too.'

'Oh shit.'

Jo stared at Chris in dismay. This was the worst possible news. The thought of someone in possession of such a compromising film, and with all the necessary information to blackmail the participant, was a total disaster. If Belinda got wind of it, it could mean the end for Fantasy and Co, and for all their plans.

'Why would anyone steal a video tape?' asked Jo.

'Because he knew what was on it, I presume,' replied her friend.

'But what will he do with it?'

'I don't know. But there's one obvious answer.'

'You don't mean blackmail?'

'It's got to be a possibility.'

'Oh no. What the hell do we do now?'

'Well, for a start we hope that it's us he tries to blackmail and not Belinda,' said Chris. 'At least that way there's some chance of keeping our reputation intact.'

'I see what you mean,' said Jo. 'Do you think he will?'

'If blackmail is what he has in mind, it's my guess that's what he'll do,' replied her friend. 'Then he's always got the option of blackmailing Belinda as well if we won't play ball.'

'Let's hope you're right. Who do you think it could be?'

'It's hard to say. It could be anyone.'

'You must have your suspicions.'

'It's not that easy. It could be someone who's been told what we do by one of our customers. Or one of the guys we've hired. Possibly even Doug or Mark.'

'You don't think it was them do you?'

Chris thought for a while, then shook her head. 'No,' she said. 'After all, they've both had plenty of opportunity to steal the videos. There was no need for them to go through this sort of charade.'

'What about one of the bikers?'

'Hardly. Jet was here when the so-called courier collected the tape. He's sure to have recognised whoever it was.'

'But he did leave at the same time.'

'You're right, although it seems stupid for him to draw attention to himself by doing that. Nevertheless, I think I'll have a word with him. Meanwhile you'd better edit another tape and get it to Belinda pronto. At least that should buy us a little time. Then we've got tomorrow's little escapade to set up.'

'Cheryl you mean?'

'Of course. No matter what happens, we've still got to stick to the schedule.'

'It could have come at a better time. Couldn't we put it off?'

'I suppose we could. After all she doesn't know it's tomorrow. When she booked she said she didn't want to know when or where, just asked us to book a day with her agency and surprise her. It just so happens that we picked tomorrow.'

'Still, I suppose it would be a shame to call it off when everything's arranged.'

'You're right. After all, our bogus courier hasn't even tried

174

to contact us yet. There's no point in sitting around just waiting for him to call.'

'So we go ahead?'

Chris thought for a moment, then nodded. 'Yes. After all we can't just down tools. We've got a business to run.'

Chapter 21

Cheryl Armour pulled the piece of paper from her bag and rechecked the address on it as she emerged from the station. She read the words 'The Angel, 126 Commerce Road' and consulted the map that accompanied the note. Then she set off towards her rendezvous.

She was still uncertain precisely why she had been called to this particular area. She worked as a temporary secretary and most of the jobs she received were in the City or the West End. To find herself called to an East End address was most unusual. The name of the company also puzzled her. The Angel. It didn't sound like the name of any company she'd ever heard of.

Still, a job was a job, and she wasn't averse to any kind of work that came her way. Cheryl had been working as a temp for some years now and she was used to the variety of establishments and roles that this could throw her into. On one occasion she had found herself handling the fan mail of a famous rock star and on another she had crossed the Atlantic on the QE2 doing office and typing work. A job in London's East End wasn't going to phase her.

Up ahead she saw the words 'Commerce Road' on the side of a building. It was a fairly wide road, lined on both sides by wholesale clothing outfits. The heart of the rag trade, in fact, and close to the famous Petticoat Lane market. She paused in front of one of the shops, its window somewhat untidily decorated by various articles of ladies' underwear. At the back of the window was a mirror and she checked her appearance critically.

What she saw pleased her. Cheryl was twenty-three years old. She stood about five foot six inches tall, her body perfectly shaped with large, full breasts and beautifully rounded hips, her long, shapely legs tapering to fine ankles. Her eyes were large and brown, her lips full. In her glasses she looked studious and stern, but when she removed them her expression changed to one of wide-eyed innocence that endeared her to many men. Her hair was brown, pinned back by combs and clips so that not a strand was out of place. Combined with the smart grey business suit she wore and her neat leather briefcase, she looked the epitome of the efficient secretary.

She checked her watch. Eleven-forty. A start time of a quarter to twelve was most unusual, but she would, as always, be on time. She moved on up the road, counting the building numbers. Then she drew up short. There, on a corner, was her destination, and its appearance was quite unexpected.

The Angel was one of those Victorian pubs that still survive in London's East End. Its outside was covered in shiny tiles, forming agreeable patterns in green and white. The windows were decorated with frosted floral designs and insets of stained glass, beneath which the words 'Fine Cask Conditioned Ales' were picked out in a ceramic mosaic. The pub had seen better days, though, and a general air of shabbiness hung over it now. The windows were in need of a clean, much of the brasswork was tarnished to a dull brown and the paint on the door was peeling.

As she approached, the door swung open and a man stepped out. He was carrying a sandwich board which he placed on the pavement in front of the pub's entrance. It bore the legend 'Live Strippers Every Lunchtime'. The man checked that the board was firmly in place, then turned and headed back inside.

'Excuse me.'

He paused at the sound of her voice and turned to face her.

'Yeah?'

Cheryl consulted the piece of paper again. 'Mr Carter?'

He shook his head. 'Nah. I'm just the barman. Sam's inside. You want him?'

'Yes please.'

'What's this all about?'

'I'm working here today.'

He ran his eyes up and down her body, taking in the prim efficiency of her appearance. 'You are?'

'Yes. I was told to report to Mr Carter at eleven forty-five.'

'You're new here, aren't you?'

'Yes, but I'm very experienced.'

Once again he examined her appearance. 'If you say so,' he said, thoughtfully.

'Listen,' she said, growing impatient. 'Could I see Mr Carter please?'

'I guess so. Step inside.'

She followed him into the pub. The door opened onto a saloon bar that mirrored the shabby appearance of the exterior. The carpet was threadbare and covered in cigarette burns. The walls had once been painted white, but the smoke of a million cigarettes had stained them brown, with dark streaks running up above the wall lights. Tables of various designs were set out about the room. Behind the bar was a dirty, cracked mirror. The sole occupants of the room were two men in labourers' overalls sitting on bar stools in the corner. They eyed the newcomer with undisguised interest.

'Where's Sam?' asked Cheryl's companion.

'Next door, checking the lights. This the new act?'

'Apparently.'

The man gave a low whistle. 'Kinky.'

Cheryl found herself blushing under the men's gaze. She turned to the barman.

'Through here?' she asked, indicating a door at the side of the bar.

'That's it. Good luck, darling.'

Cheryl opened the door and went through. She found

herself in a larger room. Like the previous one, it was long overdue for redecoration. To her right was a bar and on the other side was a low stage surrounded by coloured lights. There were a few tables set at the side of the room, but in the centre, in front of the stage, the floor was bare. A man was crouched in the corner, screwing in a light bulb. As she entered he rose and turned to face her.

'Mr Carter?'

'Who wants to know?'

He was a tall, burly man with a wide chest, though some of his weight had slipped to his stomach. He was in his late forties, balding slightly, his broken nose betraying early days spent in the boxing ring. He wore striped trousers held up by red braces, with a white shirt open at the collar.

'I'm Cheryl Armour. From the agency.'

He eyed her doubtfully. 'You're Cheryl?'

'That's right.' She stepped forward holding out a hand, but he ignored it.

'You got much experience?'

'Certainly. I've been with the agency for ages.'

'You always dress like that?'

'Of course. Is there something wrong?'

'Not as long as you've got a costume.'

'A costume?'

'Sure. You'll never get that lot off on stage.'

'I don't understand.'

'Look, I just asked if you had any experience, and you said yes. Now you sound as if you don't know what I'm talking about. Now tell me, what other joints have you stripped in?'

'Stripped?'

'Of course stripped. This is a fucking strip joint and you're supposed to be a fucking stripper.'

'But I'm a temporary secretary.'

'What?'

'A temp. I thought it was a secretary you wanted.'

'Holy shit!' Carter banged his hand over his face. 'I knew

180

it was a mistake to try a new agency. I ask for a bloody stripper and they send me some bloody pen pusher. I should have realised your body wasn't right when I first saw you.'

'What's wrong with my body?' demanded Cheryl, suddenly defensive.

'I need a girl with the right curves,' said Carter.

Cheryl dropped her briefcase and pulled her jacket open, revealing the smooth swell of her breasts and the slimness of her waist.

'Isn't that curvy enough?' she asked.

Carter paused and eyed her body as if seeing it for the first time, his face brightening.

'Now you come to mention it, you're not so bad,' he said. 'Take off those glasses.'

Cheryl hesitated for a moment, then removed them.

'Shit,' murmured Carter. 'You're quite a chick. I guess you'll do after all.'

Cheryl's jaw dropped, and she immediately jammed her spectacles back on her nose. 'Are you suggesting that I perform for you?' she asked indignantly.

'Can you dance?'

'Well, yes, but . . .'

'Then that's precisely what I'm suggesting.'

'You must be out of your mind. What sort of a girl do you think I am?'

'One who's proud of her body. And not afraid to show it off. Look at the way you're flashing your tits.'

Cheryl looked down at herself and immediately pulled her jacket shut. 'That's not exactly the same thing,' she argued.

'It's precisely the same thing, just to a lesser degree. Now come out the back. I've got some costumes there you can use.'

'No!'

Carter moved closer to her, staring down into her face.

'Now listen, Miss Armour,' he said. 'I hired you from that agency in good faith. I've got a load of very thirsty punters

181

coming in here in fifteen minutes, and they're going to want to see some action. And you're it.'

'But you can't be serious.'

'I'm deadly serious. I had an agreement with your agency and it's up to you to honour it. Or I'll sue them, and you, for every penny I can get. Now come with me.'

Cheryl stood rooted to the spot.

'Come on,' he insisted.

For a moment more she hesitated. Then she picked up her case and, as if in a dream, followed him towards a door at the back of the room.

In her heart she knew that this must have been arranged by Fantasy and Co. This was their response to her request that she be allowed to display her body to a roomful of strangers. She had agreed that they would set up the whole thing and that they would spring it on her when she was least expecting it. Yet still, in her mind, there remained a doubt. What if she really had stumbled on a genuine mistake? What would her friends and colleagues think if they knew what she was going to do? Surely she should just make a dash for it. After all if she really made a fuss there was nothing he could do. But at the same time an unfamiliar sensation was already filling her. A sense of excitement that sent thrills running through her body.

She glanced at the stage and thought of herself standing on it removing her clothes before a group of randy young men. All at once a warm wetness began to fill her sex as she followed Carter from the room.

Chapter 22

Cheryl sat in the small dressing room at the back of the pub, her heart hammering in her chest as she listened to the sound coming from the room behind her. It was a sound that filled her with trepidation and knotted her stomach, yet at the same time it roused a sense of excitement inside her that she hadn't felt for ages.

The sound was that of voices. Male voices. At first there had just been a few, talking in low tones, accompanied by the clink of glasses. But within a short time the noise had grown to a hubbub of sound, punctuated by roars of raucous laughter, and now the room was clearly full to capacity. She tried to estimate how many she could hear. Thirty? Maybe as many as fifty? She gave a little shiver as she thought of all those men, and what she was about to do.

She glanced at herself in a mirror. In the fifteen minutes since Carter had led her from the room where the stage was, she had undergone something of a transformation. Gone were the glasses and the hairclips, her hair brushed back over her shoulders in a carefree way. Her clothes had changed too. The austere business suit had given way to a short red latex dress that barely covered her thighs, the front being fastened by criss-crossing tapes through which the low-cut bra she was now wearing could easily be seen. Her legs were encased in black fishnet stockings, above which a vast expanse of thigh was visible, and on her feet she wore slim, red stilettos. She shook her head, allowing her hair to fall over her face, and struck a pose, her hands on her hips, her right foot thrust forward. There was no doubt about it, she looked very sexy indeed. What was more, she felt sexy too.

The door opened suddenly and Carter put his head round. He made as if to speak, then stopped short as his eyes took in the lovely young girl.

'Shit,' he said. 'That's some change.'

Cheryl ignored the remark. After all, she had told him that she'd got what it takes. There was no need for him to look so surprised.

'You're on in two minutes,' he continued. 'Just listen for the music.'

Cheryl nodded. She had chosen a beaty dance number to perform to. She wished she had had an opportunity to practise beforehand. As it was she would have to rely on her knowledge of the piece and the skills she had learned at dancing school when she was younger.

She went to the door and peered out. There was nobody around and she tiptoed along to the door that led to the back of the stage. It seemed ridiculous to be so cautious. After all she would soon be the centre of attention. But her natural modesty made her embarrassed by the outrageous way in which she was dressed.

She paused by the door and listened through the curtain that was draped across it. From here the sound of the crowd was even louder and she could sense their impatience as they called for the show to begin. Her stomach seemed to perform somersaults as she realised that in no time at all she would be out there, on that stage. For a second she contemplated making her escape. Then the first chords of her music boomed from the speakers and she knew it was too late. Taking a deep breath she stepped through the curtain into the room.

For a moment her mind reeled. A bright light was being shone directly into her eyes, temporarily blinding her, and her ears were filled with the roar of the crowd and the crash of the music. She stood stock-still, like a rabbit in a car's headlights, mesmerised by the assault on her senses. Then she caught sight of Carter standing at the side of the stage and she pulled herself together. She snapped her fingers twice to the beat of the music, then her body dropped into the rhythm of her dance.

She moved sensuously across the floor, her hips gyrating, and was amazed to find herself smiling broadly at the cries and wolf whistles of those watching, knowing they were in appreciation of the sexiness of her body. As she moved to the edge of the stage, she was able to stare out into the crowd beyond the spotlight. There were, indeed, at least fifty of them, all men. Most wore dark business suits and stood close to the stage, clutching pints of lager or swigging foreign beer straight from the bottle. They nudged one another and pointed as she shimmied across the stage and she started blowing kisses at them, bringing more cheers as she did so.

She continued to dance thus for a full minute, almost forgetting the purpose of her act as she enjoyed the adulation of the crowd. Then once again her eye was caught by Carter and she knew it was time to move on.

She paused in the centre of the stage, legs apart, hands on hips, eyeing the audience. Then her right hand went to her bodice and with a tug she pulled undone the tape that held the neck of the dress closed. At once the shiny material parted, revealing the white lacy bra beneath. It was cut low, lifting her breasts and accentuating her cleavage, two brown arcs of nipple peeping through on each side. She shook her shoulders, raising yet another cheer from her audience as the soft flesh of her mammaries quivered.

There were two more bows holding the dress closed and she undid these one at a time. For a moment she stood, holding the dress closed across her body, gazing coyly at the men. Then she pulled it open, uncovering her bare midriff and small lacy panties for the first time. Once again the audience shouted their appreciation as she allowed the dress to fall from her shoulders and tossed it aside, dropping back into the rhythm of the music.

Cheryl was feeling good now. The initial nerves had given way to a new confidence and she sashayed across the stage, throwing provocative glances at the onlookers, suddenly in her element before this sea of appreciative eyes. She glanced down at her body, aware of how sexy the underwear was, particularly when set off by the stockings, which reached halfway up her thighs and were self supporting.

The beat of the music suddenly increased in tempo, and she knew it was time to begin to bare her body in earnest. First of all it would be her breasts, and a thrill ran through her as she considered the idea of all these men ogling them.

Once again she moved to centre stage, turning her back on the crowd. She stood, her body swaying gently to the music for a few moments. The crowd went silent, and she remained still a moment longer. Then she reached up behind her back and flicked the bra undone. One by one she slid the straps down her arms and off, so that the garment was being held in place by her hands alone. Slowly she turned to face the audience, clutching the bra to her chest, her head down, staring up at them through lowered eyelashes, her hands trembling slightly at the thought of what she was about to do.

She took a deep breath. Then, with a sudden movement, she tossed the bra aside and stood facing the men. Her breasts were firm and succulent, the nipples hard with excitement, standing out like long brown knobs, as if inviting someone to suck them, and she thrust her chest forward proudly, a broad grin on her face.

The applause was deafening.

Cheryl began to dance as if her life depended on it, her breasts shaking deliciously now they were free of restraint. She had never felt sexier, the eyes of the men like physical caresses on her body as she shamelessly exposed herself to them. She could feel the wetness in her crotch as she danced and she wondered if it showed through the gusset of her panties. She eyed the men. Were they as turned on as she was? She imagined their cocks stiffening in their pants and a fresh tremor of lust swept through her lovely young frame.

Suddenly she badly wanted to masturbate. To free some of the sexual tension that was building up within her. And why not? After all, this was her show. Slowly, almost nonchalantly, she placed a hand on her thigh, running it up her body and brushing her crotch through the thin knickers as she did so. It was all she could do to suppress a gasp as the brief contact sent yet another shiver of lust through her barely clad body.

She stared out at the crowd. Their calls had turned to shouts now as they anticipated seeing her naked and she too felt a sense of urgency to divest herself of her panties, though she knew she must try to remain in control.

She moved to the front of the stage and stopped, her feet planted wide apart. The men began to clap in unison as she stood there, a slight smile playing about her lips, her hips moving from side to side. She dropped her hands to her waist, sliding her thumbs inside the waistband of the panties. She pulled them down to her hips, revealing a tuft of pubic hair above the silky white material.

Once again, as the moment of revelation approached, she turned away from her audience, standing with her back to them. Slowly she bent forward at the waist until she was almost doubled over.

Her hands slid round to the back of the panties and pushed them down further, until the round curves of her backside were on view to the cheering crowd. Then, in a single movement, she pulled them all the way down, kicking them to one side. She remained as she was, bent forward, giving the onlookers a perfect view of her bare behind, before suddenly straightening up and spinning round to face out into the audience, totally naked but for her stockings and shoes.

She dropped back into her dance, revelling in the cries and catcalls of the men as she shimmied about the stage, ensuring that everybody got a good look at her breasts and sex. The shouts of the men were like music to her ears and once again

187

she felt an almost physical sensation as their eyes fixed on her naked charms.

Gradually, she moved to centre stage again. Her arousal was almost total now and she knew she would be unable to restrain herself much longer. She reached up with both hands and began caressing her breasts, squeezing them and pressing them forward as if offering them to the crowd. Then her right hand left their soft roundness and began to move down her body. She ran it over the soft, downy blonde hairs that covered her belly and on to the thicker, darker thatch below, teasing out the wiry curls and delving lower. She cast her gaze across the sea of upturned faces, running her tongue slowly across her lips. Then, with a decisive movement, she thrust two fingers into her vagina.

The crowd was totally silent now. Even the music had almost completely died away and all eyes were fixed on her hand as she began to work it back and forth inside her. The only sound was of her panting, her hips thrusting against her fingers with an urgency that betrayed the genuineness of her arousal. Her sex was wetter than she had ever imagined possible, the juices flowing over her hand so that it shone in the brightness of the spotlight. Her breath had shortened, coming out in harsh grunts, and she bent her knees, pressing her sex forward to ensure that all the men could see precisely what she was doing. Then the music started once more, quietly at first, but gradually rising towards a crescendo.

As the tune reached its climax, so did Cheryl, her cries ringing round the room as she was released from the exquisite tension of her arousal. Wave after wave of pure pleasure coursed through her as the sheer joy of the orgasm overcame her. The men had started to cheer again but she barely heard them, her whole being engrossed in her climax.

Gradually, as the pleasure began gently to ebb, she dropped to her knees, her fingers slowing their movements. She allowed her body to fall backward until her shoulders were touching the floor, her legs still spread wide apart. Then she was done, her breath rasping in her throat, her hand falling to her side.

For a moment silence reigned. Then the men began to cheer.

Chapter 23

Cheryl slumped into the chair in her dressing room, panting for breath, her face flushed but triumphant. She had just completed her third and final stint on the dance floor and each act had raised more cheers than the last. Even now she could still hear the excited voices of the men calling her back to the stage. She felt exhausted. But overriding her exhaustion was an overwhelming sense of exhilaration. She couldn't remember anything more thrilling than the last hour and a half.

She had danced her heart out, loving the attention she had received from the crowd, who had cheered her every move with enthusiasm. She had come on all three occasions, violent, gasping orgasms that had shaken her frame deliciously and had brought loud accolades from those watching, all of whom were clearly aware that she wasn't faking.

Now, as she sat, still naked, in the small back room, the sounds from the crowd outside changed and she realised that Carter was saying something to them, his words punctuated by loud shouts and the occasional cheer.

She rose and crossed to the mirror, where she cast an eye over her body. Her skin was covered by a thin sheen of sweat that made it glisten in the soft lights. She examined the perfect roundness of her breasts and the smooth curve of her hips. She slid a finger down between her legs and felt the heat and wetness that was still in her crotch. She bent her knees slightly, spreading her legs and stroking her sex, taking the precise pose she had taken only minutes before on the stage, marvelling at her own shamelessness as she watched herself masturbating.

Despite her previous three orgasms, she felt the heat rising inside her once more. She gave a little moan, her eyes fixed on her wet fingers as she worked them back and forth. She thought once again of the men's eyes on her as she performed this intimate act and a new shudder of lust passed through her.

'You still randy?'

Cheryl jumped at the sound of the words, whirling round to see Carter standing in the doorway, grinning.

'Don't let me stop you,' he said. 'Enjoy yourself.'

Cheryl blushed, embarrassed for the first time since her initial foray onto the stage. She placed a hand over her crotch and wrapped her arm across her breasts, her face glowing.

'Don't you knock?' she asked.

'Why? It's my place. Besides, it's not as if there's anything in here I haven't seen already.'

'Even so. It's supposed to be a dressing room.'

'Well that wasn't dressing that you were doing. More like wanking.'

'Listen,' she said, angry with herself for allowing him to rile her. 'What do you want? I did the act for you, didn't I?'

'Yeah. And bloody well too. There wasn't a soft cock in the house by the time you'd come for the third time. Really turned you on, didn't it?'

Cheryl didn't reply.

'I reckon you could take it up professionally,' he went on. 'Just let me know if you want a job.'

'Don't worry,' she said. 'Meanwhile I assume I've finished for the day?'

'Not quite.'

'What do you mean?'

'Well at the end of the lunchtime session, we always have a raffle. It's very popular with the punters.'

'A raffle?'

'Yeah. You know, put the numbers in a hat and pull one out.'

'I know what a raffle is.'

'Good. And can you guess what the prize is?'

'No.'

Carter said nothing, simply allowing his eyes to travel up and down Cheryl's body. For a moment she stared at him uncomprehendingly. Then the penny dropped.

'You want me to . . . ?'

'That's right.'

'You can't be serious,' she gasped.

'I'm completely serious. It's all part of the deal. All my girls know that.'

'You mean I have to . . . With some guy?' Despite her previous lascivious behaviour, Cheryl found herself unable to articulate the words.

'Two actually.'

'Two?'

'Well we normally have two girls doing this slot, so they take one each. In your case you'll have to take on both.'

She shook her head. 'It's out of the question,' she said.

'Afraid not. We had a deal, remember?'

'Yes, but . . .'

'That you'd do the job you were assigned to. Well, this is part of that job. Besides, judging from the way you were frigging yourself just now, you're still in the mood for sex.'

Cheryl's mind was a whirl. She could scarcely believe what he was suggesting. It was no more than prostituting herself. Yet she knew that it was all part of her fantasy. For years she had imagined herself flaunting her naked body in order to titillate a roomful of strange men and the fantasy had always ended up with her being fucked by some burly stud. Now she was being asked to do just that. Even as the idea entered her mind, she felt the arousal inside her increase still further and she knew she would do it.

'Where are they?' she asked, the calmness in her voice

belying the excitement she felt at the prospect of what was to come.

'They're outside. You want me to show them in?'

'All right.'

'Both of them?'

She nodded.

Carter stepped out into the hallway. When he returned he was not alone. Cheryl eyed the two men breathlessly. They were gorgeous specimens, with broad, muscular chests and handsome faces.

'This is Mark and Doug,' said Carter.

Cheryl had still been covering herself with her hands. Now, as the three men watched, she lowered her arms to her sides, her legs spread slightly apart in a gesture of surrender.

Carter smiled, then stepped outside and closed the door.

Cheryl looked at Mark, then at Doug. 'So you won the raffle?'

The pair said nothing, but simply stared intently at her.

Cheryl stepped forward, placing a hand over each of their crotches. They were both hard and she rubbed them gently. Mark moved first, reaching for her breast and testing its softness. Doug followed suit, grasping the other one in his large hand and describing small circles with his palm against the nipple. Cheryl leant across and kissed each in turn on the cheek.

'Hope you like the prize,' she murmured.

She lowered herself slowly to her knees and turned her attention to Mark's fly, undoing the button and pulling down the zip. His jeans dropped to his ankles. Beneath he wore a pair of bright blue briefs against which his swollen cock strained for release. Cheryl pulled them down in a single movement, then licked her lips at the sight of his heavy, meaty cock bobbing in front of her face.

She ran her fingers slowly down its length, loving the heat and the hardness of it, feeling how the smoothness of the skin contrasted with the puckered roughness of his scrotum. She closed her hand about the tip and eased it back. The hole at the end peeped out at her, like a single eye. There was a tiny bead of moisture glistening on it and she protruded her tongue, licking it off. As she did so she sensed him stiffen and felt his ball sac tighten under her fingers. She licked again, enjoying the taste of him, her senses filled with his maleness.

She leaned forward, taking him fully into her mouth and sucking at him. His swollen cock filled her mouth completely, but still she pressed forward, wanting to take him all the way inside, excited by his reaction.

She sucked on, whilst manoeuvring his jeans and pants over his feet and pulling his shoes and socks off in the process. Meanwhile he was shrugging off his shirt, revealing the broad expanse of his smooth chest. Cheryl worked his foreskin back and forth with one hand and ran the other over his skin, marvelling at the hardness and solidity of his rippling muscles.

In her preoccupation with Mark, she had almost forgotten Doug, but she was soon reminded when a pair of hairy arms suddenly encircled her waist, the hands sliding up her stomach and closing over her breasts. As he moved closer and the hairs on his chest rubbed against her back, she felt something else too. Something thick and hard that brushed against her, betraying the fact that Doug too had stripped and was as horny as his companion.

Cheryl reached behind her, feeling for his crotch. His rod was rock hard, small pulses coursing through it as she began gently to masturbate him whilst still sucking greedily at Mark. Doug nuzzled against the back of her neck, his lips planting tiny kisses that sent shocks of pleasure through her. She pressed her body back against him, moaning softly.

Suddenly Mark was pulling her to her feet, turning her round to face Doug, so that she was able to see his slim tanned body and the main object of her desire jutting upwards from his groin. Naked he was even more desirable than before and her body ached to have him inside her.

Mark began pressing on her shoulders and she realised he

wanted her to kneel once more. She complied immediately, and when he pressed her forward onto all fours she understood his motive, moving her knees apart as he ran his hand between her thighs and sought out her slit.

Suddenly, without warning, he rammed two fingers into her, bringing a cry of surprise from her lips at his audacity. At once he began to frig her hard, nearly knocking her off balance as he thrust his hand back and forth inside her. Barely had Cheryl time to react, however, than she found Doug kneeling before her guiding his erection towards her lips.

She took him in willingly, sucking hard at him as he began to fuck her face, grasping hold of her hair and pumping his hips back and forth. At the same time Mark withdrew his fingers and suddenly there was something else nuzzling up against her vagina. Something much thicker than a pair of fingers. Something that throbbed with life as it drove into her.

But for her mouthful of penis, Cheryl would have screamed aloud. As it was she managed only a strangled groan as Mark rammed himself home, burying his thick weapon deep within her. Up until then Cheryl hadn't realised how badly she had wanted to be fucked, but she knew now, the pleasures of her earlier masturbation suddenly as nothing compared to the wonderful sensation that Mark's cock was bringing her. So aroused was she that she momentarily forgot to suck at Doug's rampant tool, but she was soon reminded of his presence by the new urgency with which he pulled at her head, pressing ever deeper into her throat.

Cheryl felt her orgasm welling up inside her as her body was shaken back and forth by her two lovers, her breasts swaying beneath her as she struggled to satisfy both. Then suddenly she was being manhandled again as Doug took hold of her, dragging her forward towards the low couch that stood by the wall.

She gave a cry of disappointment as both cocks slipped from her, but she was becoming used to the dominance of these men now and was thoroughly enjoying being in their control. She allowed herself to be led across to where Doug was prostrating himself on his back across the couch, his legs hanging over the end.

He pulled her forward so that she was straddling him, her crotch just above his rampant tool. She understood what he wanted now and reached eagerly for his cock, which was still slippery with her saliva. Carefully positioning it at the entrance to her vagina she began to lower herself slowly onto him.

Such was her lubrication that he slipped easily into her. She bent her knees lower, driving him deeper and deeper inside her until she felt the hard, prominent bone of his pubis rest against her own. It felt wonderful to be so filled with cock and she began to move back and forth, fucking him with relish, her firm breasts quivering with every stroke.

Once again she sensed the proximity of Mark and turned to see him standing just behind her, his glans shining with her love juices, a hungry look on his face. He placed his hands on her back, pushing her forward whilst Doug assisted, wrapping his arms about her neck and forcing her to prostrate herself over him. For a second Cheryl was confused, uncertain what was happening. Then she felt a finger probe her backside and seek out the tight hole of her anus, and it suddenly became clear.

Cheryl had never had her backside penetrated before and she gasped as she felt the fingers gently prise her nether hole open. They wormed their way into her back passage, easing into her, loosening her up for what was to come. Mark fingered her gently, twisting his digit inside her before withdrawing. Then she felt something much thicker and harder press against her there and she braced herself for what was to follow.

Mark began to push, applying a steady pressure against her anus. At first the flesh resisted, but Cheryl struggled to relax the muscles of her sphincter and allow him inside, and slowly he began to make headway. She cried aloud when he penetrated her, the momentary pain causing her to grit her teeth. Then he was pressing on and she felt the full thickness of his tool filling her rectum.

To Cheryl it was like nothing she had ever experienced before. There was some pain, but this was completely overshadowed by the extraordinary pleasure of being doubly penetrated. To have had a cock simultaneously in mouth and vagina had been an extraordinary thrill, but to be penetrated in this most intimate manner was quite indescribable and she gasped and moaned with lust as the two began to fuck her.

Cheryl was almost delirious with delight, sandwiched between two naked, muscular men, her nipples pressed hard against Doug's chest whilst two pairs of hips thrust against her from in front and behind. It was as if her entire body was filled with cock, and the urgency with which they pumped back and forth inside her brought her to new highs of ecstasy with every second.

Doug came first, his mouth opening in a grunt of satisfaction as he began pumping sperm into Cheryl's vagina. Moments later she had the extraordinary sensation of hot semen streaming into her rectum as Mark too shot his load. Experiencing the double ejaculation inside her was too much for Cheryl and, with a shriek of release, she felt her own orgasm overcome her, her body writhing back and forth between her two lovers as she came like she had never come before, the excitement of the striptease and the sheer eroticism of her afternoon combining with this extraordinary sexual encounter to fill her with a previously unimaginable pleasure.

The two men continued to pump their hips back and forth, holding her at her peak for what seemed forever. Then she was coming down, gasping for breath as she milked the last of their semen from them.

She gave a cry as Mark gently slipped his cock from inside her. Once he was out she remained prostrate over Doug for a few seconds before gently rising to her feet. She slumped down into the chair, her legs spread wide, small trickles of sperm escaping from her vagina and anus. She still couldn't credit the audacity of her behaviour. But she had achieved what she wanted and, in a way, that had been more pleasurable than she could possibly have imagined.

Cheryl's fantasy was now a reality.

Chapter 24

The package arrived in the offices of Fantasy and Co on the day after Cheryl's adventure. Jo was seated at her desk checking through the video footage when Chris walked in and dropped the morning's mail on her desk.

'How does it look?' she asked.

'Fine. The pictures of the striptease are great and the cameras we hid in her dressing room did the trick beautifully. You can see every detail of Doug and Mark's performances.'

'I'll have to have a look later.'

Chris settled down behind her desk and began opening the mail. It was quite an encouraging haul, with at least three prospective customers and a couple of cheques. It was only when she came to the parcel that her demeanour changed.

'Oh hell.'

Jo looked up. 'What is it?'

Chris held out the video tape that had fallen from the envelope.

'Put this on the machine would you?'

Jo slid the tape into the slot on the front of the VCR and pressed a button. There was a momentary fuzz, then the image cleared. The picture was of Belinda stretched naked on the grass whilst Jet fucked her.

'Oh hell,' echoed Jo.

'I presume it's a copy?'

'Yes. It's a completely different brand of tape from the one I usually use. Whoever sent this has still got the original.'

'There's a note as well.' Chris passed a sheet of paper across to Jo, who studied it carefully. The script was in large, untidy capitals, written in red ballpoint.

'As you can see, I have your tape, together with the name and address of the lady in question. I'm sure she'd be most put out by your carelessness in allowing them to fall into the wrong hands, even more so when the film is sent out to the press, as well as her husband. If you wish to prevent this, follow my instructions carefully.'

The letter went on to insist that one of the girls be in a telephone box in a village called Lower Hedingbury the following day. Whilst Jo was reading it, Chris pulled a road atlas from the bookcase and leafed through it.

'Here it is,' she said, pointing to a page. 'Lower Hedingbury.'

Jo pored over the map with her. It was a tiny hamlet, no more than a crossroads really, in a remote area of the Romney Marshes in Kent.

'It's certainly miles from anywhere,' said Jo.

'And whoever goes has to be alone. He's quite explicit about that.'

'Do you reckon it's safe? After all he might be a serial killer or something.'

'No.' Chris shook her head. 'It's money this bastard's after. He's too cunning to be a psychopath.'

'So we go along?'

'I don't see that we have much choice. We have to find out what he wants. If he releases that tape we're finished.'

'I suppose there's one good thing,' said Jo. 'At least it's us he's blackmailing, not Belinda. If she found out he had a copy of this tape there'd be hell to pay.'

'That's why we'll have to go along with his demands, at least for the time being.'

'So what's our next move?'

Chris read the letter once again.

'He wants somebody to be in the phone box tomorrow at

three o'clock. Then he'll call and tell her where he wants to meet her.'

'Won't that blow his cover?'

'He'll probably be disguised. After all he only needs a balaclava or something. I mean he walked in here and collected that parcel and we never saw his face.'

'So which one of us is going to meet him?'

'You want to toss for it?'

Jo smiled wanly. 'It's as good a way as any.'

Chris reached into her bag and pulled out a pound coin. 'Heads or tails?'

'Tails.'

She flicked it into the air and caught it, slapping it down on the back of her hand.

'Tails it is.'

'Oh hell.'

'Listen, Jo,' said Chris. 'You don't have to go through with this. We could always call his bluff.'

Jo shook her head. 'No. We've worked hard to get this business started and we're not going to screw it up now just because of some slimy git like this. We'll play along with him for the time being and see what he's up to.'

'Hey,' said Chris suddenly. 'I've got an idea. The guy wants you alone in the phone box, where he's going to call and tell you where to meet him, right?'

'That seems to be the general idea. I'm to be alone, and nobody's to follow me.'

'So what's to stop you taking the mobile phone with you?'

'What do you mean?'

'Well, as soon as you leave the phone box you can call me and tell me where you're going. Then I can intercept our friend and find out who he is, and what he's up to.'

'Hey, you're right,' said Jo. 'Then Doug and Mark can form a reception committee.'

Chris shook her head. 'No, I don't want to involve Doug and Mark at this stage.'

'Why not?'

'Well for all we know they might be part of the plot.'

'What, Doug and Mark?'

'It's possible. After all, whoever's doing this obviously knows very well how our business operates, and there's not that many people been involved with Fantasy and Co since we started. We can't rule them out as suspects.'

'You really think it might be them?'

'To be honest, no,' said Chris. 'But I'd like to be certain before I involve them. So for the time being I'll just follow you to where he tells you to go, then try and find out who he is.'

'How?'

'With any luck he'll have taken off his disguise by then. Otherwise I might have to tail him home.'

'So it's off to Lower Hedingbury tomorrow, then?'

'It certainly is. And meanwhile we've got some paperwork to get through.'

Chapter 25

The village of Lower Hedingbury was indeed small, consisting of less than a dozen small cottages around a crossroads. Jo stood outside the solitary phone box taking in the scene. The land was flat, dotted with small copses. She shivered as she imagined somebody watching her from one of the groups of trees. She had no doubt that the blackmailer was out there somewhere and that he could see her. She would have preferred not to be alone, but the note had been insistent. She had left Chris at a small inn about two miles away with strict instructions to sit by the phone.

She checked her watch. It was nearly three o'clock. The call would come through at any moment. She opened the door of the phone box and slipped inside. It was an old-fashioned box, with its familiar musty smell. She stood staring at the instrument, waiting for it to ring.

The sharp peal of sound made her jump when it came. She snatched up the receiver at once.

'Hello?'

Silence.

'Hello?'

Not a sound. The instrument was completely dead. There wasn't even a dialling tone.

All of a sudden Jo realised that she could still hear the ringing. She glanced about herself in confusion. Then it came to her. It was her mobile.

Hurriedly she fumbled in her bag, pulling out the small instrument. She switched it on and put it to her ear.

'Hello?'

There was a low chuckle at the other end.

'I thought you might try bringing your mobile. That's why I sent you to a phone box that's out of order.'

'Who are you?'

Again the chuckle. 'Just a businessman, wanting to talk business with you.'

'What are you after?'

'That's what I want to discuss. Now you are to follow my instructions precisely, or a certain young lady is going to receive a lot of adverse publicity, along with your company.'

'What do I have to do?'

'First of all I want you to drive to a nice quiet little place where we can talk. Now listen carefully.'

He gave Jo a series of directions, instructing her precisely where to park her car.

'Do you think you can find the place?' he asked.

'I think so.' Jo repeated his directions to him.

'Good. Now all the time I want you to keep this telephone line open. If you ring off I'll know you're trying to contact someone and the whole deal will be off.'

Jo frowned. He was clearly much cleverer than they had given him credit for.

'After you've parked the car I want you to strip.'

'Strip?'

'That's what I said. I can't afford to have you carrying any bugging devices, or anything else. If you're naked I'll know I'm safe.'

'But somebody might see me.'

'Nobody will. I chose the spot carefully. Leave your clothes on the front seat of the car, with the phone on top, still switched on. Then head up the path for about five minutes until you reach a clearing. Wait for me there.'

'How will I know which path?'

'There's only one. Now start moving.'

Jo hesitated. There was now no way she could contact Chris.

She was truly on her own as long as the man was on the other end of the telephone. She knew she was taking a risk. But if she didn't do as she was told, all might be lost. She took a deep breath, then pushed open the door of the box.

The directions he had given her proved easy to follow and her car wound its way through a series of lanes. All the time the phone lay on the seat beside her, still connected. From time to time she fancied she could hear his breathing, but she guessed she was probably imagining it.

Before long she found herself passing a thick wood. Up ahead was a right turn, then she expected to see a gate to her left and a small clearing. Sure enough the gate appeared and she braked gently, pulling off to the left and drawing to a halt.

When she switched off the engine the silence seemed to overwhelm her and she sat for a few seconds composing herself. Then she picked up the phone and listened.

'Are you still there?'

'I'm still here.' His tone was even and calm.

'I'm at the wood.'

'Good. You know what to do next.'

'Can't I just keep my undies on?'

'Not if you want your business to survive. Remember, leave the phone on top of the clothes where it can be seen.'

Reluctantly, Jo pushed open the door and stepped from the vehicle. She glanced about her. It certainly was a quiet spot, the only sound the calling of birds. The car was parked in such a way that it was difficult to see from the road. She was quite alone.

She was wearing a pair of tight jeans and a blouse. Now her fingers went to the buttons of the blouse and began slowly to undo them.

She stripped off the top, dropping it onto the driver's seat of the car. Then she unbuckled her belt and slid down the zip on her jeans. She kicked off her shoes and peeled the jeans from her legs. Soon these too were back inside the car.

She glanced around again, fearful of being seen. Then she

reached for the catch of her bra, flicking it undone and allowing the garment to slide down her arms. Her panties followed, leaving her totally nude.

She closed the car door, then opened it again and, picking up the phone, went to place it on top of the pile. As she did so she heard the man's voice.

'Are you naked?'

'Yes,' she said quietly.

'Good. You're very wise to cooperate. Now off you go and wait for me at the clearing.'

Jo put down the phone and closed the door once more. Then, suddenly feeling very vulnerable, she set off up the track that ran through the wood.

It was a hot day, the trees bathed in bright sunlight. Under any other circumstances Jo would have felt good, strolling naked in the sun in such a gorgeous spot. She glanced down at herself, aware that she made an erotic sight as she walked along, her breasts bouncing with every step, her bare skin smooth and inviting. She thought of the man she was going to meet and wondered what he would want of her. She considered the sight she would make, her lithe young body completely on display, and to her surprise she found herself oddly aroused by the idea. It was as if she was one of Fantasy and Co's customers, about to live out her desires in this leafy spot with a handsome young man. She would certainly rather be meeting Doug or Mark, she mused. In fact, the thought of being seduced by the pair brought a renewed sense of arousal to her, and she thought of the video she had edited the day before and of the image of Cheryl doubly penetrated by the two men.

It took her about five minutes to reach the clearing specified by the man. It was around fifteen yards across, with a thick layer of lush green grass that felt soft and cool beneath her bare feet. She knew at once that this was the spot where the rendezvous was to take place.

Feeling exposed standing in the centre of the area, she

moved to the edge, taking up a position beside a thick tree trunk. She leaned back against it, feeling the roughness of the bark against her bare flesh. Now all she had to do was wait.

As she stood, with nothing but her own thoughts to keep her company, her mind strayed once again to the eroticism of her situation. She thought of Fiona, the girl whose swim had ended up with her naked in the arms of the bird-watcher. She imagined herself caught in such a predicament, being forced to give herself to a stranger like that, and once again the heat in her belly began to increase.

All at once she wanted to masturbate. The feel of the air blowing over her bare cunt and the sunlight on her breasts sent tiny shivers of excitement through her. Her hand strayed down between her legs and toyed gently with the solid bud of her clitoris. She felt its wetness as her fingers slid over its surface, a new thrill filling her as she did so.

Then she snatched the hand away. The man would be there at any minute and she couldn't allow him to see her in a state of arousal. Instead she closed her eyes, trying to think of other things and to erase from her mind the desires that were trying to surface.

All at once she froze. Somewhere nearby, a twig had snapped. Somebody was coming along the path towards the clearing. Instinctively she pressed herself back against the tree, her hands trying to cover her nakedness.

She saw him before he saw her. He was a tall man, strongly built, wearing the same motorcycle gear he had worn when he had taken the video from the office. The visor on his crash helmet was up, but beneath it he had on a balaclava that concealed all but his eyes, giving him a somewhat sinister appearance.

He paused in the middle of the clearing and his eyes lighted on her almost at once. She couldn't be sure, but she fancied he was grinning as his eyes took in her lovely, naked body.

'You found this place all right then?'

Jo nodded silently.

'Now I've got to check you're clean. Come over here.'

She moved hesitantly towards him, stopping about a yard away.

'Put your hands on your head and open your legs. Then turn round slowly.'

'Is this really necessary?'

'It is if you want that tape back.'

She glared at him. Then slowly, reluctantly, she removed her hands from her breasts and sex and placed them on her head. His eyes were fixed on her crotch as she spread her legs and she hoped that he would not see the wetness there.

She turned right the way round, giving him a complete view of her charms. She was afraid that he might touch her as she stood with her back to him, though she wasn't certain what she feared most, his hands, or the way her body might respond to it. As it was, however, he made no attempt to lay a finger on her, simply inspecting her for any devices.

'Good,' he said at last. 'I see you're being intelligent about this whole thing. Now, perhaps, we can talk business.'

'What is it that you want?' she asked.

'Why, money of course. What else?'

'How much?'

'Twenty thousand.'

'Twenty?'

'That's what I said.'

'But we can't possibly afford that kind of money, you must know that. We've only just started up.'

'And you're going to be closing down again if you're not careful.'

'Look,' she said. 'This is just silly. There's no way we can possibly afford twenty thousand. You might as well send that tape off right now. Now, if you'll excuse me, I'm going to put some clothes on.'

She turned and began walking towards the path. Her heart was beating hard as she did so. She knew full well that she had to reach some kind of accommodation with this man.

But she knew too that this was not what he wanted either and she hoped against hope that he wouldn't call her bluff.

He didn't.

'Hey, come back here.'

She paused. 'What's the point?' she asked. 'I've got better things to do than stand and let you gawp at my tits.'

'Ten thousand, then.'

'It's still too much. It'd just put us out of business. We'd have nothing to gain.'

'Five then. And that's my final offer.'

She eyed him. It was impossible to tell what he was thinking behind the mask.

'When would you want the five thousand?' she asked.

She saw his shoulders relax. 'Tomorrow.'

'You're pretty impatient.'

'I need the money.'

'All right then. Five thousand. How will I deliver it?'

'In cash. Same arrangement as today. I'll tell you where to go on your mobile. And no tricks.'

'Do I get to keep my clothes on?'

He shook his head. 'No. I like it better this way. Besides, you do have gorgeous tits.'

She reddened. 'Where will you call me?'

'I'll let you know tomorrow. Just don't try anything funny.'

'I won't. You make sure you bring the tape.'

'Sure. Now stay here and don't move for five minutes. Any funny stuff and the deal's off. Five minutes, and then you can go. That clear?'

'Yes.'

'Good.' He took a final look at her, then turned and headed back down the path. Jo watched him as he disappeared. Then her hand slid down to her sex and she began to masturbate.

Chapter 26

'You awake?'

Jo rubbed her eyes and gazed blearily up. A figure was standing over her with a steaming mug. For a second she couldn't remember where she was. Then her vision cleared and she recognised the spare room in Chris's flat. She dragged the sheets up over her naked body and sat up.

'What time is it?'

'Nearly eight o'clock. Time to rise and shine.'

Jo took the mug of coffee from her friend and sipped at it whilst Chris picked up her own from a table at the side.

'Thanks for letting me stay last night,' said Jo. 'I really didn't fancy going home.'

'That's okay. You had a pretty traumatic time.'

'Oh, it wasn't all that bad. It's not as if he threatened me or anything.'

'But making you strip off like that.'

'I could live with that. Actually it was a bit of a turn-on. And he was pretty horny too, I could see his crotch bulging.'

'Even so. You're sure you're up to seeing him again?'

'Perfectly. But we've got to think up some kind of plan.'

'I guess I could follow you this time. Try and keep myself out of sight.'

Jo shook her head. 'It's too risky. We've got too much to lose. We've got to think of something a bit more subtle. Some way of really trapping him.'

'That's going to be tough. He's obviously thought this whole thing through pretty carefully.'

'Yeah. There was no way I was going to pull a fast one on him yesterday.'

Chris sat down on the bed beside Jo. She was wearing a sheer negligee through which Jo could clearly see the curves of her young body, her breasts pressed against the material so that the dark brown of her nipples was starkly outlined. She began to stroke Jo's neck.

'There's gotta be a way that two girls like us can get one over on a slob like him,' she said. 'After all, what is it that most men are after?'

Jo grinned. 'Sex of course.'

'And that's precisely what we have to offer. I mean look at you.'

As she spoke she took hold of the sheet that was covering her friend and pulled it back, revealing Jo's naked body. 'I mean what man could resist that?' she said, idly caressing Jo's breast.

'He could, apparently,' said Jo. 'He never made a move after me yesterday.'

'I know, but I bet that if you'd made an advance he wouldn't have said no.'

'Are you suggesting I offer him my body in place of the money?'

Chris toyed with her friend's nipple, which was already hard. 'Of course not,' she said. 'But I bet he'd be tempted if you did.'

Jo smiled. The sensation of Chris's caresses was beginning to have an effect on her and she was having difficulty lying still. 'So you reckon my body's the key to this?'

'It could be. What sort of a guy did you think he was?'

'Cocky, arrogant, self-assured. I guess he thought he knew it all.'

'So we've got to play to those weaknesses.'

'Yeah, but how?'

Chris transferred her attention to Jo's other breast, her fingers squeezing and caressing the soft flesh and encircling

214

the tight, puckered knob of her nipple.

'I'm beginning to get an idea,' she said.

'Go on.'

'Well, we're pretty certain this guy must have worked for us at some time.'

'Yes. How else would he have known so much about us?'

'How many people have we taken on part-time?'

'I don't know. Ten? Maybe a dozen? That's if you don't count the bikers.'

'I don't think it's one of them. Besides the only one we really worked closely with was Jet. The others hardly knew who we were.'

'And Jet was in the office when this guy took the tape. And it was him that got suspicious when the guy pretending to be a dispatch rider didn't even know what kind of bike he was riding.'

'So we've got about ten suspects.'

'That's about it.' Chris continued to stroke Jo's breast, whilst her other hand ran down over the girl's stomach and lower, towards the dark bush that covered her mound.

'How are we going to tell which one it is? After all, the guy was covered from head to toe.'

Chris slid a finger between Jo's legs, feeling the girl start as she did so.

'Perhaps you could persuade him to take off some of his disguise,' she said.

'You mean seduce him?' Jo was finding it increasingly difficult to concentrate on what was being said as Chris's fingers sent sharp pulses of pleasure through her body.

'Do you think you could do it?'

'Sure I could do it. But I'm not sure he'd remove much more than his pants. And all the guys who've worked for us are so well hung I don't think I could be certain of telling one cock from another.'

'Still, there must be a way.'

'I suppose . . . Oh, shit, Chris, this is really making me

horny. Why not take off that nightie?'

Chris ceased her caresses and rose to her feet. Then, grasping hold of the hem of her skimpy garment, she pulled it over her head and dropped it to the floor.

Jo never tired of the sight of her friend's slim figure. Or of her magnificent breasts which were revealed in their full glory now, the flesh quivering slightly as she gazed down at her. Jo reached out a hand and placed it on her thigh.

'I want to taste you,' she said quietly.

'Sounds good to me.'

'Come on then.'

Jo drew the blonde girl down onto the bed, manoeuvring her so that she was kneeling behind her head. She pressed her friend's knees apart with her fingers, then eased her body up the bed so that she was gazing up at the pink flower of Chris's sex.

She ran her hands up the girl's inner thighs, feeling the trembling anticipation in her. Moving them still higher she slid her thumbs into the slit and eased it open, studying the pink, moist flesh inside. Chris's clitoris was in full view now and Jo pressed it between her thumbs. She was rewarded by a shiver than ran through her friend.

'Come lower,' she whispered.

Chris spread her legs still wider and lowered her crotch down over Jo's face. Wrapping her arms about Chris's thighs, Jo raised her head and protruded her tongue, lapping tentatively at Chris's love bud.

The effect on her friend was electric, a gasp of pleasure coming from her at the intimacy of the contact. Jo moved her tongue from side to side, suddenly more aroused than ever by the smell and taste of the lovely young woman who knelt over her, her head thrown back, her eyes tightly closed as she revelled in the sensations that Jo was bringing her.

Jo slid her tongue down the full length of Chris's sex, the tip just inside her, feeling the way the muscles contracted at the contact.

'Oh god, that feels good,' murmured the blonde girl.

Jo protruded her tongue further, penetrating Chris's vagina and bringing new moans of pleasure from her companion. She began working the muscle back and forth, lapping at the juices in her friend's quim, her senses filled by the intimacy of the situation. She could feel the arousal in her friend now and it was beginning to transmit itself to her, so that she felt the heat begin to rise in her own sex.

Chris must have sensed it too, because she suddenly leaned forward, lowering herself over Jo's body. Jo felt the hardness of her friend's nipples as they brushed against her stomach, then a tongue was working its way down, around her pubic bush, licking at the creamy flesh of her thighs.

'Oh!'

Jo's cry of delight was muffled by the folds of skin that covered her mouth, but the shudder that ran through her body betrayed her arousal as Chris's tongue came into contact with her sex. She grasped the other girl's thighs even more tightly, her fingers digging into the soft flesh of Chris's backside as she pressed her sex up into her face. Chris responded by extending her own tongue still further, delving deeply inside the moist cavity and bringing more spasms of lust from her companion.

The girls continued to roll about on the bed, first one on top, then the other, their faces locked in one another's crotches as each lapped enthusiastically at her friend. Every now and again a groan would arise from one or other of the pair as her companion found a particularly sensitive spot and worried away at it with her tongue. Each had her thighs wrapped tightly about the other's head, forcing her sex forward, encouraging the other to probe deeper and deeper as they lost themselves in each other's bodies.

Chris came first, her body going suddenly tense, then relaxing as her sex muscles tightened about Jo's insistent tongue. She was still writhing in ecstasy when Jo too succumbed, her backside banging up and down as she was overcome by the pleasure of her orgasm. The girls remained locked together, their tongues still deep inside one another's bodies, their stifled moans forming a strange low-pitched chorus as they rolled back and forth on the bed.

At last though, sensing that her companion was spent, Jo raised her head from between Chris's thighs and toppled off her, lying back on the bed, her chest heaving with the exertion of the session. Her mouth was covered with a mixture of saliva and love juice, as were her thighs, but she didn't care. The orgasm had been wonderful and she knew that Chris had enjoyed it just as much.

She sat up and reached for her coffee cup, placing it to her lips. Then she grimaced.

'Ugh! Cold.'

Chris reached out and stroked her thigh.

'You certainly weren't.'

Jo laughed. 'Neither were you. You give great head, Chris.'

The blonde girl suddenly leapt to her feet.

'To hell with coffee,' she said. 'We can make some more later. Let's shower.'

She took Jo by the hand and pulled her off the bed, dragging her towards the bathroom. In no time the pair of them were standing together in her shower cubicle whilst she fiddled with the taps.

The water in the shower was cool and Jo let it run over her body, her flesh tingling at the caress of the strong jet. Chris picked a bar of soap from the rack and began to apply it to her friend's breasts, her fingers sliding over Jo's smooth flesh as she worked the lather into her. Jo reciprocated, loving the feel of Chris's soft, pliant flesh as she slid her hands round in circles.

The pair scrubbed one another's backs, chattering and laughing as they did so, the problems of the blackmail forgotten for the moment as they enjoyed each other's company.

At last they staggered out of the shower, still giggling like children, their lovely bodies dripping with water. Chris opened the airing cupboard and pulled out two thick, luxurious towels, throwing one to Jo. They began to dry themselves off.

'Have you got a comb I can borrow?' asked Jo.

'In the cabinet over the sink,' replied Chris.

Jo pulled open the door of the cabinet. It was set quite high in the wall and she had to stand on tiptoe to reach the top shelf. As she fumbled for the comb her hand caught a small bottle which tumbled down into the sink, losing its cap as it did so. Jo jumped back as the dark brown liquid began to glug down the drain. She went to right the bottle, but Chris's hand came down on her wrist.

'Don't Jo. That's iodine. You'll never get it off your fingers.'

'Iodine?'

'Yeah. That bottle's been in there for years. I keep meaning to throw it out. It's awful stuff. Stains your skin something dreadful. I'll be glad to see the back of it.'

'Is it really that difficult to get off?'

'Yeah. It stays around for days, no matter how hard you wash it.'

A smile began to spread across Jo's face.

'What are you thinking?' said Chris.

'Maybe we can catch our blackmailer after all.'

'I don't understand,' said Chris. 'How will a bottle of iodine help?'

'It won't in itself,' replied Jo. 'But it's given me a great idea.'

Chapter 27

Jo stood by her car, slowly removing her clothes. She was parked in a clearing almost identical to the one she had been in the day before. Once again she had been forced to go through the rigmarole with the mobile phone, and once again it lay on the seat of the car, still hissing with life, the line open to the mysterious blackmailer.

She undid the buttons on her blouse and slipped it off. Her skirt followed. Beneath she wore matching underwear and a pair of black hold-up stockings. Glancing about her in a final check that she was alone, she unclipped her bra and dropped it onto the seat, then stepped out of her panties. The stockings she kept on. The move was deliberate. She knew only too well how they enhanced her nudity, drawing attention to her small, neat pubic triangle and the paleness of her bare skin. Her shoes, too, were scarcely suitable for what she was doing, being a pair of slim, black high heels, but they served further to emphasise the eroticism of her situation. As she set off up the path she knew that, in this state, few men would be able to resist her charms.

Once again the path was a long one, winding between the trees. The man had chosen the wood well. It was deserted, the only sounds the swish of the wind in the trees and the call of the occasional pigeon. Jo strode alone like a woman with a purpose, her firm, pert backside swinging as she did so.

As before, the meeting was to be in a clearing, and as before she found it easily. She sought out a patch of grass and sat down, leaning back on her elbows and arranging her body carefully, ensuring that her legs were slightly spread so that the man would have a clear view of the soft white flesh above her stocking tops, and the darker, pinker gash that was her sex.

He arrived about ten minutes later, stomping up the path, his breath rasping. She could see that his outfit was totally unsuitable for the heat of the summer's day and it was clear that he was sweating heavily beneath the helmet and balaclava.

He stopped short when he saw her, clearly unprepared for the sexy way in which she was displaying herself, stretched back in the lush green grass, her breasts thrust upwards, the brown-tipped nipples hard.

'You took your time,' she said.

The man said nothing for a moment, his chest still heaving from the heat and exertion of his walk. Jo suspected that some of his breathlessness might also be due to her own appearance, and she noted with satisfaction the bulge that was rapidly growing in his trousers. She gazed down at herself and began idly toying with her nipples, rolling them in her fingers and increasing their hardness.

'I thought I said you were to be naked,' he panted at last.

'Oh, don't you like the stockings?' she asked, her eyebrows rising, an expression of innocent surprise on her face. 'I'm told they look rather sexy. I'll take them off if you want.'

He stared at her for a second, his eyes glued to her crotch, then shook his head.

'No, leave them.'

'I thought you'd like them.' Jo shifted her position slightly, spreading her legs a little wider and cupping her breast from beneath. 'You must be hot in all that gear.'

'I'm all right. Let's talk business.'

'If you like.'

He looked about the clearing. 'Where's the money?'

'I haven't got it.'

Through the slit in his balaclava she saw his eyes narrow. 'What?'

222

'I haven't got it. I thought I could get it, but it was too short notice.'

'But we made a deal.'

'I know we did. And I'll stick by it, I promise. There just wasn't enough time to draw that sort of money out in cash. Our assets aren't all in one place, you know. Anyhow we're doing a big job at the end of the week and that'll bring in enough to be able to pay you.'

'But I can't wait until the end of the week.'

'You'll have to. We're only starting to audition for the job in a couple of days and we're going to need a male extra. Then we've got to get him rehearsed. There's no way we can do it sooner.'

His eyes darkened. 'It's not good enough,' he said. 'I'm going to have to release the tape.'

'It's only a few days. You can't be that impatient, surely?'

'We had a deal. And you've failed to deliver. Now I'll show you that I'm not a man to be fooled about with.'

'I never suggested you were. Come on now, this is silly. Once that tape is released we've both lost everything. And all for the sake of a few days.'

'But how do I know you're not planning something?'

'Like what? Nobody could possibly have followed me here with all the precautions you took, and I'm hardly likely to be carrying anything am I?' She glanced down pointedly at her naked body.

'Look,' he said, 'if I did agree, how soon would I have the money?'

'By the end of the week. I told you.'

He grunted. 'I don't see why I should agree. After all you dragged me all the way out here for nothing.'

'It needn't be for nothing.' Jo slid a hand down over her stomach and through her pubic hair, her forefinger coming to rest over her love bud. Looking up at him through lowered eyelashes, she began to move the finger round in small circles.

'What do you mean?'

'I mean I don't have any money, but I could give you something else on account.'

His eyes travelled down to her crotch again and she could sense that he was starting to sweat once more.

'You mean . . .'

'You know what I mean.' She glanced down at her body, then back at him. 'Don't you fancy me?'

'Yeah but . . .'

She eased herself up onto her knees, so that she was kneeling just in front of him. She stretched out her arm and ran her hand over his crotch.

'I can tell,' she said. 'Why don't you let me get closer acquainted with you?'

He said nothing, but made no complaint when Jo pulled down his zipper and slid a hand inside his pants. As she had expected, they were barely able to contain his massive erection and his cock felt hard as iron through the thin cotton material. As she cupped it in her hand she felt it pulsate.

She looked up at him. He was standing rigidly, his hands by his side, his fists clenched. She had the impression he was trying to suppress his emotions, but it was clear from his erection how he really felt.

She eased down the front of his pants, uncovering the inches of thick, meaty flesh beneath. She wrapped a hand about the shaft and pulled the material down further, marvelling at the strength with which his cock forced itself erect. Running her hand up its length, she slid back his foreskin. His glans was shiny with lubrication and she licked at it gently, making it twitch violently once more as she did so.

She opened her mouth, taking him inside and sucking hard at his massive erection. At the same time her hands went to his belt, yanking it undone and unfastening his top button so that his jeans dropped to his ankles. She pulled his pants down after them, then, relinquishing her throbbing mouthful for a moment, sat back to admire his tackle.

His cock was certainly a big one, the tip bulbous and shining with her saliva. His balls hung low, stretching his capacious ball sac and swaying slightly with each twitch of his organ. She closed her fist about his length once more, working the foreskin gently back and forth and watching the expression of pure ecstasy on his face as she did so. Then she was fellating him again, loud sucking noises escaping from her lips as she ate greedily at his shaft. He was grunting now, his eyes closed as he pumped his hips back and forth against her face. Jo felt for his balls, caressing them gently as her head worked energetically up and down.

Glancing up at him, Jo could see that he was totally absorbed in his own pleasure, his eyes tight shut, his head thrown back. Keeping her eyes fixed upon him, she dropped her right hand to the ground and reached back to her shoe.

She felt around her heel for the small catch that she knew was there, and pressed it. At once a cavity opened up and something dropped out. She picked it up. It was a small felt-tipped marker pen, no more than an inch long. Palming it in her hand, she reached round behind him, ostensibly to take hold of his backside as she moved her mouth back and forth against his knob. Then she ran her nail up the crack of his behind, drawing the pen with it, praying that it was having the desired effect of tracing an indelible black line from the top of his legs to just above his anus. Having done so, she dropped the pen behind him and concentrated once more on sucking his cock.

'That's enough of that.'

For a second Jo thought her ploy must have been discovered as he grunted the words, pulling her head back from his glistening tool.

'Get on your hands and knees.'

The words sent a wave of relief through her and she obeyed quickly, presenting her perfect backside to him as she spread her legs, knowing what was to follow.

She felt his cock press against her behind and for the first time realised how aroused she was herself. She moaned as she felt him position his glans and begin to press, forcing himself into her.

He slipped in easily, despite his size. The wetness in her crotch saw to that. He thrust his cock home and began to fuck her at once. There was no finesse in his technique, he simply slammed his erection hard into her, his stomach slapping loudly against her backside as he took his pleasure. For her part, Jo was perfectly happy with the unceremonious shagging she was receiving, content to feel a hot cock slip in and out of her whilst she steadied herself as best she could.

He was fucking her hard now, his heavy balls slapping against her sex lips, his hands gripping her thighs so tight it almost hurt. He was taking her with an animal passion, like some rutting stag servicing one of his harem of does, and Jo could hear him grunt with every stroke, his long, thick penis carrying her to new heights of pleasure so that she knew that she must come soon.

He came in a rush, his cock suddenly ejecting great spurts of semen into her. She tried to hold back her own climax, to control her lustful desires, but it was no good. All at once her orgasm was upon her, pulses of pleasure sweeping through her as he continued to shoot his seed into her vagina.

His orgasm went on and on, until she felt she must be filled to the brim with his semen and could feel it leaking out of her and trickling down her thighs. Still he pressed on, triggering a second climax in the wanton girl as she surrendered herself to his lovemaking, suddenly careless of everything but the hefty cock that rammed itself into her so insistently.

For a while Jo thought that he would never tire, that she was destined to kneel in this quiet wood indefinitely whilst he pounded against her. Then she sensed him slowing and knew that he was spent.

He withdrew as he had started, without ceremony, yanking his cock out of her and pulling up his pants. She rolled over onto her back, squinting up at him as he tucked his already detumescing penis away.

'I'll call you on Monday,' he said. 'And no tricks this time.'

'No tricks,' she replied.

He snorted, then turned and set off back down the path.

Jo waited a minute until he was well out of sight, then rose to her feet and picked something up from the ground. It was the marker pen. She walked across to a tree and ran it across the pale grey bark. It left a distinct black line. Nodding with satisfaction, she took off her shoe and slipped the pen back into the cavity in the heel. Then, whistling softly to herself, she set off down the path.

Chapter 28

'How's it going, Chris?'

The question was almost a casual one as Jo strode into the office and dropped her bag onto her desk. Chris was sitting behind her own desk, a neat pile of envelopes stacked in front of her. She looked up sharply as Jo entered.

'Jo! Are you okay? How did it work out? Did he take the bait? You're not hurt are you?'

'Hey, slow down,' laughed Jo. 'One question at a time, Chris.'

Chris had risen to her feet and come out from behind her desk.

'Seriously, Jo,' she said, taking her friend's hand. 'Are you all right?'

'Never better.'

'And the plan?'

'Worked perfectly, just like you said it would.'

'So he went for you?'

'Could any man resist me?' Jo gave a little twirl that made her friend giggle.

'And the pen was all right?'

'I hope so. Unfortunately our friend wouldn't let me inspect his backside. But I'm pretty certain it did the trick.'

'So he now has an indelible black stripe running down his bum.'

'That's right. It'll be there for days. And unless he's in the habit of inspecting his own crack, he'll never know.'

'That's just great, Jo.' Chris kissed her on the lips. 'It wasn't too bad was it?'

Jo shook her head. 'Quite a good fuck, actually. And all in the line of duty of course.'

'You're a wicked woman, Jo,' said Chris. 'And I love you for it.'

'What about you?' said Jo. 'How's the great talent hunt going?'

'Well, as we agreed, I left out the bikers,' replied Chris. 'I make it nine guys apart from Doug and Mark who've worked for us since we started.'

'And you've asked them back?'

Chris indicated the pile of envelopes on her desk. 'I was just about to post them,' she said. 'The auditions take place on Wednesday.'

'And do you think our man will come?'

'With his vanity? It's a cert.'

'Well, let's go down and get them in the post then.'

And grabbing the letters, Jo took Chris's hand and the two girls headed for the lift.

Ed Mercer sat in his flat gazing gloomily out of the window. Things weren't exactly going to plan. By now he'd expected to be taking a well-earned holiday in the sun on the proceeds of his ill-gotten gains. Instead here he still was, no better off than before.

Perhaps he should have been more forceful and insisted on getting the cash immediately. After all it wasn't as if the girls could be that hard up. He should have at least demanded a down payment. He glanced across at the bookcase, where the precious tape was stored. Maybe he should just try and sell it to a newspaper. He had done a little research into Belinda since discovering her address and what he had uncovered was very interesting.

It turned out that her husband was a merchant banker and very well known in the City. Something of a celebrity in fact. There was no doubt that some of the tabloids would pay well for the tape. Which was precisely why he was glad he had taken two more copies. Originally he had told himself that this was merely an insurance against the original being damaged, but now it was becoming clear that he could clean up twice on this particular deal. As soon as he got the money from the girls, he would put Plan B into operation, take one of the other tapes to the press and make some real money. After all, why should he care about those bitches who ran Fantasy and Co? They were just like the rest, completely unappreciative of his talents. Well, he'd show them who was boss, and he'd make a good deal of money at the same time.

A noise from outside the room distracted him. The mail must have arrived. He rose to his feet and made his way through to the small hallway. There, lying on the mat, was a small pile of letters. He sorted through them. Two bills and some junk mail. He snorted with disgust. There was one other letter though. It was a large white envelope, addressed by hand.

Curious, he tore it open and unfolded the letter. At first he was taken aback, since the letterhead bore the words 'Fantasy and Co' in large red letters. Could it be that they were onto him? Had he made some kind of mistake? Then, as he went on to read the letter, his expression of consternation was replaced by one of relief, and a smile began to spread slowly across his features.

'Dear Ed
'You must remember us. We gave you a job recently of a slightly unusual nature, and you performed very well. We now have need of someone of your talents again, and would be grateful if you would call in for an audition.'

The letter went on to define time and place for the audition, which was to take place the following day. Ed put down the letter, still grinning broadly, and settled back in his chair.

So they still wanted him. He had to admit that he wasn't surprised. After all he had put on a brilliant performance on the previous occasion, so much so that he was surprised they hadn't called him back earlier. This was, at least, proof of his superior acting powers, as well as his prowess as a lover. He had a good mind to call the agency and tell them what fools they were to have let him go.

But for Ed, the supreme irony was that the very firm he was blackmailing was the one calling him back for more work. In fact this must be the job to which that dimwitted girl was referring when she said they needed to raise more money. So, not only would he be paid for the job, but he'd be collecting all the profits as well. It really was poetic justice.

He settled back in his chair. This was one audition he was really going to enjoy.

Chapter 29

Jo emerged from the shower and towelled herself dry whilst Chris stepped under the hot spray and began to wash away the sweat and semen from her body.

'Only one more chance,' she said, rather gloomily.

'Don't despair,' replied Chris. 'Our man's got to be one of these last two.'

'Not necessarily. There were nine of them altogether, remember, and only six replied to the invitation. It could be that he's not coming at all.'

'I tell you this bastard's too vain for that,' said Chris. 'I'm certain he'll be here.'

'Well, we'll know in twenty minutes,' said Jo.

'You feeling up to another audition?'

'Just about. Are you?'

'I could do them all day.'

Jo giggled. 'It's a tough job, but someone's got to do it.'

They had decided that Chris's flat was the best place to carry out the exercise, the office being a little cramped for what they had in mind. The first audition had been at ten o'clock that morning, and the two girls had put the men through their paces with enthusiasm, though neither of the pair had had the telltale black stripe for which they were searching. The second two men had proved equally energetic, but equally unsuccessful. Now they were expecting the last two who had responded to their letter, and Jo was understandably nervous at their lack of success hitherto.

Chris climbed from the shower and stood beside her,

rubbing herself down with the towel.

'What are you going to wear?' she asked.

'I thought maybe some sexy lingerie,' replied Jo. 'That should get them going.'

'What I'm looking at should get them going,' replied her friend. 'You look good enough to eat.'

She dropped her towel and moved across behind Jo, who was standing at the mirror brushing her hair. Jo felt her friend's nipples press against her back as the girl wrapped her arms about her waist and reached upwards for her breasts, taking one in each hand and squeezing them gently. She leaned back her head so that it rested on Chris's shoulder, kissing her on the cheek as she did so.

'Mmmm. You smell wonderful,' murmured Chris. She continued to squeeze Jo's breast with her right hand, whilst her left dropped down, her fingers skimming lightly over the soft, downy hairs that covered Jo's stomach, then lower, towards the thicker, wiry ones at her crotch.

Jo gave a stifled cry as she felt Chris's fingers tease her clitoris into life. She pressed her body back against the other girl's, loving the sensation of flesh against flesh.

'We shouldn't be doing this,' she murmured. 'They'll be here in ten minutes.'

'You're right,' said Chris, her fingers continuing to play with Jo's most sensitive places. 'Perhaps afterwards. I've got a feeling I'll need something a little gentler after yet another pair of hefty studs.'

'It's a deal,' said Jo.

Ten minutes later both were in the living room, waiting for the doorbell to ring. Jo wore matching underwear – the black lacy bra lifting her breasts and exposing her luscious cleavage whilst the knickers were trim and brief, with transparent panels up the side through which her pale skin could be seen. About her waist was a matching suspender belt that held up a pair of sheer black stockings. The whole outfit was finished off by a pair of high, black stiletto heels that accentuated the slender shape of her legs.

'Wow, Jo,' gasped Chris. 'You look stunning. No red-blooded male could possibly resist that lot.'

'You look pretty sexy yourself,' replied her friend.

Chris turned and admired herself in the mirror. She had chosen a bright red basque that was barely big enough to contain her full, succulent breasts so that they bulged over the top. She too wore stockings, coloured red to match the basque, with a pair of red knickers completing the outfit. Her red shoes were of patent leather, the heels as high as Jo's.

'We're not exactly dressed for a church tea party are we?' she laughed. 'Do you think the guys will get the message?'

'We'd have to hang a sign round our necks with the words "Fuck Me" written on it to make it any clearer,' giggled Jo.

'Well let's hope they appreciate us.'

At that moment the doorbell rang. Chris turned to Jo.

'This is it,' she said. 'One of these is our man.'

'I hope so.'

Jo went to the door and opened it. On the doorstep stood a young man. He was about twenty-five years old, slim with fair hair and deep blue eyes. Jo registered at once the look of surprise and embarrassment on his face as he eyed her outfit.

'Hello,' she said.

'Hello. I'm Rick.'

'Come inside, Rick.'

She held the door open for him. He stepped in rather hesitantly and she could see he was nervous. She led him into the living room where Chris was waiting.

'It's Rick,' she said. 'I'm Jo, by the way, and this is Chris.'

Chris smiled. 'I remember you, Rick,' she said. 'You were the guy who serviced the girl on the train.' She turned to Jo. 'Don't you remember Rick?'

Jo nodded. 'Oh yes, I do now. An encounter with a stranger

in a first-class compartment that ended up with her getting screwed. I saw the video. I have to say you performed pretty well, Rick.'

'Thanks.' Rick had gone a deep shade of pink and was clearly rather put out by the appearance of the two girls.

'Have a drink,' said Chris. 'It'll help to settle your nerves.'

She poured the young man a measure of Scotch and handed it to him. He sipped at it nervously. Chris threw Jo a glance and raised an eyebrow. Her friend gave a little shake of the head. Rick did not appear to be the man.

The doorbell rang again.

'That'll be our other candidate,' said Chris to Rick. 'Get the door will you, Jo.'

Ed was standing on the doorstep, a grin on his face – a grin that widened when he caught sight of Jo.

'Hi,' he said casually.

'Hello,' Jo eyed him up and down. He certainly had the right build for their man, though she couldn't be certain.

'Remember me?' he said.

For a moment Jo thought he was referring to their encounter in the woods, though she couldn't think why he should admit to it so quickly. She looked at him curiously.

'I once did an act as a bird-watcher for you,' he explained. 'I had a beard then.'

Jo blinked, then forced a smile.

'Of course,' she said. 'You're Ed.'

'The very same. You going to invite me in, or are you showing off that underwear to the neighbours?'

Jo stepped aside and Ed strode confidently in. Jo followed him through to the living room, where Chris was chatting to Rick.

'Two gorgeous ladies,' exclaimed Ed. 'This must be my lucky day.'

'This is Ed,' said Jo. 'He used to have a beard.'

'Oh yes, the bird-watcher,' replied Chris. 'I'd hardly have recognised you. Have a drink?'

'The same as him,' said Ed, nodding in the direction of Rick's whisky.

Chris poured the drink, and the four of them sat down, the two men in armchairs and the girls together on the sofa opposite.

'I guess you know why you're here,' began Chris. 'We've got a rather special job coming up and we need a special guy for it.'

'Look no further,' said Ed. 'I'm your man.'

'Yeah, well, there's one or two things we need to check first,' said Chris.

'What kind of things?' asked Rick.

'We just want to be certain you're physically up to it,' said Jo.

Ed flexed his biceps. 'They don't come much more physical than me,' he boasted, looking pointedly at Rick's slimmer build.

'That's not the part of your anatomy we're really interested in,' said Chris.

Ed grinned. 'I think you'll see I've got all you need.'

'That's what we're here to find out,' said Chris. 'Would you mind stripping off please?'

The two men placed their drinks down and climbed to their feet. Ed began unbuttoning his shirt at once, but Rick looked more nervous than ever.

'Something wrong, Rick?' asked Jo.

He shook his head. 'No, sorry,' he said, reddening. He reached for the hem of his T-shirt.

'Come on,' said Ed. 'Don't be shy in front of the young ladies.'

The two girls sat back and watched as the men undressed. Rick stripped slowly, carefully placing his clothes across his chair. Ed, on the other hand, tossed his casually aside onto the floor. In no time he was naked, his heavy cock dangling from a thick mat of black pubic hair, as he stood, hands on hips, grinning at Chris and Jo.

Rick dropped his pants at last, revealing a surprisingly large penis. He stood awkwardly, his arms at his side, whilst the pair took him in.

'Come over here, Ed,' said Chris. 'And Rick, you go to Jo.'

The two men moved across the room until they were standing in front of the sofa, close enough for the girls to touch them if they wished.

'Turn round.'

The pair turned their backs giving the girls a view of their behinds. Chris reached out and took hold of Ed's cheeks, pulling them apart. There, slightly faded, was the black stripe put there by Jo only a couple of days before. Chris nodded towards it and winked at her friend.

They had found their blackmailer.

'Nice arse,' said Chris casually. 'Turn back again please.'

Obediently, the pair turned to face the girls once more.

Jo looked across at Chris. Really their job was complete. But she knew her friend too well to imagine she would turn away a pair of hunks like Rick and Ed, particularly now that they were naked, and she had to admit that the sight of Rick's thick weapon *was* rather tempting.

'Let's see what you look like ready for action,' said Chris. 'Jo. You want to do the honours?'

Jo was reminded of the similar situation when they had first met Doug and Mark, and how shocked she had been when Chris had brought both men to an erection. A lot of time had passed since then though. Now, what she was about to do seemed the most natural thing in the world.

Jo sat forward, so that her face was only inches from Rick's crotch. She reached out a hand and closed it about the soft stem of his cock. He bit his lips, but said nothing.

She pulled him closer to her, then opened her mouth and took him inside. His cock had a slightly salty taste and she could feel it beginning to swell as she sucked tentatively at it. Out of the corner of her eye she could see that Chris was giving a similar treatment to Ed, who stood with his hands

...ned the Spice Girls ...est pop group Brit-...produced since the ...nes and Beatles.

...t it surprise you that ...ee them being inter-...on TV or radio? ...g they do is pre-...nd the cutting ...nust be full of ed-...their obscenities. ...sh, Scary and Co. ...autiful and drive ...with their horny ...if you heard their ...'d think you were ...day night lager ...rawl.

Vile

...m interviewed on ...show where they ...ored . . . and their ...s absolutely vile. *...zine interviews ...crammed with ...words and com-...sanitary towels.* ...iend of mine who ...s' TV shows why ...rls haven't been

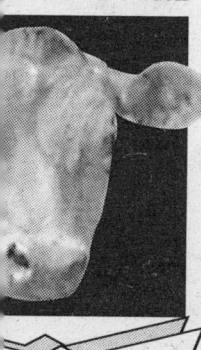

on children's programmes

He confirmed what I'd suspected, replying: "I don' know what they'll say. The just want to cause outrage."

They know more swea words than I've learned in 4 years and if my daughte Sophie grew up to spew ou foul language like them, I'd be appalled.

Many children model themselves on these girls and if their parents could hear them speak, they wouldn't have a Spice Girls CD in the home.

Question

Johnny Rotten got slaughtered for this behaviour yet they get away with it. The success behind them is manager Simon Fuller and the brilliant marketing team who keep them going.

But the burning question is: How much longer can they last at the top?

I'm sure they won't roll on like Mick Jagger and the boys, who brought New York to a

...ECAUSE of my ...mitments with ...

☀SEASIDE stunna Angela Lea doesn't hav

behind his head, his groin thrust forward, a look of quiet satisfaction on his face.

Jo ran her fingers down to the base of Rick's cock, her hand stroking his balls as she continued to suck. He was semi-erect now, his organ swelling all the time as she fellated him enthusiastically. She glanced up at his face. His eyes were closed, his expression one of deep concentration. She began to masturbate him slowly, her hand working up and down his shaft whilst she sucked hard at him. This made his organ stiffen even more, forcing her lips wider apart. She wrapped an arm behind him, pulling him closer to her, so that he plunged even deeper into her mouth, his glans nearly touching the back of her throat.

'Right, let's take a look,' said Chris suddenly. 'Stand back, fellas.'

Somewhat reluctantly, Jo released Rick from her mouth and he took a step backwards to stand beside Ed. Both men's cocks were fully erect now, the tips glistening with the girls' saliva. Jo watched, fascinated, as they bobbed up and down. Ed was grinning proudly at them, still thrusting his groin forward, like some peacock displaying to his mate. Rick was rather less confident, although Jo noted with interest that his penis was the larger of the two.

'Well, you certainly both measure up,' said Chris. 'Now, let's see if you've got the wherewithal. Jo, you happy to stick with Rick?'

'Fine.'

Jo stood up and moved forward. As she came close to Rick she reached between his legs, taking his balls in her hand. Her other arm she placed about his neck, pulling his face close to hers. He was much taller than her and even in the high heels she had to stretch upwards as she placed her lips over his.

Rick was clearly aroused – the pulsating of his cock told her that. When her tongue slid into his mouth, he responded by grabbing her and pulling her to him, so that her bra pressed against his chest. She began to run her fingers up and down his shaft as they kissed, touching him only lightly and sensing his arousal as he held her tighter, his cock fairly jumping under her touch.

Jo drew her lips away.

'Do you like the taste of pussy?' she asked quietly.

He nodded.

'Come and taste mine.'

She pulled him back towards the sofa, then sat down indicating that he was to kneel before her. He did as he was bidden, his eyes fixed on the crotch of her panties. She spread her legs apart and looked at him questioningly.

He hesitated for a second, then stretched out a hand, running it over the gusset. He pressed hard, his fingers tracing the outline of Jo's slit. She lay back, watching him as he rubbed her there. She knew her wetness was already starting to show through, but she didn't care.

Across the room, Ed had pulled down the front of Chris's basque and had his head buried in her magnificent breasts, the sucking and slurping sounds clearly audible as he made a meal of her.

All of a sudden, Jo's thoughts were brought back to her own partner with a jolt. He had slipped a finger into the leg of her panties and it was now directly in contact with the soft flesh between her legs. She was unable to suppress a moan of pleasure as he slipped it into her, moving it back and forth as she writhed beneath his touch.

He slid the finger from her and reached for the waistband of her panties. He pulled them off in a single movement, dragging them over her shoes and tossing them aside. Once free of them, Jo spread her legs again, sliding her backside forward in the chair so that it was right on the edge of her seat.

Rick placed his palms flat on her inner thighs just above the knee. Then he began slowly sliding them up over the soft, smooth skin towards her love hole. Jo found his pace maddening. She was dying to be touched there, lifting her backside from the sofa and pressing forward. Yet still he was in no hurry, his fingers inching toward the centre of her desires.

'Ah!'

He arrived at last, his thumbs sliding up her sex lips, prising them apart at the same time so that she could feel the coolness of the air against the warm wetness within. Then he leaned forward and protruded his tongue.

'Oh!'

The moment his tongue touched her slit, Jo's body bucked upward and another cry echoed about the room. He ran it slowly up and down the length of her sex, his fingers still holding the lips open so that he was able to seek out the soft, sensitive flesh within. He moved higher and found her clitoris, closing his lips about it and sucking hard, bringing Jo to new heights as he ran his tongue back and forth over the hard little knob of flesh and sending the most exquisite sensations buzzing through the girl's body.

All at once she could stand it no more. She pushed his head away from her crotch and pressed him backwards. Sensing what she wanted, he lay back on the carpet, his beautiful cock standing upright from his slim body.

Now it was Jo's turn to fall to her knees as she brought her head down over his groin, taking him into her mouth again. He seemed to have swelled even more and it was all she could do to contain his engorged penis as she began to fellate him once again. She sucked hungrily at his erection, her fingers kneading his balls as her head bobbed up and down. Behind her, Chris was leaning back over the arm of the sofa, her backside lifted high, her legs spread. She too had lost her panties and was watching as Ed guided his erection towards her honeypot.

Jo felt a hand creep behind her back and she realised that Rick had sat up. He flicked the catch of her bra undone and it fell away, leaving her perfectly formed breasts dangling beneath her. He took one in each hand and she knew he could feel the way the flesh quivered as she bobbed her head up and down.

All at once she wanted to have him inside her. Raising her head from his erection she pressed him back once more until he was prostrate before her, his hands behind his head. She straddled him, still on her knees, then moved forward.

She positioned herself just above his crotch, staring down at him. Then she reached a hand between her legs from behind and wrapped her fingers about his erection. Slowly she lowered herself, manoeuvring his thick glans towards the portals of her vagina. A shudder ran through her as she felt his hard weapon brush against the fleshy petals of her sex. Carefully, she positioned him where she wanted him and pressed downwards.

It was a tight fit, tighter than she had imagined, but she continued to press. At last, the flesh gave way and he was inside her, his great erection filling her more than she could ever remember being filled. She continued to force her body downward, gasping as he inched his way inside her. She wondered for a moment whether she could contain all of him, yet still he slid deeper until, with a sigh, she felt her pubic bone come into contact with his.

She rested for a moment, loving the way he stretched her, making her own muscles contract against the heat of his flesh. Behind her the grunts and groans told her that Chris was being shafted by Ed, but she didn't even bother to turn round. All her being was concentrated on the great spear of flesh upon which she was impaled.

Tentatively, she flexed the muscles in her legs, gasping with pleasure as she felt him move inside her. She began gently to work her body up and down, easing herself upwards then dropping back onto his shaft, every movement sending new thrills of passion through her. She gazed down at Rick. His face was convulsed with pleasure, his eyes fixed on Jo's lovely young body as she took the initiative, her pace increasing with every stroke.

She threw a glance over her shoulder at the other two. Chris was splayed face down over the arm of the couch now, her legs spread wide, her breasts pressed against the seat. Ed was just behind her, his hands grasping her buttocks as he pumped his hips back and forth. Chris's mouth was open in a soundless scream as his strokes rocked her body and Jo could see that her friend was close to coming.

She turned back to her own partner. She was fucking him hard now, her body rising and falling, her breasts bouncing with each stroke. Rick reached up and took them in both hands, massaging them hard and sending new pulses of pleasure through her. She smiled down at him, grinding her hips against his. A sheen of sweat had broken out on her body and he seemed to be massaging it into her flesh as his hands manipulated her breasts.

Suddenly she sensed a new urgency in him. Glancing down, she saw that his features were a mask of concentration, his movements somewhat jerky as he pressed his hips upwards, their bodies slapping wetly together with a noise that echoed about the room.

He came suddenly, a grunt of satisfaction coming from him as he began to pump his seed deep into Jo's vagina. She drove down still harder, loving the feel of his thick, hot spunk as spurt after spurt escaped from his mighty dick. In no time she was coming too. Her head thrown up, her mouth open, her vagina contracting about him, as if drawing the sperm from within him. Behind her the cries of Ed and Chris told her that they too had reached their climaxes, but she didn't care. All she cared about was the wonderful sensation of the cock that was continuing to fill her with spunk.

Rick's movements were slowing now and she could tell that he was spent. Gradually she slowed too, extracting the last vestiges of pleasure from him, still moaning with the pleasure he was giving her.

All at once she felt a pair of hands come round her from behind and reach up to caress her breasts. She felt a hot young body press against hers and a pair of soft lips nuzzle against her neck.

'I want to taste Rick's spunk,' murmured Chris in her ear.

For a second Jo was taken aback, but the smell of Chris's scent mixed with sweat and arousal suddenly made her want to kiss the girl. She turned to meet her friend's lips, the pair of them embracing passionately whilst Chris's hard nipples pressed against Jo's soft skin.

Chris took charge. All at once Jo found herself being dragged off Rick's prostrate body, giving a sigh as she felt his cock slide from within her. Then she too was on her back, her legs wide apart, looking up at Chris kneeling over her. Chris's hair was dishevelled and her skin, like Jo's, had a sheen of sweat on it. As Jo watched she leaned forward and licked her stomach, her tongue worming into her navel, then moving downwards towards the hole so recently vacated by Rick's cock.

Chris was kneeling by Jo's head and Jo took hold of her friend's thigh, manoeuvring it over her body until Chris was straddling her and she was gazing up at her friend's open slit. A trail of white fluid ran from the pink lips and down the creamy white skin of her thigh. Jo lifted her head towards it.

She began to lick at it. It tasted odd, the saltiness of Chris's sweat and the secretions from inside her vagina mixing with Ed's spunk in a cocktail that was both bitter and extremely arousing. Eagerly Jo licked again, her tongue tracing a silver trail up Chris's thigh. At the same time she felt Chris's tongue lap at her own love bud and a shiver of lust ran through her body.

She worked her head higher, swallowing down the trail of semen as she closed on her target. Chris's sex lips were pink and shiny and she ran her tongue over them, the taste and smell of sex becoming stronger as she wormed her way into her friend's vagina.

The two girls drank the sperm from one another with a frenzy of passion, hips grinding against faces as their passion exploded once more. Jo was vaguely aware of the two men watching, their cocks still erect, wanking slowly as they stared down at them. She wondered at her own wantonness and at the voraciousness of her appetite for sex. Not long ago she would have been mortified to have been seen like this, stark-naked, her head buried between another woman's thighs, but now the thought of an audience simply spurred her on.

The two girls came simultaneously, their cries lost in each other's pussies as they rolled across the carpet, their bodies sliding against one another as the perspiration gathered between them. When they finally rolled apart, Jo could see that her friend's face was smeared with saliva and sperm and she knew hers must look the same. She lay panting on the floor, her breasts rising and falling as she regained her breath. Then Ed dropped to his knees between her thighs, and one look at his still throbbing knob told her that there was more to come.

Chapter 30

As Ed drove out to his rendezvous with the girls from Fantasy and Co that morning he was in a decidedly good mood. He hummed quietly to himself as he manoeuvred the vehicle along the winding country lanes. All at once life was being good to Ed Mercer and he smirked as he contemplated what a great job he was doing.

The call had come the day before informing him that he had been the successful candidate for the job with Fantasy and Co. Though he hadn't been surprised, he felt pleased that he had been preferred over all those other men. That Rick had been pretty well hung, he mused, but it was figure and prowess that counted, and he had shown plenty of both. There was no doubt that he had satisfied those two chicks better than they had been satisfied for a long time. He wondered what Jo would have thought if she had known that it had been the second time in a week that he had had his dick in her. And it wouldn't be the last. He had already decided that, when they met for the handover of the cash, she would again enjoy a good shagging from him.

His grin widened. He was really outsmarting everyone at the moment. Not only was he screwing the two girls he was working for, he was blackmailing them as well. And once he'd got their cash, he was heading straight for the newspapers. By the end of next week he would have made a pretty fancy profit. He had already contacted a newsman on the *Daily World* and he had received a letter only that morning confirming an appointment the following week.

Things were certainly looking up.

He swung the car down a side road, glancing at the map that was open on the seat beside him. Not far now. It was a damned nuisance that they had to hold these things in such out-of-the-way places, but he supposed that privacy was the reason. Anyhow, the pay was good and it amused him to think that some sap was actually paying him to fuck her. He ran his hand down over his cock, feeling the hardness that was already there in anticipation of what was to come. At least she wouldn't go away dissatisfied, he thought.

He turned left up a narrow tarmac road. He'd have been better off on his bike, he knew, but he didn't want Jo to see him in his motorcycle gear for fear that she would realise who he was. So he had hired a car for the day, determined to do this thing in style.

He slowed, his eyes searching for a farm track at the side of the road. Sure enough, there it was, just where they had said it would be. He turned left through a gate and, as soon as his car was out of sight of the road, pulled up and switched off the engine.

He climbed out, locking the car. His instructions had been to return to the road and wait there to be contacted. He checked his watch. He was five minutes early. He sauntered back in the direction he had come.

Ed waited at the side of the road, leaning against a tree and watching the birds fly overhead. It was certainly a quiet spot. Ideal for their purposes. In fact it would have been ideal for one of his rendezvous with Jo. Once again he felt his cock stir at the thought of the lovely girl waiting naked for him. Next time he would give her a real seeing to.

'Hello, Ed.'

The sound of the voice made him jump and he swung round to see Jo standing right beside him, holding a large carrier bag. For a second he must have looked totally surprised and she laughed.

'You were expecting me weren't you?'

'Yes,' he said at last. 'It was just that you sort of sneaked up on me.'

'Sorry. Next time I'll send some kind of signal ahead. You all set?'

'Of course.'

'Well, come along. We'll have to get you ready.'

She set off down the road with Ed following. He had to quicken his pace to keep up with her.

'Where are we going?' he asked.

'Just down the road a bit.'

'How far?'

'Does it matter?'

'The car. I don't want it to get stolen.'

'Don't worry. It'll be safe. Now get a move on, we haven't got long.'

They walked on for another few minutes, then turned off and followed a path into a small glade. There they stopped.

'Right,' said Jo. 'Strip off.'

'What, here?'

'Of course here. You're not embarrassed are you?'

'No. It's just . . .'

'Well get them off, then. We haven't got all day. Hurry now. We've got to get your costume on.'

'Costume?'

'Certainly. You have to look the part.'

'Aren't you going to explain what I'm supposed to be doing?'

'All right. But meanwhile get your kit off.'

Slowly Ed reached up and began undoing his buttons. This whole thing wasn't exactly working out as he'd imagined. All at once Jo was in charge and he was just doing as he was told. That didn't suit him at all. He was used to being the one in control. When he met her again next week she'd pay for this. Perhaps a spanked behind would show her who was boss. Meanwhile, though, he'd better go along with what she told him.

As he peeled off his shirt, Jo began to explain the scenario.

'You see, this customer has a slightly odd fetish,' she said. 'For a start she likes dressing up in uniforms.'

'You mean like school uniforms and maid's costumes?' asked Ed.

'No. She's more into authority figures. Today she's coming as a policewoman.'

'Oh.' Ed's demeanour brightened somewhat. He'd often fantasised about screwing a policewoman. Perhaps this was his big chance. It would be ironic if his fantasy was fulfilled at the same time as hers. Quite amusing really. Especially since she was paying for the privilege, whilst he was actually being paid.

He kicked off his shoes and socks, then dropped his jeans, pulling them over his feet.

'So what's the scenario?' he asked. 'Do I dress up as a copper and seduce her in the back of the panda car?'

'Nothing like that,' said Jo. 'Actually she's going to arrest you.'

'Arrest me? That's a turn up, screwing the prisoners,' he laughed. 'So I'm some kind of mobster am I?'

'Not exactly,' said Jo. 'Get your pants off, Ed.'

He pulled down his underpants, leaving him completely naked. His cock hung down limply. Somehow Jo's authoritative air had lost him the mood for the moment, although he knew he could soon get it back. He turned to face Jo, striking a pose that he felt sure would excite her.

'Right,' she said, reaching into her bag and pulling something out. 'Get these on.'

Ed took the bundle from her and unwrapped it. Then he goggled in disbelief. The outfit consisted of a long, grey, rather dirty mackintosh and a pair of trainers.

'What the hell's this?' he spluttered.

'Your costume.'

'But what am I supposed to be?'

'A flasher, of course.'

He stared at her aghast. 'A what?'

'A flasher. You've heard of flashers, haven't you?'

'But I can't wear that.'

'Of course you can. Come on, Ed. I thought you were a professional. It's only a coat after all.'

'Who the hell thought this up?'

'The customer, of course. The scenario is that she sees you flashing and stops her police car. When she goes to try and make the arrest you drop the mac, then seduce her, and she ends up getting fucked by the wayside.'

'And that's it?'

'Yeah. A bit kinky I suppose. Still, each to his own, eh?'

Ed shook his head doubtfully. 'It's not exactly what I'd expected.'

'Well it's too late to change your mind now. She'll be along in a minute, and she's paying good money. If I'd known you were going to make this fuss I'd have given the job to someone else. What's the matter with you anyhow?'

Reluctantly Ed donned the mac. It was about two sizes too small for him, so that the sleeves stopped well above his wrists. He sat down and pulled on the trainers which, by contrast, were too large, so that he had to curl up his toes to keep them on when he walked.

Jo surveyed him critically.

'Good,' she said. 'That seems to be the required effect. Now let's see you flash.'

'Must I?'

'Of course. We've got to make sure you've got the hang of it. Go on.'

Ed had done up three of the buttons down the front of the coat. Now he undid them and, with a swift movement, pulled his coat open and shut.

'You're going to have to do better than that,' said Jo. 'Open the coat properly and let us see what you've got.'

Ed glared at her. Then he repeated the action, this time holding the coat open for much longer.

'Good,' said Jo. 'Now thrust yourself forward. That's right. Much better. We're going to have to do something about your cock though. I mean you're not exactly looking interested, are you?'

She moved closer to Ed, pushing the coat aside and taking his cock in her hand. She began to rub her fingers up and down its length, whilst her mouth closed over his nipples, nibbling and sucking at them. Almost at once he felt himself stir in her hands and she wrapped her fingers about his shaft, working it up and down.

'That feel better?' she asked.

'Yeah.' All at once the ridiculous coat was forgotten as Ed's body began to respond to Jo's expert touch. When she dropped to her knees and took him into her mouth, he gave a grunt of pleasure, feeling his cock engorge itself with blood as it came to full erection.

Jo remained on her knees for two minutes more, sucking hard at his now rampant penis, one hand wanking him slowly whilst the other stroked and fondled his balls. By the time she sat back to admire her handiwork, Ed's cock was as hard as iron, rising from his groin like a flagpole.

'That's much better,' said Jo approvingly. 'That ought to interest our client. Now, you'd better get ready. She'll be along any minute. And don't forget, the moment she tries·to arrest you, drop the coat and seduce her. She'll love it.'

Feeling a lot hornier than he had a few minutes before, Ed followed Jo back down the path to the road. She stood him on the side, in full view of any approaching traffic.

'Just wait there,' she ordered. 'I'll be in the bushes behind you.'

As he stood, gazing expectantly down the road, Ed contemplated what was to come. There was no doubt about it, getting into the knickers of a policewoman in uniform was a real turn-on. He wondered if she would be wearing black underwear. Possibly even suspenders. He reached into his coat and ran his hand up and down the length of his cock.

Well, lady, he thought as he began slowly to wank, *this is your lucky day.*

He heard the car before he saw it. So quiet was the lane that the sound of the motor reached his ears when the vehicle was still some distance away. He stopped masturbating and turned to face the direction from which it was coming, the flaps of the coat held in his hands. As the car came round the corner he waited until it was in full view, then pulled the coat open, thrusting his groin forward as Jo had instructed him.

As the car came closer, he saw that there were actually two figures inside, both dressed as policewomen. The car itself looked extremely authentic. There was no doubt that these people did these things thoroughly, he thought.

The car drew to a halt just in front of him and the two young women got out. Both were slim, one with short dark hair, the other with blonde hair tied in a ponytail behind. He wondered which was the customer. He would happily take on both.

'Stop right there!' It was the blonde who had shouted and it was she who stepped towards him as he stood, his coat still held wide, his erection there for all to see. As she came close he shrugged off the coat and, stepping forward, placed an arm about her, pulling her to him.

'I'm going to give you the best shagging you've ever had,' he murmured.

At that moment Ed's world seemed to fall apart. All other sensations were forgotten, replaced by the most excruciating pain imaginable. The woman had brought her knee up into his groin with a single sharp movement and suddenly Ed was bent double with the agony of the blow.

'Hey,' he gasped. 'You weren't supposed to get that realistic. I might not be able to perf—'

But he was cut off in mid sentence by an arm that came round his neck from the back whilst his wrist was grasped and placed in an arm-lock. For a second, the pain in his groin was overshadowed by a new one as his arm was forced high

253

up his back by the dark-haired policewoman.

'Steady on,' he shrieked. 'It's only a game.'

The blonde girl moved round in front of him.

'It may be a game to you, sir,' she said, 'but you're committing an offence. I am arresting you for gross indecency. You are not obliged to say anything, but anything you do say . . .'

Ed listened in stunned amazement as the woman went through the routine.

'Listen, girls,' he croaked as the arm-lock tightened on his neck, 'this has gone far enough, don't you think? I don't mind shagging one of you, but could you stop strangling me for a second?'

The blonde girl's only response was to pull a notebook from her jacket and begin writing in it.

'Is that two g's in shagging?' she asked her companion.

The other one giggled. 'I think so.'

The blonde policewoman eyed Ed up and down. 'I thought I'd seen it all in this job,' she said, shaking her head. 'But you really take the biscuit. Come on, Clare, help the gentleman on with his coat and we'll get him down the station.'

'But I . . .'

Then it began to dawn on Ed. The uniforms, the authentic police car, the way the pair had reacted.

'You're real coppers,' he gasped.

'No, we're a pair of out-of-work coal miners on our way to a fancy dress party. Get the cuffs on him, Clare. And cover him up. I don't think I can take much more.'

'No, wait!' cried Ed. 'It's all a mistake.'

'It certainly was a mistake to flash at us.'

'No. You don't understand. There was this girl wanted screwing. I just had to flash at her.'

'Yeah, I'm sure you thought that was all you needed to do.'

'You've got me wrong. Ask the girl in the bushes.'

'What girl in the bushes?'

'In there. Her name's Jo.'

'All right, sonny,' said the blonde. 'You've had your fun. Now you've got to come with us.'

'But you've got me wrong. I'm not some sort of pervert.'

'I understand all right. I understand that you'll compound the offence by resisting arrest. Now, are you getting in the car or not?'

Ed opened his moth to protest once more, then closed it. His mind in a whirl, he allowed himself to be led to the car and shut in the back seat. Two minutes later the car was back on the move and headed straight for the police station.

Chapter 31

Ed was still fuming when he left his flat the following Monday morning and mounted his motorcycle. He had spent most of the weekend at the police station, having, indeed, been detained for resisting arrest. But it wasn't just the arrest that bothered him, it was the humiliation. The laughter of the policemen was still ringing in his ears. Officers had come from all corners of the station to watch as he was brought in. The two policewomen's statements were listened to amid much hilarity whilst he was forced to stand in front of the desk, still clad in only the overcoat and trainers. When, at last, his demands for something to wear were answered, they found him a shocking pink shell suit that was far too small for him, and it was this he had worn in his cell that night, and before the magistrates the following morning.

The fine of two hundred pounds had stung as well. Especially since he had no way of paying it. For a while it had looked as if his stay inside was to be even longer, but, fortunately for him, the court officials had relented and had given him two days to pay. Then came the long walk out into the country to recover his clothes and car, still wearing the ridiculous suit, a walk that wasn't helped by the fact that the weather had taken a turn for the worse. A number of motorists had sounded their horns at the sight of him trudging through the rain, but none had offered to pick him up, and it was nearly three hours before he finally reached the spot where he had been arrested.

His clothes were where he had left them, soaked through

of course. He had not attempted to change then and there, fearing that he might again be discovered naked and have to begin his ordeal all over again. Instead, he had gathered them up and trudged back to where his car was parked.

The car hire company was none too sympathetic with him either. In fact Ed was lucky not to have been on the wrong side of the law once again, since the manager had been about to report the car stolen and none of Ed's protestations had dissuaded him from charging the rental for the full three days.

Now, though, Ed's thoughts were only of revenge and, as he dropped the box containing the video tape into his pannier, a grim smile crossed his features. As he had expected, when he returned to his flat the master copy of the video was no longer there. Somebody had gained entry, probably with his own house keys, and had taken it from the shelf. What they hadn't reckoned with, of course, was the two spare copies concealed under the sofa. Once again he congratulated himself for having had the presence of mind to take backups of the video. One of the spares was now safely stashed in a safe deposit box at the bank. The other he had with him. He had even taken the trouble to slip it into his video machine before coming out to ensure that all was well, and had been pleased to see the image of the bikers as they closed on Belinda's car. He had outsmarted them after all.

He checked his watch. His meeting with the journalist from the *Daily World* was in half an hour. He kicked the engine into life and headed off down the road.

It was a while before it occurred to him that he was being followed. So intent had he been on his mission, that he had failed to notice the two motorcycles that had pulled out behind him and taken up station on his tail. In fact, it wasn't until two more pulled out of a side road just in front of him that he realised something was happening, and by that time it was too late.

The first thing that struck him was the insignia on the back of their jackets. It was a picture of a striking serpent and it seemed somehow familiar to Ed. Then, as the following bikes pulled up on either side of him, he remembered. The video. All the bikers in the video had worn jackets of the same pattern.

All of a sudden, Ed was nervous. He looked from one side to the other. The bikers were now very close to him and were matching his speed exactly. He checked his mirror. Behind was another machine close on his tail. The riders in front had also closed up. Blocking the way ahead.

'What the hell are you doing?' he shouted at the biker on his left.

'Just taking you for a little trip,' replied its rider. 'Go where we tell you and there'll be no trouble.'

Ed considered his position. He was outnumbered. Any attempt to get away from these riders would almost certainly be unsuccessful and might well end in an accident. But what if he did go with them? What would they do to him? He didn't fancy being beaten up. Still, the man beside him had said that there would be no trouble if he did as he was told. That was clearly his best option, then.

Ed followed the gang as they took him across town and into one of the less salubrious residential areas. They came to a halt outside a low, rather nondescript building, the other bikers surrounding Ed's machine so that there was no chance of escape.

The man he had spoken to dismounted and stood in front of him.

'Who the hell are you?' asked Ed.

'My name's Jet,' said the man. 'This lady is called Vixen. 'We're Vipers.'

'Well, Jet,' said Ed, trying to keep the anxiety from his tone. 'What's all this about?'

'It's about what you took from Chris and Jo,' said Jet. 'Open up that pannier would you?'

'That contains my private property,' protested Ed.

'If you don't open it, Vixen will use a crowbar.'

Ed looked at Jet, then at Vixen, then at the other bikers.

They all looked as if they meant business, and he decided that discretion was his best option.

'All right,' he said. 'But you have no right.'

He took a key from his pocket and unlocked the pannier, then opened it.

'Take out what's inside.'

'There's nothing in there.'

Jet peered into the pannier. Ed stood by impassively, knowing that he would find nothing.

'It's empty,' confirmed Jet to his companions. 'All right you, come inside!'

'What if I refuse?' Ed's defiant stance belied his nervousness. If this lot decided to turn nasty there was very little he could do.

'Don't refuse. Not if you know what's good for you.'

Reluctantly, Ed allowed himself to be led through the door and down the steps to the bikers' clubroom. There, even more of their number were seated about the room, swigging bottles of beer. A general hubbub of disapproval went up as he entered, increasing his unease. He really was in the lion's den here and he wasn't at all comfortable with the idea.

Jet led him across to where a number of people were seated. With a shock he recognised the two girls from Fantasy and Co, as well as their assistants, Mark and Doug. Now he felt even less comfortable, but he determined not to show it, holding up his head and putting on a defiant air.

'Why, Ed,' said Chris, rising to her feet. 'What a pleasure to see you. The police let you out then?'

Ed glared at her, but did not reply.

'Right, Ed,' said Chris. 'Let's get straight down to business. You were on your way to an appointment, I think.'

'I might have been.'

'Who with?'

'None of your business.'

'I think it is precisely some of our business,' said Chris. 'In fact it's what our business is all about.'

'What do you mean?'

'We'd heard you had another video tape.'

'Who told you that?'

'It doesn't matter. We want it back, that's all.'

'Even if I did have one, why should I give it to you?'

'Because you have no right to have it. You have got it, haven't you?'

Ed stared about at the bikers, then turned to her once again.

'Yes. What are you going to do about it?'

'Just ask you to hand it over, that's all.'

'And if I refuse?'

'I don't think that would be advisable, do you? Where were you going with it?'

'To a journalist. On the *Daily World*. He was going to pay me a lot of money.'

'That was rather a dirty trick.'

Ed grimaced. 'So was the trick you played on me.'

Chris laughed. 'You started it.'

'Listen,' said Ed. 'If I hand over this tape, will you guarantee that I get out of here unharmed?'

Chris turned to Jo. 'What do you think?'

'I guess it's all right,' said Jo. 'After all, this whole thing's been enough trouble as it is.'

'All right,' said Chris. 'Hand it over.'

'And I have your word I won't be harmed by any of this lot?'

'You have my word.'

Ed turned to those watching. 'You heard that didn't you? I hand over the tape and you let me out of here without a scratch.'

'We heard what the lady said,' said Jet.

'All right then. I'll have to go back to my bike.'

Jet followed Ed up the steps once more and out to where his machine was parked. Once again Ed unlocked the pannier, but this time he reached into it himself. There was a click and he lifted out the false bottom. He rested this on the saddle, pressed a button on the side and a small panel fell off. From the recess it uncovered, Ed pulled the video tape.

'Very clever,' said Jet. 'Now, I think you'd better take that back down to the ladies.'

Once again Ed descended the stairs, this time holding the tape. He strode across the room and stopped once more in front of the girls.

'This what you're looking for?'

He flung the cassette on the table.

'That looks like it,' said Chris. 'Though we'll have to check of course.'

'And if it's the one, then I can go?'

'Certainly.'

Ed could barely suppress a grin. Surely they weren't so stupid as to assume this was the only copy? All at once everything seemed to be going fine again.

From somewhere at the back of the room, Jet wheeled out a trolley on which was a television and a video recorder. He turned on the television and slipped the cassette into the slot.

For a moment the screen was covered in black and white snow. Then the picture cleared and there was Belinda, filmed from behind as she sped down the road on the back of Jet's bike.

'There, you see?' said Ed. 'You've got your precious tape back.'

All the other bikers had gathered round the screen to watch and Ed stood back, his usual arrogance restored. Boy, were these people easy to fool.

All at once the soundtrack, which had been dominated by the roar of the motorcycle engines, went quiet. Ed turned to look at the television again, and his jaw dropped. There, on the screen, was not the sight of Belinda being carried off by the bikers, but a lone man, standing by a road in an ill-fitting overcoat, his legs bare beneath the hem. At the sight of Ed in his ridiculous outfit, a roar of laughter went up from the crowd.

As Ed watched in horror, his image suddenly pulled open the coat. A cheer rang about the room as the police car came into view whilst Ed stood there, displaying his rigid cock to the car's occupants.

Ed was totally numb as he watched the scene unfold. There he was in full colour, stripping off the coat, attempting to seduce the policewoman and subsequently being arrested.

If the film had reduced him to silence, it had had the opposite effect on the bikers. The room was filled with the sound of jeers and raucous laughter as the two women overwhelmed the stunned flasher and led him to the police car.

As the car disappeared down the road, the picture faded and a whoop of applause went up. Ed gazed about in dismay at the crowd, some of whom were weeping with laughter.

'You bitches!' he stormed.

'What's the matter, Ed? Don't like the show?' said Chris, wiping her eyes. 'I thought it was hilarious. The expression on your face!'

'Bitches!' shouted Ed again.

'Come now, Ed. You didn't think we were that stupid, did you? And rest assured, wherever you've stashed the other copy, it's just the same. Aren't you glad we saved you the trouble of showing it to that journalist now? Though I'm sure he'd have used it. After all it's not everyday you get hold of action shots of a real flasher getting arrested.'

'I'll get you for this,' stormed Ed.

'Oh, I don't think you will. After all, the boot's on the other foot now.'

'What do you mean?'

'I mean that if you so much as go within a mile of any of our customers, or our office, the *Daily World* will get that video and you'll be splashed all over the front page of every tabloid in the land in all your naked glory. Now, Ed, I think it's time you were going.'

'I'll . . . I'll . . .' Ed was speechless as he stared helplessly at the two laughing girls.

'I think the ladies asked you to leave,' said Jet quietly.

'Don't forget your mac,' shouted someone.

Ed looked round at the sea of grinning faces. Then, amid jeers and boos, he made as dignified an exit as he was able.

Chapter 32

Jo stared at her reflection in the mirror and made final adjustments to her outfit. When she was satisfied with what she saw, she checked her watch. Just in time, she mused. Chris was due to pick her up in five minutes.

The party invitation had come somewhat out of the blue. Chris had rung her that morning to say that one of the magazines that carried their advertisements was holding a cocktail party that night, and that it might be a good place to look for prospective clients.

'What, just ask them what their fantasies are over a drink?' Jo had asked.

'Not exactly. But you never know who's going to be there,' replied Chris. 'I think maybe we should take a look. Why, were you planning something else this evening?'

'Not exactly. In fact I was going to have a quiet night.'

'Well, we need not stay late.'

And so Jo had agreed, and had gone out to buy a new dress, a short black one that hugged her figure and displayed her cleavage to excellent effect. Now, as she admired her reflection, she wondered precisely for whom she was dressing up.

The doorbell rang and, taking a last look at herself, Jo grabbed her bag and went to the door. There stood Chris, wearing a long coat.

'It's not cold out is it?' asked Jo.

'No. It's just that it looked a bit like rain earlier. But I think it's okay.'

They climbed into Chris's little sports car and were soon on their way, the wind blowing through their hair. Jo thought it a little odd that Chris had worn the coat in case of rain but had then left the hood down on her car, but she said nothing.

The pair chatted as they drove along. The business seemed to be doing better than ever and only that morning they had taken on three new commissions. Since the episode at the bikers' headquarters they had heard nothing from Ed and Mark had announced earlier in the week that he had seen him moving out of his flat, so it looked as though they had seen the last of him. It was in a happy frame of mind, therefore, that the pair set off for an evening out.

The venue for the party was a large house in a quiet suburb. The driveway already had a number of cars in it when they arrived. Chris parked the car and they both climbed out, heading for the front door.

They were nearly there when Chris gave an exclamation.

'Damn! I've left my bag in the car. I'll have to go back and get it.'

'Okay. I'll wait here.'

'No, you go ahead. I'll catch up with you inside.'

'You sure that's all right?'

'Of course. Go ahead. Grab me a drink if you can.'

Chris set off back to the car, whilst Jo went up to the front door.

She rang the bell. She was slightly puzzled at having to do so. Normally at these affairs the doors were open and a member of staff was there to greet arrivals. She waited a moment, then the door opened.

'Doug!'

Jo almost stepped back in surprise. It wasn't just the presence of her friend and employee, it was the way he was dressed. Doug wore a sort of loincloth about his waist. He was bare chested, a sprig of laurel leaves on his head. On his feet he wore sandals.

'Come in,' he said.

Jo followed him into the house, still totally perplexed. Her confusion doubled when he showed her into the next room.

It was as if she had stepped into a Roman villa. All about were low couches with men and women reclining on them. The walls were hung with drapes, the tables covered with bowls of exotic fruits. There were about thirty people in the room, both men and women. All were dressed in Roman clothes. Some of the men wore togas whilst others, like Doug, simply had on loincloths. The women were in long, diaphanous dresses pinned at the shoulder with low necklines and slits up the side. Around the walls stood more young men and women, clearly dressed as slaves. Both sexes had on short leather skirts and the women's breasts were bare. All had collars about their necks and some carried trays of food and drink whilst others bore great feathered fans that they were waving to cool the guests.

'It's like a Roman orgy,' gasped Jo.

'That's precisely what it is. And you're the guest of honour.'

Jo swung round to see that Chris had come in behind her. Once again her jaw dropped as she saw how her friend was dressed. Her dress consisted of a single piece of sheer cloth, pinned at her left shoulder so that her right breast was bare. A belt about her waist held it together, but so thin was the material that the shape of her body was quite clear beneath.

'What the hell's this about, Chris?' asked Jo.

'A little reward for the way you handled that bastard Ed. We all owe you a great deal, and I seem to remember you once confessed a penchant for a Roman orgy.'

Jo glanced about her. All eyes were directed her way and in the corner a band had begun to play. Their instruments were hand-held harps, tabla drums and reedy sounding pipes, but somehow it all seemed authentic.

'It's like something out of Cecil B De Mille,' she said.

'You mean we haven't got it right?' asked Chris anxiously.

'Of course you have. All my orgy fantasies came from his

films,' laughed Jo. 'I'm no Latin scholar. This whole setup is perfect, except for one thing.'

'Oh damn. What have we done wrong?'

'Nothing. It's me. This dress is completely inappropriate.'

Chris laughed. 'Thank God that's all. We've got a great Roman empress's outfit you can change into.'

'Thanks, but no thanks.'

Once again Chris's brow was creased. 'What's the problem?'

'This is my fantasy, right?'

'Of course it is.'

'Then I want to be dressed like one of them.'

Jo pointed at the slaves standing by the walls.

A smile crossed Chris's face. 'Of course,' she murmured. 'I remember now. Kinky.'

'And lying on a beach naked waiting for a stranger isn't?' said Jo in a low voice.

'Touché,' laughed Chris. 'Take this slave away and see to it that she is appropriately attired.'

At once Doug took hold of Jo's arm.

'This way,' he said.

Jo allowed herself to be led from the room. Doug took her down a narrow corridor and into a small cell. There, hanging on the wall, was one of the short skirts and a collar, as well as wrist and ankle bands, all made of leather.

'So, you were equipped to satisfy my preferences all along,' said Jo.

A ghost of a smile crossed Doug's features.

'We allowed for every contingency. Prepare yourself, slave.'

Jo looked about her. The room was almost bare, so there was nowhere to conceal herself. It was clear that Doug had no intention of leaving the room.

'Are you a eunuch?' she asked.

'Do you want me to be?'

'No. But you could pretend to be one just for the moment.'

'Your wish is my command.'

'I thought it was the other way round.'

Jo lifted the skirt from the hook and examined it. Then she reached for the catch at the back of her dress.

She undressed slowly. First the dress was discarded, leaving her in her underwear. She had worn an expensive set of bra, pants and suspender belt, and she knew she looked good as she stood before Doug. She glanced down at his loincloth.

'For a eunuch you're showing more interest than I'd expected,' she said.

'Silence, slave!' His voice held an air of authority, but she sensed a degree of strain in it as he eyed her up.

She unhooked her bra, freeing her succulent young breasts. Once again she sensed Doug's eyes on her pretty brown nipples, and the thought of it thrilled her. She unhooked her stockings and rolled them down her legs, then discarded her suspender belt. Finally she slipped off her panties and stood naked before him.

Doug nodded his approval, letting his eyes roam over her slender figure, down to the small dark triangle of pubic hair. Jo felt very sexy standing there, having her body admired. For a moment she considered making a pass and having him fuck her then and there. But already he had picked up the skirt and had handed it to her.

She wrapped it around herself. It barely went all the way round, being fastened with a cord at the waist. Once she had done this up, it left a slit down her left-hand side all the way from her waist, making her lack of underwear obvious. The skirt was short, reaching no more than three inches below her crotch, so that she had to be careful to keep herself covered when she moved.

Doug ordered her to sit whilst he buckled the leather straps to her ankles and wrists. Once these were in place, he came round behind her with the leather collar and placed it about her neck. It made a snug fit and Jo ran her fingers over it. The inside was lined with the softest suede whilst the outside was stiff, with a row of silver studs running round it and a single ring set at the centre. Once he had fastened it, Doug's hands dropped to her breasts, which he squeezed gently. Jo leaned back against him.

'That's nice,' she said quietly.

He kissed her neck. 'Time to go to the party,' he said.

Jo followed him back along the corridor, suddenly feeling rather self-conscious in her costume. As she entered the room, all eyes turned towards her, and she had an overwhelming desire to cover her breasts. But before she could do so a tray, on which there were silver goblets and a large jug of wine, was thrust into her hand.

'Serve the guests,' ordered Doug.

Jo set off about the room with the tray in her hands. She went up to a young man who was chatting to a woman and offered the tray. He took two goblets, passing one to his partner, then reached for the jug. As he did so his hand brushed Jo's nipple. The contact was obviously meant to appear accidental, but Jo saw his eye catch his partner's as it happened, and her face reddened as she realised how hard her nipple was. He poured the wine for himself and the girl, then put the jug back. Jo made to move on, but he placed a restraining hand on her arm, then reached for her again. This time he made no pretence, taking Jo's breast in his palm and squeezing it, then inviting his partner to do the same.

Jo stood there, her hands occupied by the tray, whilst the girl too felt her breasts, her fingers closing about the hard knobs of Jo's nipples. To Jo the sensation was at once pleasurable and embarrassing, and she stared straight ahead, unable to meet the girl's eyes as she felt the pleasure course through her.

At last the couple let her go and she moved on to another group. Here they not only fondled her soft orbs but commented to one another about how soft and warm they were. Then one man poured a drop of wine over her nipple and licked it off. It was all Jo could do to remain silent as his lips closed over her sensitive teats.

Suddenly she felt another hand on her, this time on her

inner thigh. The man standing beside her had placed his hand on her leg just below the hem of her skirt and was sliding it upwards, bunching the material as he felt her smooth skin.

When he touched her sex, the sensation was electric and Jo's body shook, making the goblets on her tray clatter together. He ran his fingers over her soft nether lips, finding her love bud and teasing it gently. At the same time another hand was moving up the crack of her backside and Jo bit her lip as the tip of his finger penetrated her anus.

For a few seconds Jo felt almost smothered, hands and lips on her breasts, more hands up her skirt, all probing her in the most intimate manner imaginable. At the same time she found herself extremely aroused, pushing her hips forward against the fingers that penetrated her most private place.

'Come on, slave, there are people to be served!'

The voice was right by her ear and she realised with a shock that she had been standing with her eyes closed, lost in the treatment she was receiving. She opened them to see Doug standing beside her, pointing to another group of guests.

Hurriedly Jo squirmed away from the clutching fingers and made her way across the room.

For the next half hour, Jo was probed and fondled by more hands than she could remember as she continued to bear the tray about the room, regularly recharging the jug and picking up more goblets. All the time her hands were too occupied to repel the attentions of the men and, if truth be told, she didn't want to. The more it went on, the more she revelled in the treatment she was receiving, her body tingling with desire as both men and women freely fondled her gorgeous body. She knew Chris was watching her as she moved amongst the guests and she wondered what her friend must be thinking. Still, she reasoned, this was her fantasy and she was determined to enjoy it.

Suddenly Chris was clapping her hands together and the music stopped. The guests fell silent as she began to speak.

'Ladies and gentlemen. As you know, the object of this

271

evening is pure indulgence, and for that reason we have brought along a group of young slaves for your pleasure. Now you will have the opportunity of bidding for the chance to take these young ladies as your personal slaves. All monies bid will, of course, go to charity. I want all the slaves to line up on this platform for the inspection of the guests.'

Jo found herself herded, along with the other slave girls, towards a long, low stage in the centre of the room. She climbed up onto it and stood facing the crowd. On one side of her was a slim young redhead with freckled face and breasts like ripe apples. On the other was a beautiful Negro girl with dark, sultry eyes.

Doug walked along the line of girls carrying a short cane which he used to prod them into line, pressing it into their stomachs or tapping their behinds until he was happy that they were properly aligned. Then he nodded to Chris.

'Right, ladies and gentlemen,' she said. 'Please come out and inspect the merchandise.'

The inspection went on for a full ten minutes. During that time, Jo and her companions were subjected to the most rigorous scrutiny, even more intimate than when she had been serving the drinks. Not an inch was left untouched as they poked and probed at her naked flesh whilst she stood, her hands by her sides, trying as best she could to suppress her emotions at their unceasing attention. By the time they had finished, Jo had almost come twice and she could feel the wetness at her crotch where numerous fingers had wormed their way inside her.

At last, though, Chris called a halt to the examinations. As the men and women drew back from the line of slaves, Jo looked to her right and left. There was scarcely a face that didn't betray the effect the inspection had had, and one or two of the girls were literally panting, their breasts rising and falling as they fought down their passion.

'Bring the first slave up for auction.'

Suddenly Jo realised that Doug's stick was pressing into

her back and she saw that Chris was beckoning her forward. Just beside the stage was a table, and Chris indicated that she was to stand on it.

Feeling very conspicuous indeed, Jo stepped up, then turned to face those watching. She was trembling slightly as she stared out over their faces, aware that she would soon be the property of one of them and that she would have to satisfy his or her desires.

'Remove the skirt.'

For a second Jo almost protested. It may not have been much, but the skirt was the only concession to modesty that she currently possessed, and she was reluctant to lose it. Then she remembered her role and closed her mouth.

Doug stepped up to her and reached for the cord that held her skirt in place. With a single tug he pulled it undone and the skimpy garment dropped away, leaving Jo totally naked apart from the straps and collar. A murmur of approval came from the crowd as she stood there, the colour rising in her cheeks.

Chris banged a gavel down and the room went silent.

'Right, ladies and gentlemen,' she said. 'What am I bid?'

At once cries came from all around the room, hands waving in the air as bid after bid came in. Jo was stunned by the frenzy of action, scarcely able to believe that what they were bidding for was her body. So fast were the bids coming that she could barely follow the progress of the auction, the men shouting one another down in their desire to take possession of her.

As the price rose higher and higher, though, the bidders began gradually to drop out. Soon there were only two left. One was a dark, foreign-looking man of about forty-five in a grey suit. He had stood silent during the early bidding but, even so, Jo had found her attention drawn in his direction, somehow captivated by his intense green eyes. Only when the price went high did he finally join in, indicating his bids with the smallest of waves, in contrast to the earlier shouting.

Bidding against him was a younger, fair-haired man with a hungry look. Jo stood, her limbs trembling slightly, trying not to show the excitement she was feeling as the two men vied with one another for the pleasure of taking her.

At last the room went silent. Jo stared from one man to the other, uncertain with whom the bidding had stopped. Chris was raising the gavel now, and Jo knew her fate was sealed.

Bang!

The hammer came down. Jo looked at one man, then the other, and realised with an odd feeling in her stomach that the older man was smiling and nodding.

Doug stepped up next to Jo and took her arm, leading her down from the platform into the crowd. Jo looked neither right nor left as he led her through the people, the colour in her cheeks rising as she heard the lewd comments of those watching. Behind her she could hear the bidding beginning again as the second of the young slaves was auctioned.

She came to a halt before the man who had won her. He was tall and, despite his age, very handsome, with craggy, tanned features and silver hair swept back. He wore a long white gown draped with a maroon coloured toga. He was reclining on a couch, gazing up at his naked young slave.

'What is your name?'

'Jo, sir.'

'Kneel down here, Jo.'

Jo did as she was told, dropping down to her knees just in front of him. He reached out a hand and ran it over her breast. Her nipples were already hard and his fingers sent a tingle of excitement through her.

'Do you like my touching you?' he asked.

'Yes, sir.' She reddened at the admission.

'Would you like to be touched down there?' He indicated her crotch.

'If you wish, sir.'

Jo trembled as he began to run his hand down her body. She was extraordinarily turned on. This was indeed the fantasy

274

that had often kept her awake at night, a helpless naked slave amongst the Romans, forced to give them her body. As his fingers crept lower, she gritted her teeth, her hands hanging by her side, anticipating his touch.

'Oh!'

He found her clitoris, his fingers pressing against it, sending tremors of excitement through her as he discovered her wetness.

'You want to be fucked, don't you?'

'Yes, sir.'

He looked into her eyes. 'Would you rather that younger man had won you?'

Jo shook her head. 'No, sir,' she said decisively.

It was true. Whilst the other man had been more attractive physically, she doubted that he could have exercised power the way her new master was doing. This man was clearly well experienced in master-slave relationships. Jo guessed that Chris had selected him for this purpose, and that the result of the auction had always been a foregone conclusion. Her friend had chosen well. The thought of being in this man's power was the most exciting thing she could imagine.

'I have a room for you at home,' he went on, his voice taking on an almost hypnotic quality. 'I have all kinds of toys there that will bring you exquisite pain. In my dungeon I can chain you naked to the wall and make you feel the kiss of the whip. If you come back with me, you will have to submit to my every whim. Would you like to come back with me?'

'Yes, master.'

The new way of addressing him came totally automatically to her as she fell further under his spell. Behind her she could still hear the auction progressing, but she was oblivious to it, her whole being concentrating on the delicious sensation of his fingers probing between her thighs.

'You are mine then,' he murmured.

'I am yours, master.'

'Good, little slave,' he said. 'But first I'm going to share you. Would you like that?'

'Whatever you say, master.'

He smiled.

The man looked over Jo's shoulder and beckoned to someone. Jo looked round to see a young man standing beside her. He was about twenty-five, dark-haired. His eyes were fixed on her breasts and the loincloth he wore did little to hide his obvious interest in her.

'You see, young slave,' said her master. 'You've excited this young man. I suggest you give him relief with your mouth.'

'Yes, master.'

There was no hesitation in Jo's voice. She was totally in the part now, and enjoying every second of it. She stretched out a hand and tugged at the young man's loincloth. It fell away, revealing a thick, stiff cock. She glanced to right and left. A number of people were watching her.

'Let them watch,' said the man on the couch. 'Some of them will be fucking you soon. Does that excite you?'

'Yes, master.'

Jo turned back to the young man, whose cock was twitching violently, making it bob up and down in front of her face. She could see that he was in a high state of arousal.

She took his shaft in her hand. It felt hot to the touch and she could sense the blood pounding through it. The tip of the glans was exposed, gleaming with a clear liquid, and she leant forward and licked it off. As she did so she felt his whole body shudder and she feared he might come before she had started.

She opened her mouth and took him inside, tasting his maleness. He whimpered slightly as she began to move her head back and forth. From the corner of her eye she could see that all heads were turned in her direction. She sucked hungrily at his knob, her fingers working his foreskin back and forth as she did so.

He came quickly. She had known he would and, when he began pumping his semen into her mouth, she gulped it down willingly, sucking hard at him, drawing the spunk from his balls and swallowing it. His moans were audible all round the room as he shot his load into her and she kept her lips locked about his shaft until there was no more. Then she straightened up and looked across at her master.

He nodded his head approvingly. 'Good,' he said. 'Now stretch out on that couch and open your legs. I'm going to have you fucked.'

'Yes, master.'

The couch was right beside his and she prostrated herself on her back, splaying her legs apart. On the floor beside her, one of her fellow slaves was locked in an embrace with a smartly dressed young woman, who was pleasuring her with a large, whirring dildo. Jo watched in fascination as she slid it in and out of the moaning girl. Then her view was blocked and she stared up at the man who stood in front of her. He was in his late thirties, balding and with a bit of a beer belly. But it was his crotch that held Jo's attention. His knob was long and circumcised and he was holding it in his fist, wanking slowly as he contemplated her body. She looked across at her master, who nodded his head, then she reached out for his tool, taking it in her hand and drawing him closer to her.

Jo didn't waste any time. She knew her master intended her to have many partners that night, and she wanted badly to please him. So she drew the man down, guiding his cock unerringly towards her open sex.

Such was her lubrication that he slipped in easily, making Jo groan with pleasure as he rammed his stiff erection home. He clearly shared her sense of urgency as no sooner were their bodies locked together than he started fucking her hard.

Jo almost screamed with pleasure, her breasts bouncing back and forth with every heave of his thighs. He took her roughly, without consideration for her own desires, and she loved him for it, matching him thrust for thrust with her own hips, her legs wrapped about his body as she tried to draw him still deeper inside her. He pulled her close to him, their sweat-soaked bodies slapping together as they let their lust run away with them.

Like her first lover, this one came quickly, gasping aloud as he filled her with his spunk. Jo came too, screaming with pleasure as the tensions and frustrations of the previous hours were suddenly released in the glorious relief of orgasm.

Once his last dribble of spunk was released, the man climbed off her at once and she saw that her master was beside her. He indicated another man, who was stretched out on the floor whilst one of her fellow slaves fellated him.

'Take over from her,' Jo's master ordered.

Jo knelt down beside the man and, as the other slave lifted her head, took hold of the man's cock. It was still glistening with saliva and she ran her fingers down its length, testing its rigidity and hardness. Then it was in her mouth and she was working her head up and down, sucking for all she was worth.

The second slave remained where she was beside Jo, running her hands over the young woman's naked skin, caressing her breasts and thighs. Then she moved behind Jo, pulling her backside towards her and forcing her legs wider apart. She ran her fingers down and Jo felt them enter her vagina, which she knew to be dribbling with spunk. The girl took the viscous fluid on her fingers and, with a shock, Jo felt her rubbing it into her anus, her finger sliding into that tight little orifice. Then she felt something else, something thick and hard, nuzzling up against that forbidden hole.

Jo glanced up at her master, still with the man's cock between her lips. Once again he nodded.

'All your body must be given up to men's pleasure tonight, little slave,' he said. 'No part of you must remain unviolated.'

Even as he spoke, Jo felt the man behind her begin to press harder. Her natural reaction was to tighten the muscles of her anus, but she knew she must not. Instead, she bit her lip and forced herself to relax as he eased into her rear.

There was a stab of pain, then he was inside, pressing himself deeper and deeper into her rectum. Were it not for the meaty pole in her mouth, Jo would have cried aloud. Instead she closed her eyes as he buried himself inside her.

No sooner had he begun to fuck her anus than she felt something slide over her clitoris. Something long and wet. For a moment she couldn't understand what was giving her this delicious sensation. Then she realised that the slave girl was lying beneath her and was licking her cunt, her tongue moving up and down her slit, probing inside and giving her the most wonderful sensations.

For Jo, the feeling was extraordinary. Here she was, in the middle of a crowd of strangers, quite naked, sucking on a cock like a first-class whore whilst being violently buggered, with her cunt being licked out by another beauty. The image triggered another shuddering orgasm in the wanton girl and almost simultaneously she found her backside and mouth being filled by yet more gobs of hot spunk as her two lovers came simultaneously.

They withdrew and she turned to see that already the second slave girl was being fucked hard. All around her were couples, threesomes and foursomes, intent on bringing pleasure to one another. It really was a genuine orgy.

Suddenly a naked girl was at her side. It was Chris, her hair a mess, a dribble of sperm running down her chin.

'How are you enjoying it?'

'It's incredible. Fantastic.'

'Of course. It was organised by Fantasy and Co.'

Jo laughed. 'Who else?'

'What do you think of Brian?'

'Brian?'

'Your new master.'

'He's great. He's taking me back with him afterwards.'

'You're in for quite a night then. He's got a fully-equipped dungeon, you know. I hope you're into whips.'

'I'm ready to try anything.'

At that moment, Jo's master grabbed her arm and indicated two men. She winked at Chris.

'Duty calls,' she said. 'I wonder what their penchant is.'

'I think you're about to find out,' said Chris. 'They seem pleased to see you,' she went on, staring at their rampant cocks.

Then, suddenly, a tall stud grabbed Chris and pushed her forward over a couch, guiding his cock towards her love hole. Jo watched for a moment as her friend was penetrated, then arms were pulling her to the ground and she gave herself up once more to the pleasure of the orgy.

A Message from the Publisher

Headline Delta is a unique list of erotic fiction, covering many different styles and periods and appealing to a broad readership. As such, we would be most interested to hear from you.

Did you enjoy this book? Did it turn you on – or off? Did you like the story, the characters, the setting? What did you think of the cover presentation? How did this novel compare with others you have read? In short, what's your opinion? If you care to offer it, please write to:

> The Editor
> Headline Delta
> 338 Euston Road
> London NW1 3BH

Or maybe you think you could write a better erotic novel yourself. We are always looking for new authors. If you'd like to try your hand at writing a book for possible inclusion in the Delta list, here are our basic guidelines: we are looking for novels of approximately 75,000 words whose purpose is to inspire the sexual imagination of the reader. The erotic content should not describe illegal sexual activity (pedophilia, for example). The novel should contain sympathetic and interesting characters, pace, atmosphere and an intriguing storyline.

If you would like to have a go, please submit to the Editor a sample of at least 10,000 words, clearly typed in double-lined spacing on one side of the paper only, together with a short outline of the plot. Should you wish your material returned to you, please include a stamped addressed envelope. If we like it sufficiently, we will offer you a contract for publication.